———————— ★ ————————

In the late afternoon of the misty day, Stella, parking her car in the underground car park near the theatre complex, became aware of the figure in the gloom.

Her stalker. Tall, thin, in a long dark coat and soft hat. A spectre, a monster.

She didn't have to pass the figure to get out. There was a flight of steps just at hand. She could turn and run.

But a nervous fascination seemed to put a brake on her legs. So she stood where she was.

So did the man. In the dim light she saw he was holding a large white sheet of cardboard or something. Big black letters staggered across it.

I LOVE YOU. I WANT TO BE YOU.

———————— ★ ————————

GWENDOLINE BUTLER

A COFFIN FOR CHARLEY

WORLDWIDE.

TORONTO • NEW YORK • LONDON
AMSTERDAM • PARIS • SYDNEY • HAMBURG
STOCKHOLM • ATHENS • TOKYO • MILAN
MADRID • WARSAW • BUDAPEST • AUCKLAND

A COFFIN FOR CHARLEY

A Worldwide Mystery/May 1996

First published by St. Martin's Press, Incorporated.

ISBN 0-373-26200-0

Printed in U.S.A.

AUTHOR'S NOTE

One evening in April, 1988, I sat in the Toynbee Hall in the East End of London, near to Dockland, listening to Dr David Owen (now Lord Owen) give that year's Barnett Memorial Lecture. In it, he suggested the creation of a Second City of London, to be spun off from the first, to aid the economic and social regeneration of the Docklands.

The idea fascinated me and I have made use of it to create a world for detective John Coffin, to whom I gave the tricky task of keeping there the Queen's Peace.

A brief Calendar of the life and career of John Coffin, Chief Commander of the Second City of London Police

John Coffin is a Londoner by birth, his father is unknown and his mother was a difficult lady of many careers and different lives who abandoned him in infancy to be looked after by a woman who may have been a relative of his father and who seems to have acted as his mother's dresser when she was on the stage. He kept in touch with this lady, whom he called Mother, lodged with her in his early career and looked after her until she died.

After serving briefly in the army, he joined the Metropolitan Police, soon transferring to the plain clothes branch as a detective.

He became a Sergeant in 1958, and was very quickly promoted to Inspector a year later.

By 1969 he was a superintendent and nine years later became Chief Superintendent.

There was a bad patch in his career about which he is reluctant to talk. His difficult family background has complicated his life and possibly accounts for an unhappy period when, as he admits, his career went down a black hole. His first marriage split apart at this time and his only child died.

From this dark period he was resurrected by a longish period in a secret, dangerous undercover operation about which even now not much is known. But the esteem he won then was recognized when, in the late 1980s as the Second City of London was being formed, he became the Chief Commander of its Police Force. He has married again, very happily, to an old love, Stella Pinero. He has also rediscovered two siblings, a sister and a brother.

'So I said to Charley...'
Traditional theatrical cover-up when the
speech drops dead.

ONE

Monday. Towards the river

DARKNESS.

The two people stood facing each other. The girl with her back to the wall, the man looking at her, legs apart. He held out his hands.

'I never like being killed,' said the girl. She moved her hands forward as if to protect herself. She had long beautiful nails, painted bright red; on her left hand was a deep, diamond-shaped scar. Almost as if she had been branded.

'It's happened to you before?'

'Several times. I'm the type, I suppose, and I never enjoy it. It's so awkward. They never get it right.'

'They?'

'The killers.'

'Oh, I will get it right. Think of all the things I've been doing... Watching you, admiring you, loving you, hating you. I'll get it right.'

'You will?'

'I'll get it so right you'll never know you are dead.'

Quite a promise.

Darkness absolute.

'Shall we move in for the kill?'

But he wouldn't be killing her just yet. For that, she would have to wait. Wait in hunger, wait in darkness.

LIGHT.

One light, a spot above the dressing-table, focused on the lovely face of Stella Pinero, actress, now for a single rocky

year Mrs John Coffin. An up and down year. But she for-
gave her husband. As always, she had contributed her share.

I must put a bit more lipstick on; I'm looking pale. I
blame last night. Possibly blame was the wrong word, not
one to be associated with the evening before. Sex was good
for you and improved the complexion, but sometimes fa-
tigue made you pale.

The dressing-table had its full equipment of make-up,
sticks of colours, pots of creams, tubs of powder, sprays of
scent, Stella took a professional interest in her looks.

She smiled reminiscently as she considered the night. That
was a bit of the up and down. A quarrel and a reconcilia-
tion.

It had been her fault. Probably her fault.

A rocky year. Right to marry, of course, but they had
difficulties.

All the same, she'd enjoyed the twelve months and she
rather thought he had too. Not a man to want a quiet life
was John Coffin. He thought he did, thought of himself as
the reserved scholarly type more interested in editing his
rakish mother's rakish memoirs than anything else, but in
truth he liked a battle. Or anyway, a bit of a skirmish.
Wouldn't have become a policeman else, would he?

Well, he had had one big battle but not with her, and won
it. His management of his Police Force in the Second City
of London had come in for criticism on various grounds—
not of inefficiency, it was agreed that he was very compe-
tent, but because with some people he was too friendly and
with others too remote.

And then there was his relationship with her (well, that
had sorted itself out) and his connection with his highly
successful sibling Letty Bingham, property tycoon and
owner of St Luke's Theatre Complex which contributed
handsomely to Stella Pinero's income.

Or had done. This recession was biting sharply into Letty and so into Stella. It had taken a year or two for the slump to hit the theatre but it had done so now.

Property developers were not popular in the Docklands of the Second City where they had erected great office blocks and compounds of luxury flats which the local population resented. This had counted in the whispering campaign against John Coffin, but he had faced up to it, and also to the overt criticism of his Police Committee, and he had won.

But it had not made for an easy first year of marriage.

I was sensible to keep on my own flat, Stella decided. If the Queen can have a separate bedroom, then I can have a separate flat. Somewhere to hide when things got too hot. Also, she was performing this season in St Luke's herself as well as producing two plays and she liked to have her friends in after a performance or after a particularly gruesome rehearsal and her friends did not always fit in well with the murder and mayhem that was part of her husband's life.

They loved it, of course, but she found their questions difficult.

She lived in St Luke's Mansions which had been converted from the tower of an old Victorian church which had fallen into disuse. The St Luke's Theatre Complex was adjacent. The main theatre in the round was in the old church itself while a theatre workshop had been built across a small courtyard.

I am attractive, she told herself, and I am a well known, if not exactly a famous, actress. Which is why that man watches me.

Hangs around, follows me, watches me.

Like all actresses, she had had followers, men who called with flowers, met her at the stage door, wrote little notes. It was part of theatrical tradition, the Stage Door Johnny. She had liked it, even found some of the men attractive; she was no prude.

But this was different.

She went to her window to look out. The dark-coated figure was not to be seen but he was probably there. She never got a good look at his face because he wore a hat which he pulled low, and dark spectacles.

Not a pleasing sight.

So that's it, she said to her reflection. I'm a *femme fatale*. The *fatale* bit did not please her.

She could tell her husband who would certainly act. What was the point of being married to a policeman if you could not call upon him when you were alarmed.

She was alarmed.

JOHN COFFIN, Chief Commander of the Second City Police Force, looked out of his window in his office. He got a better view from the sitting-room of the tower in St Luke's Mansions, where he lived, sometimes with Stella and sometimes without her, but his view had improved since one tower block of council flats had been knocked down before it fell down so that he got a distant view of the river. He enjoyed looking out...

It was something he did quite often. Partly because it gave him pleasure to look down on this London which he loved (although he would not have admitted to the feeling) and partly because (and again would he have admitted it?) he liked to keep an eye on it.

It was a rough world down there and famously criminous. New wealth had not changed old ways. There were groups of streets where Victorian Peelers had refused to go except in pairs; there were still streets in which constables on the beat liked to feel they had good back-up. But he did not allow NO GO areas. Everywhere was policed.

It was the Queen's Peace he was responsible for keeping and he trusted she was grateful. Whispers had come to him about the next Honours List, so he supposed she was. He already had the Queen's Police Medal, awarded when he took up his present position.

If he did get an honour it would be a surprise since he had had several close brushes with his local MP and the Police Committee. The fact that they then passed what amounted to a vote of confidence in him did not mean they loved him the better.

Within his authority he had the old boroughs of Spinnergate, Leathergate, Swinehouse, and East Hythe, whose very place names testified to their antiquity. The Vikings had got as far as these four Anglo-Saxon settlements in their ravages up the Thames, the Norman warlords had swept in replacing the old English landowners, but the indigenous population had survived and their descendants, spiced with immigrants from every land within the old Empire, were there now, tough, wily and ready to cause trouble. They had never been particularly law-abiding and recent events had done nothing to change their mind. New money had poured into the district in the last decade turning old warehouses and dockside buildings into offices and luxury apartments, and the old poor still in their terrace houses or council housing were resentful. Ill-feeling had turned to wicked mirth as the new rich became victims of the recession.

He had in his bailiwick several hospitals, a university, numerous schools, and a high number of bookmakers' shops. One legal casino and one illegal gambling house that moved on and reopened as soon as it was closed down. He had at least two brothels which called themselves Party Clubs, a flourishing transvestite night club, and a variety of religious foundations including chapels, churches and one man who was building a replica of Stonehenge in his back garden. Very handsome it was too, if necessarily on the small side. Its creator, Mr James Eldon, told the local press that he was not a Druid or worshipping a Bronze Age goddess, his motives were purely aesthetic: he just fancied it. He had invited the Chief Commander to a glass of nettle wine and a view of his henge.

Coffin had not gone but he had warmed to Mr Eldon as one of the most harmless of his eccentrics.

As he continued looking out of his window, he knew that at any one time he had in his area any number of juvenile delinquents, several rapists, a clutch of child molesters, numerous sexual deviants more or less within the law, at least one murderer who was known but against whom they could not get proof, one killer who was about to be arrested, and possibly more than he cared to think about that were secret and undetected in their murders.

It was these last ones that worried him most.

He turned away from the window with a yawn. Tarts, rogues, evil-doers and saints, he had them in his care. He had known one saint himself but she was dead; it was really just as well because otherwise he might have been obliged to send her to prison.

He yawned again. Detective Chief Inspector Young looked at him with sympathy. He was tired himself having been up all night on a murder inquiry.

'It's the heat,' said Coffin. He was talking to Young because he was dealing with the case, which was a sensitive one in which an MP had been, still was, involved. 'Go on.'

'He said: "It's nothing to do with you who I fuck or who I don't. Push off."'

'Nice fellow.'

'No witnesses,' said Young briefly. 'He knew I couldn't quote. He was drunk,' he added in a neutral voice.

Job Titus, MP. He had started in one political party, crossed the floor of the House to join another, and finally set out his own stall. No settled party, continually changing his opinions, an Independent, very popular in his constituency, but as someone once said: 'Of no fixed abode intellectually.' A drinker, famous for it, violent, and famous for that too, and twice divorced. 'Where does he get his money?' people asked. 'Where does he get his energy?' others said. He had a crest of yellow curls and bright blue eyes. A political gigolo.

'And the girl's dead?'

'And the girl's dead.'

Silence for a short space.

'How was she killed?'

Young pursed his lips. 'There was a bit of doubt at first, but the informed opinion is that there was an attempt to strangle her and then she was smothered. Manually. Hand over her mouth and nose.'

Marianna Manners had been a ballet dancer, out of work, but hopeful of joining a big London company. Meanwhile she had tried for all sorts of other parts because she could act a bit and one thing could lead her to another. In her case it looked as if it had. She had a wide circle of friends and lovers, one of whom might be Job Titus, MP, but there was no proving it. She had said Yes to her friends, he said No to the police.

'Nasty... And Job Titus?'

'No evidence that points to him in a strong way. He's been seen drinking in the Balalaika Arms talking several times to one man and that makes me wonder.'

The Balalaika Arms in Spinnergate had a bad reputation. It was known as Drinking in Hell.

'And he knew her. And she claimed it was more than that. They both lived in Swinehouse in the same block of flats. And I'd love to get him for it.' He didn't say the last sentence aloud.

'Yes,' said Coffin, agreeing with what hadn't been said. 'That's it for the moment, then?'

'Right.'

'What sort of girl was she?'

'Nice-looking, of course. Well made-up, well turned out. Quite expensive clothes. One strange thing for a girl like her... she had badly bitten fingernails. Didn't really try to cover them up, either. No varnish or anything like that. Almost as if she didn't care.'

The two men had a friendly relationship which stretched outside working hours because their wives were friends. Stella Pinero and Alison, the ambitious, brilliant young wife of the Chief Inspector, had met at an official party and taken a great liking to each other.

The police service being what it was, Coffin and Young had to keep a certain distance at work (although well aware that the married lives of both had come under female discussion), but it made for friendliness.

It enabled Archie Young to say: 'Annie Briggs has been in again.'

Coffin frowned. 'What is it this time?'

'She thinks she's being watched.'

'She might well be.' He walked to the window again to look out. 'Haven't been any death threats lately, have there?'

'No. None that I've heard of. But they're a grudging lot, the Creeley clan, and they never forget. Pity they came back from New Zealand, I was a lot happier when it looked as though they'd emigrated. But they're back and in the same street, the same house. Well, the boy is, there's only him left now, he came back and moved in.'

'Wonder how he managed that?' Property being what it was.

'Never sold it. Just moved back in.'

Coffin was curious. 'What sort of household does he run there?'

'Not as bad as you might think. It was very mucky, the tenants not having been as careful as might be, but the young one, grandson Eddie, has been painting and gardening. He's on his own at the moment although the odd cousin has been to stay.'

'How do you know all this?'

'Community policing,' said Young. 'The local officer managed to insert himself in the house for a look round. He had a word with Eddie about car parking, Eddie Creeley has three old bangers parked outside and the neighbours were complaining. Eddie's a car mechanic as hobby but he's working in a hospital. Our man reported favourably on him. I think he liked him.'

'I didn't think you could like a Creeley.'

'The old lady's gone, of course. But her spirit lives on. Anyone who does a Creeley down gets it back in spades. They've never forgiven Annie, that's the story. Or you, for that matter.'

'They won't do anything now. It's too late, too long ago. Oh, writing on her front door, dog dirt through the letter-box...'

'They did all of that in the past, but not lately, not since the shift back from New Zealand. Perhaps Eddie's different, who knows?'

'I know old Mrs Creeley said one or other of them would kill Annie in the end. They never took that back. Never did much about it, either.'

'She still sees it coming.'

'She's lived a long while with that on her mind. How long is it now? Over twenty years? We can't watch all the time.'

'I've been told that Lizzie Creeley is being given parole. The brother's had a stroke, he'll get out too but go straight to hospital,' said Young. 'I dare say Annie has heard the news.'

'How old is she now?'

'She was about eight then. Thirty-odd now. A daughter of her own. The sister lives with her. She wasn't born then.'

Twenty-odd years ago when John Coffin, even then a controversial figure with friends and enemies, had been called across the river from his own area to consult on a case which seemed to have a parallel with a murder he was deal-ing with. Whether the death of old Addie Scott had a con-

nection with the Creeleys had never been established, but the
Creeleys had gone down anyway for another crime. Coffin
knew this area of old, because as a raw young constable he
had lived here in what was in those days a working-class
district of the great metropolis. Lodged with 'Mother'. She
had not been his mother, of course; nobody's mother, certainly not his.

A child, Annie Dunne, hiding in the garden of her home
one foggy night had heard strange noises, she had crawled
through the next-door hedge to watch and had seen two
people burying an old man, and his wife.

Coffin had been the man who persuaded her to talk.

The killers were a brother and sister, Will and Lizzie
Creeley. Without Annie's testimony the bodies might never
have been found nor the two convicted. The Creeley family
swore to get her.

Annie had grown up, had married, and had a child herself. But for some time the Creeleys had still lived three
streets away. Bad years for Annie, until the family had emigrated, but one by one they had drifted back. Eddie was the
latest. Creeleys had lived in Swinehouse for many genera-
tions and were embedded in the district like weeds.

'She wasn't believed at first, you know, when she told her
story.'

Archie Young nodded.

'But I believed her... And then, of course, the rumour
went round that there were other bodies buried in the garden. As if it was a kind of cottage industry that the Creeleys
had there: killing for money. But there were only the two, as
if that wasn't enough...I suppose Annie's heard about this
murder?'

'I don't suppose she thinks Marianna was murdered instead of her.'

'She did live two streets away.' Marianna had a tiny flat
in the Alexandra Wharf block, and Napier Street, where
Annie Briggs lived was only a few yards away.

'They didn't know each other. Not as far as we know.'

'I bet she hopes that if the Creeley boy did it we get him for it fast.'

'Doesn't look like a Creeley crime, they were strictly business as far as we know, and there was no profit in Marianna. Straight sex there, I reckon.' Young added wistfully: 'If I had to choose between getting Job Titus or a Creeley for Marianna I don't know which I'd go for.'

'Hard choice,' said Coffin.

'But poor Annie. I mean, she's a nuisance, always popping in with crisis calls, but you can see why.' He looked at the wall. 'She's got in a private investigator.'

'My God, who?'

'The Tash Agency,' said Young, still not meeting Coffin's eyes.

'Tom Ashworth. My wife used him on her divorce.' Stella had claimed her divorce was amiable on both sides, Coffin had only learnt later that this was not quite true.

Young, who knew this, he made it his job to know everything about his boss that he could, kept silent.

Then he said: 'Annie says she liked him, trusts him... Whatever that means.'

Stella had said the same. 'I think it means he's attractive,' said Coffin.

He had discovered that where Stella was concerned he was capable of quick and ready jealousy. He kept quiet about it and hoped she had not noticed, but it was there. To his surprise, jealousy was cold, not hot, and penetrated everywhere like a gas.

Stella was naturally flirtatious, and meeting desirable men all the time. She said there had to be chemistry, it was all part of the job. Very likely it was.

'There aren't so many people Annie Briggs trusts. Her husband left her, couldn't stand it.' Young kept in touch with his world. 'She's got a social worker who calls in, the sister gave them a bit of trouble once. Can't blame her, it's hardly been a normal life.'

Coffin said: 'She is on my mind and on my conscience all the time. I'll go and see her.'

He knew what was lined up for him in his diary, so it wouldn't be today or tomorrow, but sometime. Soon. Might get Stella to help, unofficially, of course. She was good with women.

At the door, Archie Young paused. 'Supposing the man that Job Titus was seen drinking with was the Creeley boy? Sounded like him. May be nothing in it.'

DRIVING HOME THAT NIGHT Coffin thought: Supposing Job Titus got a Creeley to do Marianna in, and then Titus promised to help the Creeleys get Annie somehow?

It was an interesting idea. He could feel sorry for Titus if he let the Creeleys get a hook in him. He might be a smart political operator but the Creeleys had millennia of criminality behind them. A Creeley man or woman, the women being fully as bad, had probably conned a Roman centurion and then slit his throat.

He let himself in, wondering if Stella would be home. Sometimes she was and sometimes not, but she always left a note around saying where she was. 'At the theatre.' 'Downstairs.'—This meant in her own flat. 'Gone to see Jay.'—Jay was her agent.

He was beginning to enjoy what he called 'Stella's little notes'. Part of his new life, he always felt in touch. They had promised never to be apart for long. When you marry late, then you cannot afford too many absences.

On his desk that day he had found a card and invitation: *Phœbe Astley invites you to celebrate her promotion.* An address in Birmingham and a scrawl: *Why don't you come up and see me?*

Phœbe had occupied a niche in his life before Stella came back into it. She was post-Stella and pre-Stella. She had moved away, joined another force and risen sharply. Clever girl, Phœbe, but I won't be coming. I shall be home with my wife.

Tonight he smelt cooking. So she was home. Here. His spirits rose. Darling Stella.

And he smelt cigarette smoke: so that meant Letty too. He liked his sister and admired her. She had been around a lot lately. She and Stella were putting together a scheme to help beat the recession in St Luke's Theatre by opening a small drama school which local youngsters would be encouraged to join. A keep-the-kids-off-the-streets scheme. There had been a lot of idle vandalism lately.

It would help the neighbourhood and, with local sponsors, would assist the theatre too. It was going to be very professional.

For so long resistant to economic stress, the theatre was now getting the full effects. And just at a time when Letty's property investments were in decline. More than decline, rushing precipitately down hill. But he backed Letty, he had noticed that nothing had stopped her buying her new autumn wardrobe in Paris and New York, and he took that as a sign, while being grateful that Stella could fund her clothes at less expensive outlets. Not that he bought her clothes. She bought her own and always had.

THE CAT AND THE DOG were home too. He knew that from the two food bowls on the staircase by the living-room. Why they chose to eat there he did not know. Stella said it made them feel free, but he thought it was because he had once tripped over their bowls and had fallen down the stairs. They were waiting for him to do it again.

Both women turned round to look at him as he came in.

'Talking about me?'

'Thinking about you.'

'Always, I hope.' He gave Stella a kiss. 'Hello, Letty.'

Letty raised an eyebrow, it was an eyebrow trained to rise. 'Oh, come on, she's got other things to do.' Letty's marriages never prospered because she always had other things to do.

'Rescue me,' said Coffin's eyes to Stella. His beautiful sister could terrorize him on occasion. He suspected she was like their eccentric, errant, delinquent mother who had abandoned her children one after the other. Letty was wearing black silk jeans with a leopard print silk blazer in which she looked sinewy and alarming. 'Help me out.'

Stella almost did. 'Well, not all the time, not when I'm learning my lines or on stage, but underneath, darling, I think about you and I expect I always will.' When necessary, Stella could deliver lines as if from a Coward play.

He sniffed the air. 'What are you cooking?'

'One of my chicken casseroles.'

He knew better than to criticize Stella's cooking efforts. 'Do you think it could be burning?' His tone was tentative, questioning humbly.

'No, I think it's meant to smell like that.'

'Ah.' He certainly hoped so, but it seemed doubtful. Was carbon an ingredient in the best meals? But they could always go round to Max's Delicatessen and eat there. He had what he called his Bar, just a few chairs and tables, usually full of performers from St Luke's Theatre grabbing something to eat. The comfort level was low but the food was excellent.

Coffin had eaten there a lot as a bachelor, as had Stella Pinero, but just lately she had decided it was her duty to be the Perfect Wife. A part for which she was not naturally gifted.

He knew he would have to live with the idea until she got tired of it, but he had preferred the former, unreconstructed Stella.

'That is, I think so,' she said. She too could smell something dark and burnt. 'I wonder if I ought to go and look.'

'Forget it,' said Letty. 'Past praying for, I expect.'

'Someone will murder you one day, Letty.'

'One or two have tried,' admitted Letty. 'But I was too strong for them.'

'Don't joke,' said Stella. Her tone was sharp. She went to the window. Nothing there. Well, even lurkers, Stage Door Johnnies, go home.

Coffin looked at his wife. 'What is it? You're worried.' He drew her away from the window. 'Come on, sit down and tell me.'

Nervously, she said: 'There's this man...hanging around. Sometimes he's outside the theatre. I have seen him near the old church hall where we rehearse. This last week he's even got as far as the TV studio.' Stella was filming a new series in which she had a plum part as a female detective. 'He was further away there because of the security patrol GTV have there, but I know it was him.'

'Is it always the same man? Have you seen his face?' *I'll kill anyone who touches Stella.*

'Only a glimpse, he wears dark spectacles and hat. A wig too, I think, not a good one, something cheap.' As an actress, Stella knew a wig when she saw one. 'And yes, I'm sure it's the same chap, same clothes, same posture.'

Coffin frowned. 'Go on talking. Give me all the detail you can. How long has it been going on?' He wanted to observe Stella. Many successful actresses (and some unsuccessful ones too) had people who stalked them: men and women who were ardent fans and wanted to get to know them. Or to watch them come and go from the theatre. Stella had had her share of those, and she knew how to deal with them. They did not make her nervous.

Now she was nervous. *I'll kill him.*

Dutifully, Stella went on, providing what meagre details she could. She had first observed the man almost a year ago, but his appearances had been sporadic at first and she had not taken them seriously. Now he was very regular. Of course, he couldn't get into the St Luke's complex of buildings easily, but he sited himself under the clump of trees across the road from where he could see her windows. Kitchen and bedroom. Bathroom too for that matter, but she had clouded glass on that so it wouldn't do him much good.

'He can see your windows too. But it's not you he's looking for. I'm surprised you haven't seen him yourself.'

'Keeps out of my way, I expect.' But from now on, he would be looking. 'I wish you had told me before.'

Stella was silent. 'I thought I was being foolish to worry. It might have been kind of flattering...' Her voice died away. 'But it's not. Doesn't feel right.'

'Why does he frighten you?'

Stella said slowly: 'I feel his concentration. It's obsessive. Not admiration...something else. Hungry.'

His sister Letty said: 'I think he's watching me too.'

'Oh, I don't believe that's likely.'

'Well, thanks, brother. You do know how to make a girl feel attractive.'

'What I meant was, men like that are usually, invariably, obsessed with one person at a time.'

'I've seen him there, too. I wish I'd said something sooner. He's just as Stella said: dark glasses, soft hat pulled over the face.'

'You're welcome to him,' said Stella. 'He's all yours and good luck to you.'

'There's another thing: I think he uses binoculars.'

'If you saw that you certainly should have told me, Letty.' Coffin was angry.

Letty shrugged. 'London's full of weirdos. New York is full of weirdos, so is Paris. The world is full of weirdos.'

I have a weirdo of my own. Charley, Stella thought without pleasure. Who would like to take on my Charley? Letty can have him.

Coffin stood up and went to the telephone. 'Stella, I should look at that casserole. There's burning and there's burning and there's incineration.'

'What are you going to do?'

'I can order a patrol car to call regularly, and the constable on the beat to look in as well. That ought to frighten the man away. If he hangs around, then we'll take him in.'

Stella nodded. 'It was a wig, you know... and the face, there was something not quite right there, I swear it.'

'You serve the meal.' If it could be served, and not put out with water. 'And after I have made this call, then I will walk around and see if he's there now.'

Stella looked relieved. 'So silly to mind, makes me feel a fool, but he has worried me.'

'Me too,' said Letty, anxious not to be left out.

Coffin called the dog. 'Come on, Bob,' attached a lead to his collar and went out. Bob was, as ever, eager and dragged ahead, breathing heavily in expectation.

It was dusky outside with a light rain falling, the street lights were on, but the pavements were empty. The theatre was dark tonight, with no performance, but that didn't mean it was empty. A read through, a rehearsal, or just a meeting of the Friends of St Luke's Theatre might be going on. There was never a really dead night. Letty and Stella encouraged activity.

He walked slowly, his thoughts anxious. He knew what the women did not: that there was a killer in the district.

He looked up and saw Stella profiled against the kitchen window. He could see her turn her head as if speaking to someone, she appeared to be opening the window and in the circumstances of the chicken casserole, he could see why; then she moved away out of his vision. He must remind her to keep the blind down. He felt very protective of her and yet awkward at the same time.

He was surprised how powerfully and vigorously that sight of Stella had affected him. Strong feelings came and

went with him at the moment. He was floundering with
Stella just now. It was odd, this marriage thing.

Although they each kept their separate apartments, and
although they had, let's face it, been lovers on and off for
years, marriage had subtly and definitely altered their relationship. He was less sure of himself with Stella than ever.
She was trying to be everything she could to him, he could
see that, but he didn't want her to try, he wanted her to be,
just to be. Spontaneous. Happy.

He walked on. No dark-spectacled figure to be seen under the trees or on the corner or in a doorway tonight. He
could go back and tell the two women that it was all clear.
Although that did not mean the man had not been there or
might be there again.

No need to alarm Stella and Letty by telling them that a
girl named Marianna Manners had been strangled and then
stifled. But he had to think about it.

It was possible that she might have been killed by Job
Titus whom they both knew.

Or Titus might have contracted for her death with one of
the Creeley family, a youngster with a violent reputation.

In both those instances, Stella and Letty were under no
threat.

Or Marianna might have been killed by just the sort of
man that was watching them.

HE WALKED BACK to St Luke's Mansions. A patrol car
passed him, slowed for a look, recognized him, and passed
on. So his orders were already being followed.

A prosperous-looking dark blue car was parked in the
kerb near by. An expensive-looking car and he thought he
had seen it before. He walked round the front to study the
windscreen and saw on it a card which empowered the driver
to park his car in the area reserved for Members of Parlia-
ment.

The last thing he wanted just now was a visit from Job Titus. There were good sound reasons for not entertaining in your home a man who might be a murder suspect.

He walked up his stairs quickly, arriving at the kitchen in time to hear Stella saying that they were going to eat at home but something had gone wrong with a casserole she was doing and she thought they would now be eating out.

Job Titus was sitting at the kitchen table holding a glass of red wine. He had been drinking already, Coffin could tell from his eyes, but had himself in hand. He was supposed to be able to charm all women and Coffin thought he was doing so now. Letty was smiling and Stella would probably be asking Titus to join them at dinner if he didn't move fast to stop her.

Job stood up as Coffin came. 'John, of course we've met, you remember?' He held out his hand.

At a large charity dinner in the Docklands, if you could call that meeting. They had shaken hands, no more. And as far as Coffin was concerned, they could leave it there.

They were not friends. Job had certainly joined in the late campaign to get his resignation, even if he had kept his name hidden. My secret enemy, he thought.

He left the outstretched hand hanging and after a second, Job withdrew it, covering the moment with a smile. 'I always believe in going to the top with a complaint. Your men have been harassing me. I don't want to make it official, cause trouble for you. I want to keep it friendly.'

'I can't discuss anything,' said Coffin stiffly. *Like to slit your throat.*

From Stella's startled look at him he guessed this notion came across to her. 'John . . .' she began.

'It's all right, Stella, Mr Titus is just leaving.'

Job Titus stood up. He put his arm round Letty who showed no sign of resenting it. 'I just love this leopard lady. You aren't listening to me, John. I did not kill Marianna Manners. You might pass that word on to your murder squad. They are ill-mannered bastards who take a lot for granted and if I swore at them, then they deserved it. This was meant to be just a friendly warning for you to pass on. Next time I will make it official.' He moved away, knocking over the glass of red wine. 'Look, I told your men that Marianna had been complaining of a man trying to get to know her. Go for him, not me.'

'I'll see you out,' said Coffin.

'Before we go, just one more thing: Marianna auditioned for a part in the amateur play in the Theatre Workshop here. She was out of work, you see, and she thought anything was better than nothing. Maybe she met her killer there. Bear it in mind.'

Coffin just held the door without answering.

Job Titus hesitated, then moved towards the door. 'Goodbye, Stella, goodbye, Letty. Mrs Coffin, I suggest you tether your husband.'

'What did he mean by that?' said Stella as Coffin came back.

'Tame, tie up, he was just being offensive. He's frightened, I think.'

Stella started to mop up the wine. 'I wish he hadn't come here. I don't like it when your work and mine cross.'

'He's a madman,' said Letty. 'Attractive, but mad. Did he kill the girl?'

Coffin shrugged. 'I don't know.' He was watching his wife: she had not failed to notice the phrase about the man trying to get to know Marianne.

'It's your job to know.'

'It takes time. He may have had a hand in it.'

Stella said: 'I think we had better eat at Max's. The casserole got away from me.' She spoke of it as if it was an animal she had been training. No wonder she had trouble cooking, Coffin thought, if she's always trying to tame the meat.

'I booked a table while I was out,' he said. 'Let's go. Coming, Letty?'

'Why do you think I am dressed in Versace? I knew that casserole would never come to the table. I too booked a table. You're my guests, by the way. I've got something to discuss.'

OVER THE PROSCIUTTO and chilled melon, Letty said: 'I wanted to tell you that my daughter has disappeared and that I have engaged a private detective to look for her.'

Coffin opened his mouth to speak but Letty stopped him.

'Don't say it. It is not a matter for the police. Elissa is eighteen, she sent a letter telling me she was going, and she has the money from a small trust fund. I don't think any police force is going to spend any energy looking for her, not even yours, brother.'

'Did she say why?'

'I am too dominating, too successful, she needs to lose me.'

'I see.' He wondered if he did. It was a fair description of Letty: successful, bossy. But were daughters supposed to mind that?

'But really, I think, she is our mother's descendant. Every so often she must shake herself free and depart.'

'You are taking it very well.'

'No, I'm not. I'm trembling with fear inside. Which is why I have engaged a private detective to find her. Just locate her . . . Stella recommended one.'

'Did I?' Stella was surprised.

'Well, you talked of him. Tash. You probably know of him?' She turned to her brother.

'He's known,' said Coffin tersely. The Tash Agency had been around for some time.

'He seems efficient and to have a good reputation. I inquired around. And he's attractive. I like him for that.

Lovely fair hair with bright brown eyes, and well groomed. I didn't want a seedy, backroom sort of man.'

'Certainly not that,' said Coffin. 'But he's pretty much a one man band. Can he cover the field?'

'I think he can do it; he has some help. I'm convinced she's still in London. He thinks not.'

Coffin still looked doubtful. In his opinion London was no place for a girl of eighteen to roam around in. Was she on drugs? Did she have a boyfriend? He considered asking Letty but decided now was not the moment. 'You can always call on me.'

Letty smiled at him and nodded. 'So now you know why I am taking the state of near-bankruptcy and the decline in the theatre with relative calm.'

Stella put her hand gently on Letty's arm. 'I too have a daughter.'

'But you know where she is?'

'Yes, she's putting together a play for the Edinburgh Fringe. She's in the family business, I'm afraid. I had a card from Fife. She was there last week.'

A small crowd was leaving the precincts of the Theatre Workshop as they came home. Most of them were young people and they were talking loudly and cheerfully.

Coffin raised an eyebrow. 'What's this?'

'The Friends of St Luke's Theatre are auditioning for their summer play. They're throwing it open to all this year because we're using it as preparation for the Drama School. See who comes in, sniff out talent, get local interest.' Money, she meant.

The Friends, a redoubtable group of local ladies, would be one of the great supports of the new Drama School if she was lucky.

'What are they doing?'

'Oh, an Agatha Christie mystery. It usually is.'

IN BED THAT NIGHT Stella turned to her husband. 'It's nice on the top of the tower like this. I think I prefer it to my place.'

Both of the animals had come up with them, Bob on the bed and the cat watching from the window through which he would shortly depart on to a lower roof.

'Open the window for Tiddles.'

Coffin, who was making a neat pile of his possessions on his bed table, coins stacked, clean handkerchief beside the pile, keys by a pad of paper with a pencil, obliged.

'Funny business about Letty and the daughter,' said Stella. 'I don't always understand her.'

'Who does?'

Letty was his much younger sister, child of his errant mother and an American serviceman. There was a third sibling called William, issue of yet another father, who was a successful lawyer in Edinburgh. The one thing you could say about his disappearing mother (who must be presumed dead) was that her offspring were surprisingly different and surprisingly successful. He himself had lived in ignorance for years of his true parenthood and of the existence of Letty and William. Even now, he found it hard to believe in them. Well, not Letty. She was around so much. But he still felt surprise sometimes when she walked through the door.

'Did you believe what she said?'

'Well, you can never tell with Letty... No, not altogether.'

'What's this private detective like?'

'You know him,' Coffin said tersely. He did not like to be reminded.

'I met him once and I paid his bill, that's all. Is he honest?'

'As far as I know.'

Stella settled back against the pillows. Without any conscious effort, she had turned what had been a bachelor's masculine bedroom into a feminine boudoir. The fourposter bed, an early extravagance of Coffin's, had been piled with pillows and silk cushions. She had brought in an embroidered bedcover and there was always a scent of rose geranium.

Coffin liked it but sometimes felt like a member of an alien species.

'John . . .?'

'Yes?'

'Why did Job Titus say that about Marianna coming to the Theatre?'

'He just wanted to vomit in my backyard,' said Coffin with some bitterness.

There was silence for a moment.

'I don't like this stalker,' she said softly. 'Charley frightens me.'

He drew her down towards him. 'Don't worry, I'll look after you.'

And Letty, and Letty's child, and Annie Briggs and all the people in my command.

But he knew that whatever he said he could not offer total protection. The lunatic always got through.

ANNIE BRIGGS, formerly Dunne, was pleased to see her younger sister home. 'How did the audition go?'

'I think I'm in. Just a small part, one of the policewomen in *Witness for the Prosecution,* was a man originally but they have more women auditioning. I've got some good lines.'

'I am glad, dear.' And glad you are home, I am always nervous when you are out late.

'I'm in the second company.' Anxious to take in as many young amateurs as possible, the ruling body, the Friends, had decided to have two casts who would appear alternately throughout the run of two weeks.

'You'd be surprised at the people who turned up. Even one of those Creeleys.'

'Ah.'

Didi did not share her sister's terror of the Creeleys, whom she regarded as harmless relics of the past. The younger Creeleys were different and of considerable interest to her. Especially Eddie Creeley.

'Lots of faces you'd know, Annie.'

'Don't tell me,' said Annie, trying as ever to shut out what she could not bear, past, present and future.

Didi drank the coffee that her sister had poured for her and ate a sandwich. Then swallowed what she was eating. 'Don't worry about the Creeleys, love. They're nothing now. The old ones were stinkers but the young lot are all right. I like Eddie.' She took her sister's hand and gave it a little pat. 'You've got Caroline in the flat upstairs.' It was true that Caroline seemed to her more of an absence than presence. 'You said yourself she helped.'

'She does,' Annie admitted. The flat at the top of the old house, with its own entrance up a metal fire escape, was let to C. Royal, it said so on a printed card. 'But she has a job. She's away a lot.'

'They were talking about the murder.' Didi had finished her sandwich. 'Marianna Manners. I wonder if we ever saw her? In the supermarket or getting on the Tube at Spinnergate maybe, but without knowing.'

She knew it was better to bring the subject of murder out into the open. 'Don't let her hide from the world,' the social worker had said. 'She can face it, she can do it, never you mind.' He was an Alex C. Edwards. Wonder what the C stands for, Didi had thought? He said he had to use it to distinguish himself from another A. Edwards, but Didi thought he liked it. Carolus, Cornell, or what?

He was a nice man, Alex C. Edwards, too nice really for this world. He's in love with Annie, of course. This ingenuous comment being her way of recording sexual attraction.

TWO

In the Arches of the Years

THREE PEOPLE REMEMBERED the story of Annie Briggs. She had been Annie Dunne then, but she married young and never dropped entirely from the police's view.

The most important memory was that of Annie herself, but she had been so young that she sometimes wondered now how much she truly recalled and how much of it was what she had been told. But some pictures were so vivid she knew they were real. Had been real, were real, would burn into eternity. That was what eternity was, she told herself, an endlessly revolving kaleidoscope of horrors.

Lizzie Creeley remembered what Annie had said because she had been the subject of it, in company with a corpse or two and her brother Will, but since his stroke he had no memory.

Coffin had special memories of it all because he had always wondered if they got it right.

He had his own remembrances of this district to contend with as well, some of them peculiar to say the least. He had lived here as a raw young copper with the woman that politely but falsely he had called 'Mother'. She had asked him to do so. At the time he had understood that she was a distant relation of his father, a cousin, because the old lady who had certainly been his grandmother and the woman who had probably been his aunt and who had superintended what there was of his childhood, had assured him she was and that he should take rooms with her. People did that sort of thing then, now they lived in bedsits. She had been his mother's dresser, or so she said, and was a bit mad.

She had given him ham for his supper and called it kippers and given him kippers and called it ham. But they had rubbed along all right. Every day he had travelled across to South London where he worked.

After a bit she had moved there to a flat above a shop in the Borough. Soon after this he emancipated himself. But he sat with her when she died in Guy's Hospital. Died with some pain, still calling herself Mother. He had been the only mourner at her funeral and out of charity he had sent several wreaths in different names.

Never my true mother, but more of a mother than the other one.

He had come back to this district, then part of the Met, called in as a seasoned detective who was working on a similar case across the river, in time to hear Annie's story and receive Lizzie Creeley's confession. Where had Stella been then? Not with him, one of their early bitter partings.

His picture differed from both Lizzie's and Annie's because he had seen Annie and heard her tale, he had seen Lizzie and listened to what she had to say, while those two had never spoken face to face.

Annie remembered creeping out of the house on a foggy November night to go down the garden to what had been an old privy and now housed some pet rabbits to inspect her favourite Angora whom she suspected of eating her litter.

In the dark she had heard voices and movements. She had crawled to the hedge, kept wild and uncut, to see two people, a man and a woman, dragging out from the house the old couple who lived there. Before her terrified eyes, they were tumbled bloody and perhaps not even dead (so the pathologist had reported later) into a pit and the earth thrown over them.

It had taken her a week to tell what she had seen and longer still to identify Lizzie and Will. She had done so from behind a special window that allowed her to see them while they could not see her. She had been flanked by two social workers. One, a girl whose name she had forgotten, and the other a very young man, Alex Edwards, whose name she had never been able to mislay because he visited her often to this day. Several policemen had been present, one of whom was John Coffin.

Lizzie Creeley remembered hearing Annie's written testimony read out in court and biting her lower lip till the blood ran. Her counsel hardly bothered to raise a question. She knew she was done for at that point. She wanted to kill him as well, and see that Annie got hers too if she could. She had signalled as much to her father sitting watching.

In court, she had cried out: 'She's lying, the little bitch,' and been reprimanded by the Judge.

Coffin remembered Annie's pinched and terrified face, and Lizzie's fox-like fury, and never doubted the child's truth for a moment.

But as he knew, there are truths and truths.

THREE

The same Monday evening

THE HOUSE WHERE Annie Briggs now lived and where she had spent her short married life and from which her husband had left her (not for another woman but for what he called another life) was not far away from her childhood home from whose garden she had witnessed the two Creeleys bury the old man and woman. Looking back, she thought she could remember them striking blows as well. Hitting them on the head. Skulls splitting like eggs. Had she heard that?

Two deaths it had been, people forgot that, she told herself, when they talk about letting those horrors out. Talk about pity and compassion and people having served their time. Those two cannot serve their time; for what they did such time does not run. I ought to know. I was the one who saw, who heard.

And who testified.

She had hoped they would die incarcerated, but remembering.

Annie certainly intended to do her best to see that they did: on the anniversary of the killing she always sent them letters, one each, describing that night. People said that they did not get the letters, that the letters were intercepted, but she knew better. She knew they got to their destination, not to the heart, those two had not got hearts, but to their liver and guts where fear dwelt. She knew, she sensed it.

She was always sick herself on that day. It was interesting and might be no coincidence that on that anniversary day in her eleventh year she had started to menstruate and still kept that celebration with blood.

After hearing the killing in the garden of the two old people, she had been a 'disturbed child', a name she still wore like a label round her neck. A disturbed child is a disturbing child. Her parents had discovered that fact almost at once.

'Not that I went in for any of that poltergeist nonsense,' said Annie to herself. 'Although I could have done, I could have worked it, but it's stupid, that sort of thing.'

She had been anorexic, had tried a little thievery and gone in for a bit of arson. Nothing big, she wasn't a big person, but certainly 'disturbing' if you had to live with it.

Then someone, a boy, told her she was pretty and she shed all the 'disturbed' symptoms overnight and grew up.

You cannot be a disturbed adult, not if you are looking for sympathy, you are meant to pull yourself together, or they give you pills or electric shocks or put you away, or a combination of all three, and Annie wasn't having any of that. So she put that portmanteau of disturbance behind her, recognizing that it had been self-induced and not wholly satisfying.

Marriage she had enjoyed while it lasted. She was sad when it ended, not blaming Jack Briggs or herself, thus proving to her own satisfaction that she was grown up at last.

The house in Napier Street where Annie and her small daughter and her young sister, Didi, now lived was one of three tall, narrow houses. The top two floors had been formed into a separate flat, while Annie inhabited the bottom two. The top flat had its own front door reached by means of an iron fire escape of solid Victorian construction.

Miss Royal had rented the flat from Annie about eighteen months ago and had been an object of interest to Annie ever since. To the neighbours as well when they got a chance to view her.

Miss Royal was blonde, leggy, wore trousers almost all the time, which caused the unkind old neighbours next door, Nancy and Bob Tyrrett, to say she must be a lesbian, and they didn't mean it as a compliment. The Tyrretts had watched her move in and kept their eyes open since but had not managed more than the odd fleeting glimpse. Miss Royal was a buyer in fashion for a large chain of department stores and not home a lot.

'She has to travel a lot on business,' Annie had explained to her sister. 'But she finds it fascinating and loves it.'

'She never says a word to me, just shoots past.' Not that she had done that lately either. Must have wings, thought sister.

'Well, she does to me. On occasion. When she feels like it.'

'And she's asked you to call her Caroline?'

'Oh, everyone does that now.'

'Does she call you Annie?'

'Sometimes,' said Annie, unwilling to admit that Miss Royal never did.

'Does she have a man up there?'

Annie blinked. 'Well, I'm her landlady, not her keeper. So what if she does? She's adult.'

Didi frowned. 'Thought I'd ask.' She drank some coffee. 'What sort is he?'

'The usual sort, I suppose. Why?'

'He looks,' she hesitated . . . 'different. I saw him once.'

'Keep out of things,' advised Annie. 'She lives her life, let us live ours. Laissez-faire.' A new phrase on Annie's lips; she had left school too young and was now getting an education as a mature student. She knew who Metternich was, and Lord Palmerston, and had heard of Adam Smith.

Annie was doing a course at the local university, the new one, upgraded from a polytechnic. She had a small grant which just allowed her to eat while she studied Law and History but the great plus was that Maida, her child, went to the university children's group daily.

She had read all about Marianna Manners's murder even if she did not admit it. How could they think I was not interested in murder, I who know more about it than most.

'I wonder if she'd talk to me if I went up,' Didi speculated, more to see what Annie said than because she intended to try. 'I need to talk to someone about fashion if I'm going in for drama. I haven't got my image right.'

'She told me she specialized in fashion for the older lady,' said Annie. 'But you could try.'

That means don't bother, assessed Didi. As if I was going to, anyway.

The front doorbell rang.

'Late,' said Annie. 'I shan't answer.' She began to tremble.

'Not that late. Depends what sort of life you have.'

The bell rang again.

'I'm going to answer it.'

'Look out of the window first.'

Didi said: 'Oh, it's that man.' She moved fast. 'I'll open the door.'

'Who?'

'Tash.'

Tom Ashworth.

'What does he want so late?'

'Like I said: it's not so late if your life is like that.'

Didi let him in, she had been looking forward to meeting him ever since Annie had told her that she had employed a private detective. She thought it was a waste of money but it certainly gave them status. No one else in her set had their own detective. Makes me up there with the Princess of Wales. Not that she'd boasted about it, of course, but she had certainly let the news creep out.

Tom Ashworth was a tall, easy-mannered young man who must have used the gentleness to advantage in his work. Not quite as young as he looked, he was genuinely polite and did genuinely like people.

'Saw your light on so I thought I'd pop in. I have something to report.'

'Oh, good. I mean it is good, is it?'

'I think it's good news. Or most of it. You always get a mixture, don't you? It's how life is.' He smiled at Didi who smiled back. Annie watched nervously, wondering if she ought to offer him a drink. Detectives drank, didn't they? There was some gin and a bottle of aged sherry if it hadn't dried up. Caroline liked gin, so she always kept gin and tonic in case Caroline came down here.

'Would you like some coffee? Or something stronger?'

'Coffee would be lovely.'

'I'll get it,' said Didi. She went out to the kitchen, using her special stage walk.

'So what's the news?' asked Annie. After the news would come the bill and she wondered if she would be able to pay it.

'What do you want first... The good news or the bad?'

Didi was listening at the kitchen door as she heated the coffee. She liked him.

'Well, I've checked out the Creeleys, the young ones, and they seem clear. Eddie anyway. No debts, credit is good, no record. And there is no reason to believe the boy is hanging around you to no good purpose.'

'He knows me,' said Annie grimly.

'Yes, he knows you, but I think you can stop worrying about him.'

'Here is the coffee,' said Didi, swivelling in, hand on hip, mug of coffee in the other.

'Eddie couldn't settle in New Zealand, that's the story. And he had the house, owned it, so he came back. You can't blame him for that.'

'It was let to perfectly decent people.'

'You didn't know them,' said Didi in surprise.

'That was what was decent about them,' said Annie with feeling. 'I didn't have to know them. I have to know the Creeleys, they live inside me.'

Ashworth and Didi exchanged looks and Didi gave a little shrug.

Tom Ashworth took his coffee from Didi before she spilt it. 'Houses are important.'

Annie had seen the glance and resented it. She decided to give Didi a slap. 'You ought not to bite your fingernails if you want to succeed on the stage.'

Tom looked at Didi appreciatively. You're the sort of girl I'm looking for, his glance said. Both the sisters were pretty, with thick dark hair and blue eyes, but Didi did not have Annie's perpetually apprehensive expression. She would not have frown lines on her forehead so soon.

'Actress, are you?'

'No, not yet. No Equity card or anything.'

'She's only just left school.' Annie's voice was sharper than she meant it to be: Didi's chosen career was a source of friction between them. 'She could be at a university, she got very good A-level results.'

'I will be at the university, in the drama department, and that will be working with the St Luke's Theatre School when it's set up.'

'Which it isn't yet.' This was the real rub.

'Miss Pinero says it will be. Soon.'

'Pinero, Pinero, that's all we hear now.' Annie turned to Tom. 'And meanwhile she's working in a Delicatessen shop selling brioches.'

'And coffee,' said Didi, who knew how to needle her sister.

'Not acting at all?' Tom looked at Didi.

'I'm auditioning for a part in an amateur production. It's a kind of pre-run for getting a place at the drama school.

Annie doesn't realize how competitive it is. I've got to fight for a place.' Didi shook her head. 'Do anything.'

Tom looked at her admiringly. 'Good for you.' It was the sort of thing he might have said himself. 'I seem to know the name Pinero... Isn't she married to the chief of police here?' The vagueness was professional discretion, he knew Stella Pinero, had acted for her but one did not mention one client to another.

'Yes. Do you know him?'

'Not to say know. But in my business you run across the police so you have to know names at least.'

'Is that how you started out yourself... in the police?'

Tom did not like answering personal questions; it was the wrong way round. He asked, others answered. So he skipped answering automatically.

'And the bad news—' he turned to Annie—'since you didn't ask, is that Will Creeley has had a stroke and is being given parole, so Lizzie gets the same. She'll be out. Probably out now.'

Annie had heard a rumour of this but had chosen not to believe it.

'Going home? Back to Wellington Street?'

'Reckon she'll have to. She isn't going to live long, Annie, she's no danger to you.'

'Yes, she is, you'll see.' Annie's voice was a wail. 'And what about him? Will?'

Now for the bad bad news. 'He's tucked away in hospital, can't walk or talk, he's in a worse state than she is. So they are both out. Natural justice, I suppose that's the reasoning.'

'He'll kill me,' said Annie, white-faced.

'He's an old man now, Annie. I don't think he's a threat.'

Annie stood up, she could be as dramatic as Didi when she liked, and swept to the window. 'There's a murderer out there. A killer. Marianna Manners lived not far from here.

It could be young Creeley. Family business. You say he's not been hanging around. I think he has.'

Tom took a deep breath. 'Well, maybe I haven't been quite straight with you there. I think he's looked around, seen the house. Even rung the doorbell.'

Annie stared at him.

Tom turned to Didi. 'Come on, Didi, you know the boy, don't you? It's you he's after. And not to kill.'

Annie turned on her sister. 'Is this true?'

'I told you I liked Eddie, he's decent. He wants to act too. We rehearse together.'

'Good for you,' said Tom.

'I trust him,' said Didi.

'You can't trust a Creeley. You're a fool, Didi.'

Annie made a dramatic gesture with her hands. 'You know what you're doing, you two? You are talking to a woman who is dying. I am going to be killed.'

TOM MADE AN opportunity to speak to Didi at the door. 'Keep an eye on her.'

'Oh, she'll be all right. She's got her social worker looking after her.'

He considered. 'Still?'

'I think he's off the job, it's personal now. He's in love with her.'

'That's not ethical.'

'What's ethical? Life's not ethical.'

Tom laughed. 'You're right there. What's his name? I'll look into it.'

'Alex Edwards. I don't know his address.'

'I'll find it.' He saw she was more anxious about her sister than she wanted to admit.

'Don't worry too much, kid. I think your sister will have a long life.' He was not in a position to be sure of this, who could be? But he wanted Didi to be happy.

'She does get so upset.'

'Don't we all?'

'Not you.'

'Me too. When I'm keen on something. Or I like a person.'

He smiled, and after a pause, Didi smiled.

'I'm serious.'

AS HE DROVE AWAY, he wondered if he ought to have told her to be careful with the Creeley boy. But that might be over-egging the pudding. He would seek a chance to have a word with the Chief Commander, John Coffin, and say something quiet. Go into one of the pubs he used and take his chance. Like a careful man, he had taken the trouble to run a check on the life and habits of John Coffin. Meaning him no harm, he told himself, but it is as well to know what you can.

After all, he could say, I am looking for your sister's missing daughter (although in my opinion the mother knows more about the child than she is letting on, and they just don't want to meet for reasons all their own but which I intend to know) and I helped with your wife's divorce and that was a fudged-up affair as I expect you know. Or didn't you know?

And as he drove, he said quietly to the traffic lights as they turned red: I have put my foot in that pool and I am not taking it out.

FOUR

Tuesday through to Wednesday. In Spinnergate

STELLA PINERO, as she went about her business for the next day or two kept a watch for her obsessive admirer. If that was what he was. Stalking a star, that was the phrase, wasn't it?

She seemed to be free at the moment. In her life she had been the object of passionate love, of jealousy, and of dislike. Even sometimes, almost harder to bear, of indifference. But there was something uncomfortable about being the object of an obsession.

She considered what she knew of the figure in the shadows, Charley, she called him. There was never any attempt at contact. She had never been touched, had had no letters, never been sent a photograph, had no telephone calls.

She had seen the man in the courtyard outside the St Luke's Theatre after a performance. In the road outside St Luke's Mansions, looking up, just the flash of dark glasses turned her way. Once she had seen him on the station at the Spinnergate Tube, but he didn't get on the train with her. There may have been many occasions when she had simply not seen him. Certainly in the beginning, before she became alerted, there must have been such times.

I am just watched. Perhaps admired, perhaps hated.

At Coffin's request she had made a list of the physical characteristics as she had had a chance to make them out. 'Tell me all you can,' he had said. 'Every detail helps, just jot it down.'

So she had made a list. As much for her own comfort as for his. To make the observer observed took away some fear.

So: a thin figure of medium height. A hat pulled down over the face. Dark glasses. Hands covered in gloves. Wears boots, and a wig.

A secretive man.

It came to a slim catalogue and not likely to help identify the man. She knew enough of her husband's colleagues to know that they might suggest it was all her imagination. A fantasy blown up in her mind. They would not say so directly to John Coffin, but they had their ways of showing scepticism. She wasn't sure, indeed, how much even her husband had believed her.

He must be a secret man, but someone somewhere knew him and was protecting him. That was what they always said, wasn't it? But perhaps no one knew this man's face?

I am having a hard time. I am frightened, she told herself. And that is a fact. My fear is a fact.

So she looked about her as she went out and kept an eye on the street. She spent hours at a rehearsal of a TV series in which she was involved, she visited her agent's office and signed a contract, she kept an appointment with her hairdresser in Beaumont Place.

'You're fidgety, love,' said her hairdresser. He had known her for years, and had placed a signed photograph of her on the wall above the washbasin. He had other stage ladies there too. 'Keep your head still or I can't get the cut right.'

'Sorry, Kenny.' Stella took a deep breath. 'Bit on edge.'

'I can tell . . . Why not go downstairs and get some massage? Saw you on TV last night. You were lovely.'

'Oh, good.' He was cheering her up deliberately and she knew it, but it was his pastoral skills as well as his brilliance as a cutter that kept his shop in Knightsbridge in the top league of hairdressers.

Kenny watched her walk away (without having gone downstairs to his new and expensive health and fitness salon for a soothing massage of the neck and back). He watched her passage past the hatter's window display and the jeweller's boutique and the little couture house where royalty shopped, all with their flowered window-boxes and bright front doors, and shook his head. He had known her for years. *That woman's worried.*

Stella turned round to see him looking, she gave a wave, and stepped into a taxi.

'Spinnergate,' she said. 'And don't tell me it's too far.'

One of the disadvantages of living in the Second City was that taxi-drivers complained about taking you there. Not safe, they said, or no fares back.

But this one gave her a grin. 'Lady, for you, anything.' He leaned out of the window. 'Saw you in *Candida*. Great acting.'

She had recently done a back to back couple of productions of *Candida* and *A Doll's House,* first on TV and then taking them to St Luke's Theatre on a wave of public interest to boost audiences. It had worked.

'My wife liked it too,' he shouted as he drove away.

Well, that's two of them that like me, thought Stella. Then she went home for a meeting with Letty Bingham and the rest of the committee which was setting up the Drama School, they would be discussing the constitution and the difficult matter of charitable status.

And on the mat outside her door was the cat and the cat was sitting in a wreath of white roses.

So he admires me this observer? And sends me white roses? Stella said to herself. By God, I'll get him. I don't have to be passive, I'll go after him myself.

Inevitably by this time the story that Marianna Manners had thought she was being watched had gone the rounds and Stella was told about it by Mimsie Marker as she bought a paper from the stall by the Tube station and by the chemist when she bought some aspirin. (And if ever a woman needed it, I do.)

She had not heard about Annie Briggs's similar fears. She had hardly any knowledge of the Creeley family.

MURDER IS ALWAYS noticed locally. People come to stare at the home of the victim, some take photographs. The media is always there, although they melt away as a new story breaks. The police take their time in measuring, photographing, and taking samples for forensic investigation.

The body of the victim seems forgotten.

Not in this case, however, since she had a beautiful and much photographed body and that body had been loved by a well-known MP.

Used, said the local feminist organization, used and abused and finally sacrificed. This group of women who had a club room in Spinnergate admired Stella Pinero, deplored her marriage to John Coffin (A policeman, just think! She was better free!) and disliked Job Titus, MP. They were pretty libertarian, this group of Feather Street ladies, and did not advocate sexual austerity for men, women or beasts; they liked sex themselves, they just hated Titus's way of going about it. They thought he was a coarse fellow.

Coffin was soon made aware that the murder of Marianna Manners was not going to be an easy one to handle. The appearance of Job Titus on various TV news flashes, of Job Titus as he left his flat to go to the House of Commons or walked his dog in the park, reminded him of this even if he had felt like forgetting. Apart from anything else, Titus was demanding police protection from the harassment of the media while issuing threats of legal action if his name was mentioned as a suspect.

Because of the sensitivity of the case, Coffin kept himself informed of all that went on in the Murder Room which had been set up in a church hall in Swinehouse on the border of Spinnergate, close to where she had lived and been murdered in the block of flats in Alexandra Wharf, near to Napier Street where Annie Briggs lived.

There had been a good many changes in the Serious Crime Section in the last year or so as Coffin had worked through his senior police officers and weeded out the weaker members of the team by means of early retirement, sideways promotion, and in one case by death. The unit was now smaller and more efficient.

Archie Young headed all important cases, and had taken personal charge of this one. It was important for Young as well as John Coffin, he was a very ambitious man. His wife, Alison, knew this trait and used her influence on him to moderate an open show of it. She was cleverer than he was and knew that ambition had to be masked. She valued her friendship with Stella Pinero which both of them used to communicate worries about their husbands and to put a brake on the men when it seemed wise. Both of them were convinced that without their efforts their spouses would be dead of overwork.

'She was strangled and stifled but there was no rape, no semen traces, nothing like that . . . All the same, the pathologist thinks there might have been some sexual satisfaction involved.'

'Why?'

'He thinks the killer took his time about it, that's all. Getting some kicks.'

'How does he know? About the going slow?' It was not a picture he was going to cherish.

'I don't know. Something to do with the bruising, the flow of blood. Or perhaps he's just guessing. Percy's good at guessing.' Professor Percy Peters had worked with them, on and off, for some years now. They knew him well enough to value his intuitions. He had been at it so long that he seemed to have developed a sympathetic link with both killer and victim.

It was that or black magic, Young said, and he was a rationalist by long habit. Inside himself, he admitted that Percy could make his flesh creep.

'Been turning up some things about her lifestyle. She was a good dancer and an actress as well, apparently they all have to do everything now, even a bit of singing. She was unemployed a lot.'

'Aren't they all?' Coffin had been well schooled in the politics of The Profession by his wife.

'She took what work she could get.' He paused. 'Did a stint at Karnival in Ladd's Alley.'

Coffin raised an eyebrow.

'Yes, the transvestite club. No evidence that she was into that, for her it was work. Or probably.'

He said probably because, unlike Percy Peters, he was no mind-reader and how could you know what went on inside people? Maybe Marianna had found it agreeable to dress up as a man. She was a tall, muscular girl and would have looked the part.

Karnival was a club for those who wanted to dress up and dance. It also offered a cabaret.

Fun, Fizz, Frou-Frou and Frolic, it advertised.

It was well run and although probably seedy-looking in the hard light of day, in the evening managed to be most of the things it promised.

'Ever been there, sir?'

'Yes, once. I was watching a female impersonator. He was good, the whole act was good, even I thought he was good and I knew who and what he was.' He had had to arrest him, though, but for theft not for dressing up. 'Of course, I think some of them get the most kick out of a man who doesn't manage to look quite like a woman. Or a woman who doesn't quite fit together as a man, however butch she is. The other sex still hanging out seems to give more of a thrill.'

'And that's where Titus seems to have met her.'

'Good lord!' Coffin breathed in sharply. 'Now you have surprised me. What was he doing there?'

'He's straight as far as we know.' And the Special Branch usually did know that sort of thing and had been approached by Young. 'He may be a bit of a voyeur. I think he visited for the hell of it. Just to look and pry.' He didn't like Job Titus. 'Anyway, he picked up Marianna there. So maybe they both had something in common.'

'A lovely man.' Coffin considered. 'How did you get this?'

'Judy Kinnear, Special Branch. She keeps an eye on him, just in case. I knew she'd be on to whatever there is to know, it's her job. And I've known her for years. Worked together once. Before she moved over to Special. Do you know her, sir?'

Coffin shook his head. 'Know the name.'

'She looks like a hard-faced bitch, but when you get to know her she's one of the best.'

'I don't suppose Titus is a security risk?'

'No,' said Archie Young regretfully. 'Not much chance. He's not in the government nor likely to be. He might be a killer, though.'

'Worth having a look round at Karnival. Marianna might have run into someone there who killed her.'

'Or she could have met a man anywhere and taken him home. Or it might be an old friend that we know nothing about yet. Or she might have been watched and followed, as she said. If Titus didn't make that up.'

'Interesting that he was seen talking to young Creeley.'

'I'm told that the young Creeley is a reformed character and could never harm a woman. That's the latest word on him.'

'The entry book is wide open,' said Coffin, 'and we don't know the names of the runners.'

'She auditioned for a production at the St Luke's Theatre; an amateur affair. Do you think Miss Pinero would know anything about her?'

They were all careful how they brought in Stella's name; the Chief Commander had been known to be savage, and he was not a man whose bark was worse than his bite.

'She has nothing to do with that production,' said Coffin. 'But I did ask her.' He added: 'I'm worried about her.'

'I had heard. Don't you worry, sir. We won't let anyone touch her.' If there was an 'anyone' and it wasn't Job Titus.

STELLA HAD SAID NO, she had not been present when Marianna was auditioned, the producer of the play with a colleague from the Drama Department at the University had that task. A lot of hopefuls were coming to be auditioned because it was known a Drama School was being established and that this was a kind of pre-run.

The news had been on the local radio, and she herself had been interviewed on Docks TV. In a time of recession it was good news. Yes, she was able to say all the groundwork had been done, the constitution of the school settled: it was to be registered as a charity, the Rector of the University was going to be one of the trustees, and Lady Barningham, another. The school had already been accepted by the local education authorities so students would be eligible for grants. Yes, they expected some mature students also. The name was going to be the Pinero School of Dramatic Art.

Yes, they had the premises: the old Rectory of St Luke's which had housed a private secretarial school, now defunct, would be converted. Later, they would build.

'Might be a lot later,' said Letty gloomily. She flexed her hands nervously, she had long delicate fingers which she loaded with rings. She favoured heavy smooth gold. 'Money's tight.'

Her gloom might have been entirely due to the economy but Stella knew her sister-in-law better. 'No news about Elissa?'

'No, I am having an interview with Tash tomorrow and he's going to report progress but from what he said on the telephone there isn't any.'

'I am sorry.'

'I do miss her so, I loved her even when we quarrelled.' A tear appeared in her eyes.

'Here.' Stella went across to the drinks table and poured out a gin. 'Drink it up, mother's ruin but I reckon it helps.'

Letty looked at the glass. 'Is there any ice?'

'Oh, you Americans. Yes, I'll get some.'

She came in with a bowlful of ice lumps and some sliced lemon. 'I'll have one with you. I don't feel too jolly myself.'

'Your daughter? How is she?'

Stella's daughter was in The Profession but had recently married.

'She telephoned from Edinburgh this morning to say she is expecting twins. I can't believe it. I didn't even know she was pregnant. I've only just got used to her being married.'

Letty dabbed the tears from her eyes and managed a grin. 'Hello, Grandma.'

'Yes. I won't be called Gran or Granny.'

'What will John say?'

'Grandpa?' Their eyes met and they both began to laugh. 'Serve him right for marrying a woman of my age.'

She was slightly, very slightly, older than her husband whom she had first met as a raw young detective, had loved, quarrelled with, and left. Only to meet him again and repeat the process. They had met for the third time and this time had married. It had to last.

'He'll probably be very, very pleased.'

'He's lucky, very lucky, to have you,' said Letty. 'You keep him this side of sanity.'

'Oh, he's very sane.'

'I don't think his is a job you stay sane in, you see so much that's corruptible and devious and horrible. I've seen him have terrible rages.'

'Not so much as he used to have.'

'They were nearly all inside, I don't suppose he let them show. We're a very odd family.'

'That diary,' said Stella.

'Exactly.'

A few years ago a diary kept by the mother of the three, John, Letty and brother William, had been discovered in an attic. It revealed a life even more full of lovers, strange adventures and alarming anecdotes than anyone had suspected. None of the three had memories of their mother, whose habit had been to see each child was looked after by someone else as she moved on. Moving on was her speciality.

Letty had handed it over to Coffin to read and edit with the idea of publishing it. A film had been talked about. She might put money in herself. That was when she had money, she thought regretfully, that lovely liquid stuff.

Stella had her regrets too. 'I read some of it when there was this idea of a film. I wouldn't have minded getting the part of Ma but I thought she was a liar. Did you believe it?'

'Believe, what's believe?' Letty nodded tolerantly. 'But it was fantastic and a marvellous read. I thought: Well, if that's my mother, I hope I have inherited some of her flair. She could live, that woman.'

'Several lives at once,' said Stella.

Letty leaned forward. 'You know the thing I dread most . . . and it's why I gave up the idea of a film: she might still be alive. She might be alive and come forward and say, That's me. I began to have dreams, nightmares, in which she came back; she tapped me on my face and I woke up and there she was, standing by my bed. That was when the nightmare began.'

'I think John has a nightmare like that,' said Stella. 'Perhaps that's why he married me.'

'No, oh no.' Letty's lips curved in a smile of great sweetness which yet echoed some expressions of her brother's face. 'He married you for one reason only: that he loved you and could not see life without you.'

Stella shook her head. 'We all have our own nightmares, and mine is that one day he will say, Well, that's it, Stella, sorry it didn't work. Goodbye.'

'He's worried about you at the moment,' said Letty abruptly. 'But he's taking measures.'

'Yes, I've seen the patrol cars going past. But they can't watch me all the time. One day I might go round a corner or get in a lift and there he is with a knife or a gun, and no one to stop him. And sometimes I have an even worse fear: that he horribly, terribly likes me.'

This time it was Letty who poured them both a strong gin.

Then they turned to discussing the appointment of the Principal of the School of Drama for which they had several good candidates.

It was not until Letty left that Stella went back to look again at the ring of white roses found on the mat before her front door.

It was a small ring of blooms, more funeral than celebratory, with a chewed and torn appearance as if it had been about the world a bit. Tiddles the cat had been on it and may have been responsible for the depressing, even menacing look.

As she took the roses in her hand, she thought: And they're not even real roses. A card fell out on to the mat. A small old card which, like the flowers, looked as if this was not its first use. It said: LOVE.

THAT EVENING, up the stairs in Coffin's tower, she handed them over to her husband. He had an apron on and was in the kitchen.

A pleasant smell as of savoury chicken greeted her. They had arranged to cook in turns and her husband was now doing his part. Even acting the part with his striped butcher's apron. She guessed the food had come from a famous store which specialized in providing prepared food. She congratulated him, she would do the same. She did do the same, had been doing so for weeks. No good pretending that they were an orthodox domestic pair.

Dinner was quiet and attended by both animals, cat and dog, who received their own bowls of food with suspicious pleasure. The cat had taught Bob to inspect what he ate before touching a mouthful in case it was poisoned and the dog had taught Tiddles to eat fast or the chap next to you in the feeding line might get it.

'I shall be staying the night.'

'I should hope so.' He was surprised it had to be mentioned. On the whole, their nights were spent in his tower. At first Stella had called it romantic, now she just called it home which he liked even better.

The wreath of plastic roses rested on a bookcase by them.

'I feel more nervous than ever. What can you do with the roses?'

He poured her some more wine and looked across at the wreath, sitting in a melancholy way is if it had a life of its own on the bookcase by the window where Tiddles often sat.

'I don't suppose the roses take fingerprints well, although you never know, but it shall go off for forensic examination.' He drank some wine himself. 'No one saw it delivered?'

'Who could I ask?' said Stella. 'Letty didn't know anything.'

'People from the theatre... coming and going?'

Stella shrugged. 'I'll try. But I don't think so.'

'Don't worry too much.' But he was worried himself.

'But don't you see, he's coming closer. Closer. He knows my face and I don't know his.'

'Come to bed. It'll seem better in the morning.'

Stella smiled. 'The nice thing about being married is that there is the morning as well as the night.'

Coffin traced his finger delicately down her profile. 'You have a very charming nose, did you know it?'

Without warning he remembered the face of Marianna Manners, seen in the police morgue that morning. She too had a nice nose but one now suffused with dark colour.

An actress, like his Stella, but not so talented or successful with her chewed fingernails. Trying, though, to justify her Equity card, taking whatever part she could get.

'Did you ever hear of the Karnival Club?' he asked Stella.

Stella looked surprised. 'Yes, I know about it. Why do you ask?'

'Marianna Manners had an engagement there. She was at the Karnival a week. It was where she met Job Titus.'

'I went there once,' said Stella.

'You did?'

'I was producing a play about a transvestite. I wanted to get it right.'

'Did it help?'

'So-so. The production was scrapped anyway.'

He wouldn't question her now, but tomorrow, in the morning, he would get out of her the date and details of her visit.

But he couldn't resist one question. 'What did you wear?'

She considered. 'Well, it was work. I didn't dress up.' Hastily she added, 'Not that way, or any way. It was summer. Jeans and a shirt, I think.'

One more question had to be asked now after all. 'Which summer?'

'This summer. When it was hot, in June.'

This summer, not so long ago. Not too long ago for a person to have seen both Marianna and Stella.

Damn, he thought. Damn and damn and damn.

FIVE

Thursday. Down Napier Street

MORNING DID NOT ALWAYS bring joy. Annie woke up with a headache and a gut feeling of worry. 'Always worse in the morning,' she told herself. She battled against misery, always had, she was a fighter.

Annie cleared away the breakfast and took her daughter to nursery school. Didi was still asleep, she seemed to use more than the average ration of oblivion. Annie couldn't remember if she had been that way herself but she thought not. Sleep, surely, had been a commodity hard to come by after that episode in the garden. Moreover, there had been a generation change and it had happened between Annie and Didi, a matter of some ten years. Girls were different now.

Her thoughts veered away to Caroline Royal. Caroline, the tenant upstairs, was someone she thought about often. As soon as Caroline had rented the flat, Annie had known she was going to be important in her life. There was something different about Caroline.

CAROLINE'S FLAT at the top of Annie's house was always beautifully in order but with an empty feeling to it, as if Caroline left nothing behind when she went out to work. It was hardly her home because she travelled so much. Perhaps Heathrow was where she really lived.

Annie went up the outside staircase next day, the day after her conversation with Tom Ashworth. Didi was out doing whatever Didi did every day. She said she was working at Max's Delicatessen near St Luke's Theatre and much frequented by those acting at the theatre and their hopeful hangers-on who thought there might be an agent or a company scout drinking coffee and nibbling Max's special almond brioches, but Annie doubted if she was there all the time.

Annie had a key which she used so that she could see if any post was accumulating for Caroline. She had an address to which to send it and if she felt like it, she did so send it. Occasionally, if the place looked dusty she would give a quick flick round with a duster but she didn't bother much. Caroline would not notice. One of the things that Annie had observed about Caroline was her relative indifference to the appearance of where she lived and the freedom this gave her. Annie saluted her for all her freedoms.

There was no post.

Annie looked around. The flat felt empty but no one knew better than Annie that appearances were deceptive. She stood on the threshold and let the silence of the flat sink into her.

'Caroline, Caroline,' she murmured, half aloud. 'Keep Charley tethered today. Don't let him out.'

Is Charley a dog, Annie said sadly to herself, as she locked the door behind her and went down the stairs, that I must talk about him so?

ANNIE WENT BACK to her sitting-room where she settled herself at the table with her books to do her essay of the week on the Treaty of Vienna. She was a slow worker, but thorough.

Didi came back at lunch-time. She was late and tired. 'Had a rush,' she complained. 'I had to help at the counter as well as the tables and my feet ache.' She kicked off her shoes. 'Can I get you something?'

'Some coffee if you're making it,' said Annie, her head still bent over her notes.

'Can do.' Didi padded off to the kitchen. The sisters were fond of each other and happy in each other's company most of the time.

'Why didn't you stay to eat at Max's?' Annie called after her.

'Wanted to get away. More of a break.'

'I suppose so.' Annie wondered sceptically if Didi had an arrangement to meet someone later that day and wanted to change her clothes. She had noticed the phenomenon before. Better not be the Creeley boy.

Didi came back with two mugs of coffee.

'I prefer a cup,' said Annie.

'You get more in a mug and mugs it is.'

It was a generation thing again, thought Annie. She was the cup and saucer generation. When had the division arisen? The mugs of infancy now carried on for ever. Perhaps today's adults or near-adults like Didi were trying to stay as children.

Profound thought. She made a note of it to tell her tutor.

Didi sipped some coffee and was ready to gossip. She had decided what she would change into for tonight. Red and black. Dramatic. 'Miss Pinero had a wreath of roses left on her door.' Stella had come in to Max's for breakfast where she had chattered away to her sister-in-law who was also there. Didi had listened in without shame. Sometimes she thought she was meant to, those in The Profession like to be heard.

'Well, lucky her.'

'She didn't think it was well meant. It sounded tatty. Chewed up. Plastic anyway. Didn't Caroline have one like that? I seem to remember.'

'Goodness, I don't know.' As it happened, Caroline had had such a wreath. 'Didn't know you went up there.' Annie put her head down and tried to get back to her books.

'Well, I don't. Not now. But I went up there to help when Caroline first moved in. I liked her then . . . that was before . . .'

'Before what?'

'Before she got so peculiar.'

'She's not peculiar.'

'Well, away so much. I know you like her.'

'Admire her,' said Annie. 'Career woman, good job. I'd like to be what she is.'

Didi said: 'I'm going to audition at St Luke's tonight.'

'Thought you'd done that.'

'Yes, I did. But I was too modest. Only auditioned for a small part. Cough and a spit, you know. I'm going for a bigger part. So don't worry if I'm late back. Lot to pack in.'

Annie got up. 'I've got to get the child from nursery school.'

'Thought she stayed all day on Thursday,' said Didi.

'You manage your life and I'll manage mine.'

'All right, don't be cross. I only said it, didn't mean anything. I'll collect her for you if you like.'

Annie left her coffee unfinished and went on. 'Sorry, mustn't be late.'

Didi waited until Annie banged the door behind her, then she took the mugs into the kitchen and left them in the sink. Then she changed her clothes as she had planned. Her face needed repair too, and she was slow about it. Her nails were beginning to grow but too many auditions and she might start chewing again.

Finally, she closed the front door behind her carefully, you couldn't be too careful in this district.

She hoped Caroline upstairs was careful.

WHILE THEY WERE OUT, Caroline, if it was Caroline, came in. She couldn't stay, she was in her usual hurry.

The place was tidy, she always left it tidy and there was no need for Annie to come in and dust.

She went into her bedroom, looked over her clothes. They were not many in number because she liked quality, and they were what she called 'mood' clothes. She stroked one or two pieces with a smile.

I always look good in that. Lovely cloth. She held the jacket up against her. Mustn't put on weight. Not much chance of that, the way she worked and kept on the move. It needs a press, though.

Well, it could wait. She gathered up her hat, and her big despatch case which marked her out as a person who had important business to attend to every hour. This person is me, she said to herself, and sex doesn't come into it.

She was very conscious of that other presence, even if a quiet one. Asleep, must be asleep, she supposed. Not drunk, although she kept a bottle of whisky in the cupboard. All the same, accepting his sobriety as taken, sometimes more of the whisky was gone than she would have expected. Then she would replace the bottle without allowing herself to think too much about it.

She went to the window. A lot of lunatics out there. There was a man who was building Stonehenge in his garden, and for all she knew he was putting up a pyramid in the back yard. Symbols, she supposed, of something or the other.

Then there was the woman down at Spinnergate Tube Station who sold newspapers. She herself bought a paper there if the headlines looked interesting, although she tried to have the change always ready and be unobtrusive about it in case Mimsie noticed everything as she was reputed to do. Mimsie Marker always wore the same sort of flowered hat in summer and one with feathers in the winter, she kept loose change in a leather pouch like a kangaroo, and lived in a basement near the police station. And yet the story was she had a mansion in Epping and owned a Rolls. If that wasn't mad, she didn't know what sanity was.

The police were out there too. As a protection, of course. But also as interfering, sceptical, unbelieving, nosey-parkers.

And murderers also walked.

She was really undecided what to do for the best, but time was short. She could get him up, see if he was still alive. But she knew he was. Had to be. There is death and death, and she knew Charley was not dead. Better if he was, maybe. She decided not to question the matter.

As she left, she said: 'Don't move today, Charley. Better not, stay where you are. I've read your horoscope and I know it's best for you. I have business to attend to.'

Sadly she thought that this person that she was, that she had become, had to say that kind of thing.

NAPIER STREET led into Fedan Street and Fedan Street turned right into Dockland Road, the busy artery which had the headquarters of the Police Authority, where the Chief Commander had his offices at one end and Karnival, the transvestite club, stood at the other.

John Coffin drove down Dockland Road early on the afternoon of that Thursday. He was on his way back to his own office after a boring morning on a dull but necessary committee. Not even any quarrels, which usually livened up the desert of three hours' staring at an agenda on controlling London's traffic when everyone knew that nothing could be done short of banning all traffic or knocking the capital down and starting again. You cannot control the uncontrollable and road traffic these days seemed to be a force of nature: always growing faster than you allowed for. His own district had its own particular problem of just one big artery in and out. Dockland Road joined this artery at an angle and then made its own way, as it had since Saxon times, out towards the Estuary.

He remembered the road well with all its junctions and blockage points. He never minded going slowly because it made for thinking time, something he was seriously short of.

As he drove, he was considering the death of Marianna and wondering what part, if any, the Karnival Club played in it. He had to pass where it was and might look in. Stella had been there too; he had a personal interest now.

Dockland Road was long and winding, nothing straight about it. Karnival was in Leathergate, at the western end of his bailiwick. A little bit further west and Karnival would have been sitting in the lap of the Tower of London and been the responsibility of the City of London Police. As it was, it was for him.

A narrow passage, Ladd's Alley, turned off to the west; this cul-de-sac was where the club had been for the last twenty years. No name, no one needed a name. It was marked, however, in its own way. A big lavender-coloured urn stood in a recess above the door. At night a single light shone on it. This was how you knew it. 'Going down the Lav,' was how the frequenters put it. An old joke that no longer caused a giggle.

The club was housed in what had been a garage and the cul-de-sac had been its cobbled forecourt. There was nothing smart about the Karnival but at night it looked cosy and friendly.

Closed and shuttered as it was now, it looked depressing. He sat in his car surveying it from the road. Then he got out and walked down Ladd's Alley. Presumably in the distant past it had been Ladd's Garage.

On the other side of the alley was another door, painted red with a legend curving round the top of the door: STAND UP AND SHOUT FOR JESUS. He wondered if there was much shouting and what Karnival thought about it and what happened when both clubs were in full shout. But Karnival had the reputation of being a quiet and well-behaved club.

There was a car parked on the cobbles. In the gloom he could see a man sitting in it. Men sitting in parked cars in blind alleys arouse the instant interest if not downright suspicion of the police, and from long training John Coffin reacted.

He went over, rapped on the window and stared inside at the man.

Tom Ashworth pulled down the window. He recognized the Chief Commander at once, it was his job to know that sort of thing, and jumped out of the car. 'Just taking a look.'

Coffin said nothing.

'As you are yourself,' Ashworth added. 'It's closed. No one there. I've tried the bell.'

He wasn't nervous, Coffin thought, but self-conscious.

'One of your clubs?' he asked.

'Only in the way of business. If I've got to watch someone.'

There are people in this world you have to know but don't want to go on knowing, and I think you're one of them, Coffin decided.

'Are you watching anyone at the moment?'

Ashworth was silent, his eyes thoughtful. He looked across the road at the SHOUT FOR JESUS.

'Wonder if they ever do?' he said. 'And if the Karnival crowd join in?' He decided he would talk. 'I've been looking over Job Titus. I didn't come here to watch him the first time, another job altogether, but when I saw him here I was interested. Not that he did anything. He behaved himself, sat there drinking and talking, just like a constituency meeting, didn't get up to dance or anything. Not with anyone or by himself, a few do that.'

'No law against it.'

Ashworth grinned. 'No, but an awful lot of prejudice.'

'In certain quarters,' said Coffin in a neutral tone. He had nothing against anyone who danced with himself. Stella had taught him to be open-minded and generous in certain important ways. It was part of the gift of living that she had brought with her.

But Job Titus, he did not like.

'All over the front pages today, isn't he? On some mercy mission, heaven help the poor sods who get him. I reckon you really know you're in trouble when Titus flies in.'

Coffin was aware that Job Titus had flown from Heathrow that morning, his departure and return had been quietly agreed upon. He'd be back tomorrow.

'He knew the girl that was killed. I expect you know that? If you're doing your job, you should.' He took Coffin's silence for assent. 'Don't know if he met her here or came here to see her. They were talking away.' He added carefully, 'Quarrelling, I think. Yes, I think you'd call it quarrelling. Not shouting or anything but bitching quietly.'

His eyes went distant again. 'You see some faces there all right, dressed in this and dressed in that, some you know, some you don't. Anyway, now I'm watching him for a client, because he's seeing someone I don't care for very much. Scion of a murderous clan.'

He talked like that sometimes.

Creeley, thought Coffin. This is where our paths cross. And again he thought of Stella. Had Titus and Eddie Creeley seen her there? Creeley had been back from New Zealand by last summer.

He looked at his watch. 'I'm going back to the office. Follow me, let's have a talk.'

'I've got an appointment,' said Ashworth hastily.

Coffin ignored this. 'And you can tell me why you are here now today.'

'Watching,' said Ashworth, as he got back into his car. 'Looking around. Just like you.'

Coffin sat him in a chair with a view of the river if you sat tall and had good long sight, and poured him a drink. 'You look nervous,' he said kindly.

'You make me nervous.'

'So what took you into Karnival? The first time?'

'Another bit of business,' said Tom vaguely. He wanted to keep his secrets.

'And you saw Titus there with the girl? Well, we know about that. But you've also seen Titus with Edward Creeley? You get about a bit.'

'I'm looking after things for Annie Briggs if you remember who she is.'

'Oh, I remember all right.'

'So she's nervous, and she has this idea that young Creeley is out to get her. Revenge, you know, family honour. Of course, Auntie's coming out, plus Uncle who's not with us in the world any more, so perhaps he doesn't mind too much about the honour, if he ever did.'

'And you've been keeping an eye on him.'

'Sort of.'

'And while doing that, you saw him drinking with Titus? Are you suggesting he was a hired killer?'

Ashworth looked nervously around the room. 'Is this being taped? That'd be slander or libel or something, wouldn't it?' He was acting more naïve than he really was. He saw Coffin's sceptical look and decided to tone it down a bit. 'It struck me as odd, that meeting. But Titus has interested himself in the Creeley case and may even have been responsible for getting Lizzie out.'

'You're well informed.' Coffin wasn't quite so kind now.

'I listen to things.'

'And what were you doing in the alley today? Apart from looking around, of course.'

Tom Ashworth felt the scepticism in the Chief Commander's voice and shifted uneasily.

'I had a contact there. Chap I knew. I was going to ask him if he'd seen the Creeley boy there.'

What a liar you are, thought Coffin. One day I'll find out what the lie is. But he was half indulgent: he knew well that secrets are a private detective's stock in trade.

'With or without Job Titus, MP,' Tom went on. 'I was interested, it establishes character, doesn't it? The sort they are. I wanted to know.'

'And what sort is young Creeley?'

'You don't know him?'

Coffin shook his head.

'I've got a photograph.' From an inner pocket, Tom took a coloured photograph which he handed over.

He waited quietly while Coffin studied it. A tall, plump-ish, fair-haired young man was leaning forward over a bar-room table talking to Job Titus. He had a pleasant boyish face without a lot of expression. Titus seemed to be doing the talking.

'I don't think he's a killer,' said Ashworth, 'but I'm not sure.'

'You're doing our job for us.' Coffin handed over the photograph. 'Let me have a copy, will you?'

'Sure.' He reached inside his pocket. 'Here's another.'

'You're worrying me,' said Coffin, as he reached across to take it. 'What else is on offer?'

He didn't wait for an answer.

This time the photograph was of the same young man still wearing the expression of empty good humour as if he couldn't take it off. He was seated at another table in an-other bar with a young woman. He had his arm round her shoulders.

'Who's the girl?'

'Didi, she's the sister.'

Coffin raised an eyebrow.

'Annie Briggs's sister. Years younger.'

'She's a beauty. Creeley's seeing her?'

'I think she's in love with him. Could be. If she's not in love with someone called Charley.' He sounded thoughtful. 'I can't get clear on that.'

'Who's Charley?'

'It's a name that crops up.'

'Where?'

'You could ask that and get different answers. Here and there. Movable man, is Charley. The Karnival for a start. Odd bars. You know the picture.'

'Was Charley the reason you went to the Karnival?'

'Let's say I was interested.'

Was he into blackmail? 'Does Titus know Charley?'

'I haven't been able to establish that,' said Tom with obvious regret.

'Why were you interested?'

'I am interested. It's my job. You never know what will be useful. Like the kid, Didi, with the Creeley boy. What's the relationship there? Boy and girl? Or something else? Anyway, they meet a lot. My client is the kid's sister, I don't think my client knows too much about it. Should I tell her? Well, maybe I will and maybe I won't.' He held out his hand for the picture but Coffin was still studying it. 'Meanwhile I'm keeping an eye on him which is what I'm paid for.' Not that Annie had paid him yet. Not a penny. But she would do. Tom knew how to get his bills settled.

'A copy of that picture too, please.'

'Right.' He put the photograph back in his pocket and as he did so, another fell out. Coffin picked it up. This time the picture was of a middle-aged man holding open the iron gate to a tall house up whose side ran an iron fire staircase, an escape route from the top floor.

'And who's that?'

'I had to do a bit of research there. He's a social worker, helped in Annie's case as a youngster. I think he's in love with her. That's her house. He calls on her.'

'You *are* doing our work for us,' said Coffin.

A DAY BEGUN without joy does not always improve. This day did not.

In the late afternoon of the misty day, Stella, parking her car in the underground car park near the theatre complex, became aware of the figure in the gloom.

The basement was badly lit and she had long meant to complain to Letty who she believed owned the place. Letty had various bits of property around the district, more than she would admit to.

Her stalker. Tall, thin, in a long dark coat and soft hat. A spectre, a monster.

She didn't have to pass the figure to get out. There was a flight of steps just at hand. She could turn and run.

But a nervous fascination seemed to put a brake on her legs. If she moved them it would be like walking through sand. So she stood where she was.

So did the man. In the dim light she saw he was holding a large white sheet of cardboard or something. Big black letters staggered across it.

I LOVE YOU. I WANT TO BE YOU.

She felt as if he had said he wanted to eat her. Stella turned and ran. As she ran she believed she could smell the man, smell his clothes, sour and stuffy as if he was made up of them and they only got into the air when he put them on.

Letty was in the forecourt when she got there and gripped her by the arm.

'He's back there,' Stella was shivering. Her brave resolution to get him torn away from her was dragging skin and blood with it.

'I'll go and get him,' said Letty. 'I'm not afraid.'

'I am, you might get killed.' Stella hung on to Letty and made her go into St Luke's Mansions with her. She had taken on an assailant once, had no choice really, it was that or be raped, but once was enough. She knew now you never got over it.

She didn't take in Letty's white face, being too engrossed with her own state. They each had a strong drink and then another.

When John Coffin came in they told him about the episode and he went to the telephone to send a blast down the line. Where was the watch over Stella?

A major bank raid had drawn all local patrol cars off, he was told.

ANNIE SAT OVER some coffee, she was tired, it had been a wearing day. She felt she had made no progress.

Didi was late. All this auditioning was a waste of time, but if it made her happy that was something. She was happy these days.

She poured herself some more coffee. Didi was very edgy about Caroline these days, with her question about the man in the upper flat.

I'd better explain things to her. Tell her that the man is one of those people that have agoraphobia. Can't bear to go out. Have to stay shut up.

Like in a cupboard.

Didi was still late. Too late.

SIX

Where the river runs

'GOOD,' said the killer. 'You've got it absolutely right. You've got a real feel for it.' He stood back from the wall, it was dripping wet anyway and he hated getting rain on his clothes. He could see she was flattered.

'Well, I'm new to it. Never done it before.'

'I couldn't have done it better myself.'

'Technically it's difficult, isn't it?'

'Technically, it's very difficult. These physical things always are, of course.'

'Mm.'

'You've got to think of it in terms of comedy, farce even. You've got to get everything in the right place at the right time or it won't work. Not the way it should. Smooth, easy. But natural, nothing forced.'

'Play it for real.'

'That's right. Good girl. You've got it.'

She shivered. 'It's cold here.'

'We're *in situ*. Always better to get the place correct.'

'Does the river come into it? I don't remember the river.'

'We have to think of it as a symbol... The river is time, isn't it? Running backwards and forwards. That's how it is.'

'But the river flows one way.'

'The Thames is tidal,' he reminded her. 'It ebbs and flows, back and forth.'

She was prepared to be awkward; her mood was always prickly when she was cold. Everyone who knew her knew that much, but he didn't know her well enough. Some things about her he had observed well, how she walked, how she wore her clothes, her legs, good, her hands, not so good, he always noticed hands; these things he had taken in, but not the way her moods swung.

'Time doesn't go backwards, though.' She was shivering. And the mud was marking her new shoes of suede, nearly suede, almost suede. After all, you wouldn't wear the skin of dead animals, would you? She looked down at the pale stone-coloured sandals and the stain on the toes sharpened her tongue. 'Bloody cold.'

'We think of the past,' he said gently.

'I'm cold.' It was cold and she wasn't dressed for cold weather. Not only were her shoes suffering but mud was spotting her nylons. He felt sorry for her.

Poor child, he felt sorry for her. Better get on with it.

'Shall we try again? Are you ready? Just lean your neck forward for me.' He stopped. 'You don't mind?'

'I think I do a little bit.'

'I can understand it. It's tricky, difficult the first time, but I'll go carefully.'

'I know you will.'

'Gentle. Think of it as making love.'

She giggled. 'Don't say that. My sister would die.'

'Then don't think about her.' There was a small pause while he fiddled with a machine.

'What are you doing? You're not taping this, are you? I don't like the idea of that. I mean, I'm not ready for that.'

'No, I promise, just the last bit. For technical reasons. Timing, you know.' He bent down again. Better get the sound level right. 'Just a small adjustment. I've got it. Say Eddie.'

She hesitated. 'Eddie, is that it?'

'Just say it.'

'Eddie . . . Eddie.'

She said nothing further. All that was necessary had been said.

SEVEN

Better not to think of the river

ANNIE SAT WAITING for her sister to come home. Didi was already late, seriously late. She did stay out late and her sister recognized her right to do this. There were no strict rules in that house, she had been out herself earlier that evening after all. With the life they both led there could not be timetables. But Didi was a considerate girl who told Annie if she was going to be very late, or else telephoned to let her know.

She had a strong suspicion that Didi was out with Eddie Creeley, one of the enemy. Perhaps at the moment *the* enemy. In her mind, Eddie seemed omnipresent; he might be with Didi, or he might be the figure seen earlier that night lurking in the shadows down the street. Annie knew it was mad and could not be fact and there might not be anyone there at all, just shadows in her mind (and goodness knows, there was reason for that), but sometimes the Creeleys seemed to her to have the power to be everywhere and to inhabit several bodies each.

But after all, it might just have been her own shadow against the street light.

Didi, where are you?

Annie watched the last television programme on the BBC and then switched to the all night channel. She sat there looking at an old film of Bob Hope without a muscle in her face moving, the laughs just wouldn't come.

She got up, took three deep breaths, then screamed. Not loudly but with a quiet strength. One of the psychologists she had seen, and plenty had had their hands on her, had said to her: Let it out. Scream. As loud as you like.

Annie had followed the advice in a modified, Annie kind of way. She very rarely followed advice in the way it was offered: it didn't seem to suit her body somehow. In the same way she never finished a bottle of medicine. In fact, usually she never took a dose. She had her own ways of effecting a cure for whatever ailed her. Not exactly faith cures but something very like it. She would say a little prayer to whichever god attracted her at the moment: Jehovah, Zeus, Buddha or even the anonymous just addressed as Thou.

The three quiet screams let out something inside her, never mind what, and did not disturb the neighbours who were old and slept badly but saw most things, as Annie knew to her cost.

After her three shouts, Annie went through to the kitchen to switch on the kettle. Hot tea always helped. It was a family tradition, indeed a national one, that hot tea was a help in time of crisis.

The kettle began to steam while she watched. *Heavens, I'm not keeping a prison here.* She warmed the pot, another myth probably but not one she was going to discard, you never knew. *Why shouldn't the girl be late home?*

But Annie knew, none better, the dangers that night and darkness could bring. There were some things that even hot tea could not assuage.

She drew back the blind to look at the day. A full moon sailed high but it was blotted every so often by thick clouds, the air was wet.

Didi doesn't like the rain. And I bet she'd got on those pale shoes that show every mark. I told her when she bought them that they would show every mark.

On that moonlit night so long ago Annie herself had been wearing bedroom slippers. Her parents had not looked out of the window to see her, so that they had known nothing until morning. They knew she had been in the garden because of the mud on her slippers and pyjamas. She got a beating for that. 'Naughty girl, naughty girl.'

Annie kept quiet about what she had seen for several days after that, nor was she believed at first when she spoke. 'Little girls shouldn't tell fibs.' They believed me in the end, she said grimly to herself.

She left the kitchen to go to the room in the front, taking her cup of tea with her. She might see Didi just opening the gate. If she went to the gate, then she might see Didi just turning the corner of the road, hurrying home.

Surely she would not be on her own? He was bound to see her home. Even that rotten Creeley boy would see Didi home. Eddie Creeley, I hate you.

As she stood there, her daughter crept into the room. 'Why are you still up, Mummy, and not in bed?' She managed to make it sound like a reproach. She was sometimes more in charge of her mother than Annie was of her. She dropped her voice a tone. 'Naughty Mummy.'

Annie put her arm round the child's shoulders, thin bony shoulders they were, but giving promise of growth. Wings might sprout from those shoulders and let her flutter away. Annie herself had thought as a child that she could fly.

'Looking for Didi, still out. She's the naughty one.'

'I heard you call out.'

'You might have done. Just one of my shouts. You ought to try one yourself. Shall we shout together?'

'I don't think so, thank you, Mummy.'

She was a quiet child who gave the impression that she found her mother a puzzle. Annie was not surprised, she found herself a puzzle.

'Back to bed, love.' She hoisted the child on her shoulder and took her upstairs, her long legs in trousers making nothing of the steep stairs. She was not a strongly maternal type, although a loving parent. She had to be mother and father both and somehow the father had the best of it. 'Up the wooden hill to Bedfordshire.'

Her daughter gave her a wary, sceptical, but friendly look as of one who had never found that particular bit of whimsy amusing yet could see her mother enjoyed saying it: the two loved each other.

Annie tucked the child comfortably in the blankets, they never used duvets, but the full outfit of sheet and blankets with an eiderdown in winter. 'Close your eyes and go back to sleep.'

The child dropped her eyelids obediently but with every intention of staying awake. She took a quick look.

'Quite closed,' said Annie.

She watched from the door with amusement, guessing her daughter's intention but knowing that sleep would win. Soon, she saw the light, regular breathing.

I never was a child like you, my dear, life caught up with me too soon, but you I will protect. I may not be the best of mothers or the most normal of mothers but I will see you get what is rightly yours. Be a child.

She left all the lights on to welcome Didi when she came in, then lay down, fully dressed in trousers and sweater, on her bed.

IT WAS MORNING when she awoke; she knew at once that Didi had not come back. Her room was empty, clothes thrown around just as she had left it yesterday, the bed untouched.

The sun was shining, the dampness drying from the air, she had slept longer than she had known.

Downstairs she faced her choice; she could telephone the police, she could get in touch with Alex Edwards, her social worker friend who knew the ropes and would be glad to help, too glad she thought sometimes, but you had to trust him. A creep, she sometimes castigated him inside herself, but a nice creep.

Or she could leave it, do nothing.

The dirty empty teacup and pot in the kitchen sink had to be washed before they could be used again. Once more to the ancient remedy, hot sweet tea but nothing to eat.

She was drinking it when she heard the newspapers drop through the letter-box. In pursuit of her new aim to be an educated woman, and at the same time prove she was more of a man than her husband (who read the *Sun,* if he read at all) she took *The Times* and the *Independent.*

As she picked up the papers, the doorbell rang.

She had the door open before she knew she had touched it. On the step was the street's community policeman, she didn't know his name but she knew his face.

'Didi,' she said. 'You've come about Didi.'

He picked up the milk which was sitting on the step. 'Can I come in? Here's the milk, want it in the kitchen?' He was on his way there with Annie following. 'No, not Didi. Nothing about her, she's your sister? No, it's the old couple next door, they say that they've seen lights at night in that flat of yours upstairs and they think you've got squatters.'

Annie was both relieved that he hadn't come to tell her that Didi was dead or in hospital and irritated by her neighbours. 'No, they're mad. What rubbish.'

'Not mad but a bit anxious. And since I'm on the look-out for a lad who absconded from a care home, I thought I'd have a look-see.' He put the milk in the refrigerator. 'The flat is empty?'

'No, it's not empty. Caroline isn't there very much. She travels on business.'

'She's away now?'

'I think so. Yes, she is.'

'Lights have been seen. It's upset the old pair next door.'

Then they shouldn't have been watching. 'She has a man friend, he's there sometimes.'

'Oh.' An appraising nod of the head. 'All right if I take a look? Next door says you have a key.'

Next door ought to mind their own business.

'I don't know if Caroline would want that.'

'She'd be grateful if we flushed out an intruder, wouldn't she?'

'Yes, I suppose so.' Annie produced the key reluctantly. 'I'm coming with you. But I mustn't be long, my child is asleep upstairs and there's no one in the house. My sister hasn't been home all night.'

He followed her out of the house and up the outer staircase to the flat above. 'Young is she, your sister? She'll be back. All night party, I expect. There was a big one on a boat on the river last night, I'm surprised you couldn't hear it.'

Annie stood back while he looked over the flat which was empty and quiet as she had known it would be.

'Told you there was no one here.'

The policeman opened doors and cupboards. 'She keeps it tidy.'

'I do that.'

'Housekeep for her, do you?'

'Sort of.'

'One of those career girls, is she?' He opened a cupboard door. 'He's been here, though.' Inside were male clothes and shoes. 'That jacket is wet. Damp anyway.'

Annie said nothing.

Politely he took himself off, whether satisfied or not, she did not know. Experience had taught her that policemen did not always tell you what they were thinking.

WHEN HE HAD GONE she telephoned Tom Ashworth's office, only to find his answering machine explaining that the office was not yet open but she could leave a message.

She left no message, but tried to call Alex Edwards. His office was open and answering but he was not there. She left no message.

At last, angrily, she telephoned the Creeley house.

'I want to speak to Eddie.'

'Speaking,' said a sleepy voice. 'Who's that?'

'I want to know where you've been all night and where my sister is. Is she there? Ask Didi to speak to me.'

There was a pause. 'Look, I don't know what you're on about. I've been in bed all night. I'm still in bed if you want to know, and I haven't seen Didi. A nice girl and that, but she isn't here with me.'

He banged the telephone down and Annie, after standing still for a moment, raged around the house calling upon her numerous gods for help, especially the unknown called Thou.

She was releasing into the world a stream of energy channelled into violence and anger. It would stir up something, it always had done.

DIDI TRIED VERY HARD to be found. She was dead but she kept on trying. The wind blew round her body, the damp underneath seeped through her pretty light dress, pieces of paper and autumnal leaves from the trees by the river settled upon her.

There was no life in her but she meant to be found.

Who will find Didi?

She was lying under a railway arch close to the river, where a narrow patch of rough ground ran down to the water. As train after train travelled overhead bearing commuters into London, the old archway shifted.

Didi rolled forward out into the open air. She was going to be found.

A MAN GOING TO FISH for anything that moved and would bite in the Thames saw her body and thought she was someone sleeping in the rough.

Poor cow, he thought.

Two lads, bunking off from school, skipped past Didi next but took no notice. Only as it began to rain again and they decided school might be best after all, did they give her a second look.

They stared at each other, then one of them galloped over to the man fishing. 'Mister, there's a dead 'un there.'

'Never,' he said, not raising his eyes from his rod. 'She's just getting her beauty sleep. Leave her be.'

But Didi was strong to be found and he rose up to take a look. He had served in the army and knew death when he saw it; he had also seen violent death and knew that too.

He considered quietly sloping away and not getting mixed up but neither the boys nor Didi would permit that.

'Well, lads, it's a technical problem here: which of us stays and which of us goes for the police.'

He saw the answer in their eyes and sat down. 'Right, you go. One of you go and the other stay with me.' He turned to the one with red hair. 'What's your name?'

'Peter.'

'And yours?'

'Darren.'

'Right, Darren, then you go. And my name is Bill Beasden ... Got that? Then tell the duty officer, he knows me.'

'You a copper, then?' asked Darren, preparing to move.

Beasden grinned. 'Just known to the police.'

DARREN KNEW THE ROUTE to the nearest police station, boys in his way of life always stocked that sort of knowledge as a necessary item, but he had a certain natural reluctance to setting foot inside. He had been in there once and the man on the desk had said he didn't want to see him in there again and no more nonsense about Aliens Landing. So when he saw a tall man walking towards the entrance accompanied by a rangy-looking dog, he thought he had an ally.

'Sir, sir?'

'Yes, what is it?'

'Are you a policeman, sir?' If he said sir as often as possible, he felt safer.

'Yes, I am. So what is it?'

The words were said kindly if absently as if the speaker was concentrating on something else. It was not on the dog who was sniffing round the trouser edge of Darren's jeans with devoted attention.

'Sir, there's a body down by the river.' He edged away. 'Nice dog,' he said nervously. 'What's he called?'

'I call him Bob,' said John Coffin. 'He has been called other things.' He wasn't completely convinced about the body. Not all prone figures were dead or grateful to be reported. 'Sure it's dead?'

'Her, sir, her. It's a girl.'

'Right.' All seriousness now, Coffin got a firm grip on Darren's arm. 'Let's go inside and get the details. Where is she?'

'Near the arches, the bit near the river. I can show you.'

Darren thought he would rather be on the road, showing, than inside, talking and giving details. He knew details, they got you into trouble. Such as Why weren't you at school? and What's that in your pocket?

'Yes, you shall do.' Although he knew where Darren meant, knew the rough ground littered with the detritus of urban living like old bedsteads and dead cats. Every so often a group of homeless would set up camp but it was too hostile and bleak even for them. 'Anyone with you?'

'My friend Peter. He's still there, with her and Mr Beasden. He was fishing. He said to say it was him and you would know him.'

I've heard the name, thought Coffin, but know him I do not. Beasden had his place in the police world as a highly successful villain, now retired. Allegedly retired.

The officer on the desk was not the one Darren knew, which relieved him. After all, he was doing a public service, wasn't he? Reporting a crime.

Judging by the reception he and his new friend got (he felt this chap could be a friend, but not the dog), he judged he had picked himself a high ranking copper. He began to feel positively pleased with himself.

Excited by his moment of importance, he told what he knew, and found himself sitting in a car driven by his new friend leading a procession riverwards. That dog was there too.

Then suddenly he did not exist any more. They had his name and address, they were getting Peter's, they could both go away home. Would they like a lift? No? Better get back to school, then. The next question was inevitable, you could see it coming, and it speeded their departure: Why weren't they at school?

John Coffin walked over to them both as they left. He patted Darren on the shoulder and murmured something friendly, but the boys could see that his mind was not on them but on that still figure on the ground. A figure already being photographed.

'I expect we shall want to ask you some more questions, what you saw, if there was anyone around, that sort of thing, but don't worry. You behaved well. Tell your parents and your head teacher. Now hop off.'

Darren looked at Peter and Peter gave him one of his famous expressionless looks back.

'Come on,' said Darren. 'Better go.'

They climbed up to the road and turned schoolwards. Darren looked back. Several more police cars had arrived, as well as an ambulance. It was the most exciting scene he had ever been involved in; but he wasn't enjoying it as much as he would have expected. He had a sick, heavy feeling in the pit of his stomach.

There she was, the quiet centre of it all.

'Interesting, isn't it,' said Peter. 'I might go into the police, detective work, I'd like that. Shall we stay around?'

'No, let's go back.'

'Go into Woolies for a Coke?'

'No.' He shook his head. 'Let's get back to school.' He wanted to set his world to rights, to be, for once, a boy in good repute.

Darren walked away. It was all nothing to do with him. They had said so and it was the case.

No one had asked him, but he did know her. He had seen her around with Eddie Creeley and she was called Didi.

IN STELLA'S FLAT the telephone rang and rang. But Stella was asleep upstairs in her husband's bed.

Upstairs in Caroline's flat Charley put the telephone down.

EIGHT

The day continues

DIDI WAS SOON IDENTIFIED. One police officer knew her face, thought she came from Spinnergate but couldn't put a name to her. But that was soon cleared up because Didi had her name with her, almost as if she guessed it might be wanted.

Her handbag rested in the mud beside her. In it together with a lipstick and piece of tissue was a diary with her name and address in it. With carefully protected hands, an officer opened it, then quietly showed it to the Chief Commander. If the Boss was there, then he had better see.

Diana Dunne, 6, Napier Street. She had signed her name, given her date of birth, and provided her telephone number.

Coffin nodded. Just at that moment, he did not connect her with Annie Briggs, his mind was on the girl herself.

She had been strangled, but there were bruises on her face which might indicate she had also been smothered. Like Marianna.

John Coffin waited, silent but observing, as the police surgeon worked. Dr Foss was a wiry, youngish man. He nodded at the Chief Commander, whom he knew by sight.

'Well, she's dead.'

'And?'

'Strangled manually.'

'Yes, it looked like that. Hand over her face too, I'd say.'

A protective shield had been set up around Didi's body which was not yet readied for removal to the police mortuary down in Swinehouse, a new building opened only this year. Photographs were still being taken while other policemen walked carefully with eyes down examining the ground all around her. The full police investigating team headed by a detective-inspector had arrived. They were very aware of the presence of the Chief Commander among them.

The police surgeon, being an independent professional, felt more relaxed: he had his own territory in which he was lord. Accordingly, he felt comfortable enough to take out a cigarette in Coffin's presence and light it.

'I thought you people were against smoking.'

'I am. But it helps.'

The two men moved away a few yards into the shelter of the arch. This area too was being examined and they were careful where they trod.

'How long has she been dead?'

Dr Foss was professionally cautious. 'Matter of hours. Last night sometime, I'd say. But when they get her on the slab and open her up they will know better.'

Coffin winced slightly, making a note that delicacy was not a feature of Dr Foss's working life. What sort of bed-side manner did he have?

The second young woman strangled in the Second City within weeks. A repeat of this sort was something nobody liked. Marianna Manners and now Diana Dunne. 'The second one this month,' he said.

'Yes, the Manners girl. She was one of mine.' Dr Foss took a proprietary interest in the victims whose death he was paid to certify. The more important and interesting work on them might be done later by forensic pathologists but he was one who saw them first. 'Same MOD as the other girl. Manual, neat job.' He sounded almost admiring.

Coffin said nothing, Dr Foss did not grow on him.

'She didn't struggle.' He added: 'I had a quick look at her hands. Unmarked. Even the varnish isn't chipped. Of course, she chewed her fingernails so there wasn't much scratch in them.'

Nasty way he had of putting things, thought Coffin. 'So the killer probably won't be marked?' Marianna Manners hadn't struggled either.

'No. Pity.'

'A willing victim?' Coffin said.

Foss nodded slowly. 'You could say so.'

He delivered himself of a judgement: 'Looks as if we've got a serial killer here.'

'Fashionable beasts at the moment,' said Coffin absently. Get a run of killings and everyone cried serial killings. But they were not always. Killers imitated each other.

He could see the time had come to be tactful. It wasn't exactly that he had no business here, all police matters were his business, but the investigating team would prefer him to go away.

He eased himself away from Dr Foss who showed signs of giving a lecture on serial killers and their ways, and got into his car. To his surprise he found Bob there, asleep in the back of the car as he drove off.

'Forgotten you, old chap.' He hesitated. He was late already for a meeting and Bob was a problem. 'Right, you can go into the club.' He put a leash on Bob's collar, and led him across a courtyard to a white-painted building.

ONE OF THE Chief Commander's innovations had been a club, open to all ranks. A small building on the edge of the complex of offices and communication centres which made up his headquarters, growing all the time, had been turned into this club. Although on the small side, it was well set out with good carpets and comfortable chairs, nothing cheap or sordid. You could drink there, beer, whisky, fruit juice, anything (and at a lower price than in a pub) and get a light meal.

Although Coffin had no illusions that it would wean his Force from their favoured pubs, it was a place to which they could bring their wives and where he could drop in.

He did not do this often, he knew he had to keep certain rules, but he did so now and again. Coffin couldn't have mates and must never get drunk but he could meet people there and talk like a human being.

The club manager was a retired CID officer with a nose for good wines and the food came from Max's Delicatessen which now had a catering subsidiary. Despite competition from bigger concerns, Max was proving that a well-run family business could flourish.

Bob was deposited here with the manager, together with the promise he would 'be collected'.

POLICE WORK CAN BE like a thick soup, you get stuck. Coffin had a deputy but he did not delegate as much as perhaps he should have done. As the day went on Coffin got stuck in several committees, dictating one report, and talking to the high ranking civil servant from the Home Office. At the back of his mind all the time there rested the deaths of Didi and Marianna Manners like a dark shadow.

He went home, late as usual, forgetting all about Bob as he so often did. He pushed open his front door, and knew at once by the smell of Guerlain that Stella was there. Home. He still found it hard to believe that they were married and this was his home.

He ran up the stairs. She was sitting on the floor in suede jeans and a silk shirt enjoying the crackling of a log fire. It was blazing away merrily, smoking as well, he noticed, in defiance of the clean air zone in which St Luke's Mansions rested.

'How did you manage to light the fire?'

'Just laid it,' she said dreamily. 'One of my landladies taught me ages ago.'

'That chimney hasn't been cleaned for decades.'

'I know that, it's why it smokes, but wood smoke is lovely.'

He was so pleased to see her happy and relaxed that he buried all thoughts of newspaper headlines proclaiming POLICE CHIEF BREAKS SMOKE REGULATIONS and also of the voice of the architect who had helped create his apartment pointing out that the fireplace was decorative and that the chimney, what there was of it, had once led down to the furnace in the crypt of the old church.

Then he saw Bob, sprawled at her feet, and remembered 'How did he get here?'

'Walked.'

'On his own?'

Stella put on a large pair of spectacles and picked up the month's copy of *Vogue*. 'Well, I didn't carry him.'

'Ah, so they telephoned you to say I'd left him?'

'The great detective. Yes, that was it.'

She stood up, threw her arms round his neck and kissed him. 'You work too hard.' She took one look at his face. 'What sort of a day? No, don't tell me, I can guess.'

He told her anyway, it was what wives were for, hearing the moans and grumbles, as he had discovered to his comfort when he married Stella. Of course, she had the right to grumble back and if he got too boring, then she did. The way it worked was they took turns: tonight it was his turn.

He didn't tell her about the day's routine of letters, reports and meetings, but went on in some detail about what had really galled him: the behaviour of the mandarin from the Home Office.

'He taped the whole conversation, the bastard.'

'I suppose I'd better not ask what the conversation was about?'

'Oh, the fashionable butt of the moment: police handling of evidence, suppression of evidence and lying and backing each other up.'

'And that doesn't go on, of course?' She made the inquiry gentle as if she knew the answer must be no in the case of the Second City Force. Loyalty demanded it of a wife. In one of her more politically active periods, Stella had marched, waved banners and shouted at meetings against all forms of prejudice and corruption: Men against women, women against men (she was open-minded), ageism, racism and tokenism. She had enjoyed herself but now she was quiescent, with just the odd ripple of scepticism appearing on the surface.

'Not in my lot.' Or not while he kept his sharp eye on them. He had gradually managed to weed out those of the old flock whom he had reason to distrust. But there were always a few that were doubtful, you couldn't count on everyone even in the best of Forces. People cut corners, got lazy or were just tired. The naturally corrupt were easily sussed out and got rid of, much harder to pick out the good man who had had a bad day.

Stella's political activity had been due to the influence of her most ferocious and marvellously talented actress friend, brilliant child of a theatrical dynasty, but out to reform the world. She was in Moscow now, acting in a new International Theatre and probably creating havoc.

I'm just naturally lazy, thought Stella.

'But that's not what's really nagging at you?' she said.

'Oh, there's always this and that,' he said evasively, not willing to talk about Didi yet, relegating her to the back of his mind. Almost he could feel himself pushing her face back into the mud. 'Shall we eat?'

Was there anything to eat? No smell of cooking.

Triumphantly Stella took him downstairs to the kitchen. 'Bob and I drove over to the special fish and chip shop in Greenwich when you were so late, and we brought back a helping each.' Four helpings, one for Bob too and for the cat Tiddles, already on the alert. 'They have special boxes now that keep it hot and crisp... but I thought we'd eat in the kitchen because it does smell so.'

She was setting out the meal and handing out their portions to cat and dog. She stood back to admire her work. 'I could make some bread and butter and a pot of strong tea, that's the classic accompaniment, but I expect you would prefer wine?'

'I think I'd rather have beer.'

'You shall.' She opened the refrigerator. 'And I shall have wine.' She pushed Tiddles's face away from Bob's dish. 'Eat your own food, you monster, and leave his alone.' Bob licked her foot. 'Oh, Bob, you sycophant.'

Coffin accepted his beer and sat down. She was talking too much, nervous probably.

'Would you like the cat's chips?'

'No, thank you.'

Nor Bob's, no, she put them in the bin. They didn't eat all their chips. No one ever does. The last clump of them have usually descended into sogginess. Probably that was what the bread and butter had been designed for in the classic menu: to mop them up. And then the tea took the taste away.

Still, she was talking too much. And he was too silent.

'And what's the special worry, the one you don't want to talk about?'

'Is it so obvious?'

'To me.'

The fish was settling heavily on his stomach. 'Another body turned up today. A girl. Strangled like Marianna Manners.'

'Oh, that's bad. Where was she?'

'The body was found near an arch, near the river in Spinnergate. She was probably killed underneath the arch. It would give shelter, you see.' Now he was talking too much.

'A local girl, was she?'

He hesitated. 'Yes. You might know her: Didi Dunne. Diana Dunne.'

'No, don't think so.'

He had acquired a few facts about Didi before coming home. He felt he owed something to her sister Annie.

'She auditioned for a part in a play, part of the Drama School's warm-up.'

'I haven't had all that much to do with that side of it. Letty and I have been so busy setting up the essentials... Poor kid.'

'Yes, she's a member of a famous family in a way. Her sister saw the Creeleys burying their body and gave evidence. She was just a child at the time, so it made legal history.' As well as filling the newspapers and inflaming what was left of the Creeley family.

Stella was quiet as she made some coffee. She had lately got the art of it quite nicely. It was quite easy if you bought the best and freshest coffee you could and used plenty of it. 'Did the same person kill them both?'

'Too early to tell yet.'

'But you think so?... There's a name for that sort of killer, isn't there?'

'Yes, serial killing. Jack the Ripper was a serial killer.' Probably not the first but the first to make the headlines.

'Do you think one of the Creeleys did it?'

'There's only one possible suspect from that family now,' said Coffin. 'And I have to say his name is up there.'

'I suppose that lets Job Titus out?' Stella said. 'A pity. I rather fancied him for the killing. But that's because I don't like him.'

Good, thought Coffin, because I have every reason to believe he likes you and I am as jealous as hell.

'Let's go upstairs.'

Stella looked around the kitchen. 'I suppose I ought to wash the dishes.'

'There is a machine. And aren't we too grand and important these days to wash up cups?'

'You're never too important once you're a married woman,' said Stella. 'That's something I've discovered. I expect even the Queen has put the odd cup under the tap.'

Still talking too much, he thought. 'And what about you?' He looked at her. 'All clear today? No one hanging about? I'll carry that.' He took the tray of coffe-pot and cups from her and went ahead up the stairs. All was peaceful up there, the fire had settled down to a red heap and the dog and the cat were already asleep by it.

'I had a wild, wild telephone call from Letty,' said Stella, not really answering. 'I mean, we've been working on setting up the Drama School and she's been as good as gold but she rang up and said she was in Bruges. Bruges, I ask you!'

'Nice town,' said Coffin. 'What's she doing there?' He was not seriously worried about Letty, a tough lady who had proved herself well able to look after her own affairs. Also she wove in and out of his life as it suited her.

'Looking for her daughter. But she wasn't in Bruges, she was lying.'

Another family absentee, he thought. Perhaps she'll meet up with our maternal grandmother. Or Granny's ghost. Granny had been a notable wanderer too.

'I need Letty here, there's business things to settle.' Stella sounded anxious. 'We must have good teaching staff or we won't get accreditation, and if we don't get accreditation, then the students don't get grants and we don't get students. And if we don't get students then good teachers don't come. It's a circle.' She took a deep breath. 'And that's not the end of it: Max's Deli is putting in a bid to do the food, but should I consider it? We might need a bigger outfit.'

'This isn't the sort of business you should be bothering with.'

'Well, who else?'

'Letty never neglects business.'

'Well, she didn't sound at all like herself.'

There was a pause. 'There's something else, isn't there. The hanger-on, your watcher? Been around today?'

'Didn't see anyone,' said Stella. 'I've been in and out and all clear.'

'Good.'

'I suppose your patrol car may be keeping him away.'

'So? There is something worrying you.'

'Not exactly worrying me,' said Stella carefully. 'But the telephone rang once or twice and no one spoke. Someone there, though, I could hear breathing.'

He stood up and started to walk about the room.

'Calm down, it may mean nothing. Don't get too upset.'

'Because it's you. Because it's you.' He was possessive and jealous and anxious and frightened for her, all the emotions boiled together into anger.

'I'll have the number changed.'

'Thanks.' But it seemed no solution to Stella. 'I'd rather meet him head on and have it out.'

Coffin took her hand. 'He might be a killer. Marianna thought someone was watching her. Annie Briggs, the other girl's sister, thought the same thing. I can't risk it, Stella.'

The telephone rang; he felt Stella flinch. 'I'm safe here,' she said quickly.

'Of course you are. I'll answer it.'

It was Archie Young, trying to forget the Chief Inspector and be the friend.

'Could we have a meeting?'

Something in his voice. 'Yes.' Keep it social, unofficial. 'In the club. Tomorrow.' He thought rapidly. What was happening tomorrow? 'Around midday.'

HE WAS EARLY at their meeting but Archie Young was already there, standing talking to the barman. He had a folder of papers tucked under his arm.

'You need to break it, a good sharp break, then beat it hard. One won't be enough, two or three at least.'

'What was all that?' Coffin asked as they sat down.

'Omelette... I was telling him how to make an omelette, his wife's gone on a cruise with his daughter. She'd left him a freezer full of food but he wasn't sure how to defrost it. I explained that too.' Young laid the folder of papers on the table before him.

'I didn't know you were so domestic.'

'Had to be.' His wife too was a career woman, a police officer of higher rank than his own, and cleverer. Archie knew it and did not resent it. There had been a time when some of his more macho colleagues had encouraged him to resent it, but Archie had seen the danger and drawn back. He was lucky to have a wife like Alison.

'I thought I'd rather have a talk here, sir. Wanted to talk the Manners and Dunne cases over with you.'

'You think they are related?'

Archie drank some beer, noting that the Chief Commander had restricted himself to tonic with lemon in it. 'Yes, I do. We haven't got the forensics in on the Dunne girl, and I don't know if they will give us anything but I'm hoping. But yes, there has to be a link.'

'Not a copycat killing?'

'I dunno. Could be. But neither victim seems to have struggled and that's got to mean something. They went willingly. So they knew the killer. Or trusted him.'

'Or it was a person they could trust,' said Coffin. 'Like a doctor or nurse. Or someone in uniform like a policeman?'

'It has been said.' Young was dour. 'And uniforms can be hired.'

'Yes, theatres do it all the time. So are you looking for an actor?'

'We aren't ruling anything out, but frankly we're floundering. There are differences as well as likenesses. Manners now, well, she mixed with a wide range of characters, not all wholesome. And she had quarrelled with Job Titus.' There was no love lost between Titus and any member of the Second City law enforcers. Titus had attacked them too often.

'But the Dunne girl had no enemies that we can find. Then Manners was killed indoors and the other outside, probably under the arch near where her body was found. And for the killer that's running a risk.'

'And why didn't she scream or shout?'

'Well, she may have done, we don't know that. We may get a witness yet.' He was not hopeful.

'Same method of killing but different settings,' said Coffin. 'So those are the differences. May not be important but must mean something about the killer.'

'No motive, sir, not that I can see. The girl had no enemies and only one young man she went about with.''

Coffin drank some tonic water and tasted the lemon. 'So if there is no motive it looks like a killer who does it for fun.' He thought about it. 'Who's the boyfriend?'

'You've got it there, sir.' Young banged on the table. 'Eddie Creeley.'

Coffin mopped up the tonic water that had spilt. 'Go on. Let's add it up.'

Young did so. 'Eddie Creeley was mentioned in connection with the Manners death. He comes from a criminal family with an inherited feud against the girl's sister. You might think he would be one person the girl would avoid. But no, he's the lad she's been seeing.'

'He hasn't been in any trouble, has he? No record?'

'No.' Archie Young shrugged. 'But coming from a family like that, who knows? They've got crime bred into them, that lot. Auntie is coming home this week. Parole.'

Coffin nodded. 'Yes, Job Titus helped there.'

'Yes, that seemed the link-up with the Manners girl: Titus helped with Auntie and young Creeley got rid of an encumbrance that Titus didn't want around.'

'I had wondered myself.'

'Well, that was one set of thoughts, although no evidence. But I had a look at the Creeley boy and he seemed, for one of that family, to be of good character. Getting the house ready for his aunt, looking for a job. And so he seemed less and less likely, somehow.'

'So?' Coffin was patient, he knew that Young liked to think aloud but he seemed to be taking his time.

'That was until the Dunne girl's body turned up. Even then, I thought: Serial killer, or copycat crime. It wasn't that I didn't want it to be Eddie Creeley, but once I'd seen him face to face, he didn't seem like a killer.' Young opened the folder of papers, reports, a photocopied page or two, then put his large hand firmly on them as if that wasn't where he was starting.

He took a drink, and said: 'I know you've worried about Miss Pinero.' It was universally accepted that this was how they referred to his wife. Mrs Coffin wouldn't do for Stella, even though he had been at their wedding. Alison called her Stella and so did he on more private occasions. 'She's had trouble from one of these starwatchers, so-called.'

Coffin nodded. 'Get on with it, Archie.'

'We know that Marianna Manners had the same complaint or she thought so; Annie Briggs also... Well, that may have been Eddie Creeley or it may not, but...'

He laid a sheet on the table in front of Coffin. 'Photocopy of a page in the sister's diary.'

Half way down the page was a pencilled name with a question-mark.

Charley?

Young laid his finger against it, then moved down a line.

Miss Pinero.

No question-mark this time, just Stella's name.

'No connection maybe, but all in all, I wanted to show you before you got the official report.'

'I don't know what it means. I don't know if Stella knows anyone called Charley.'

'She wouldn't have to know him, sir, would she? Not by name. But it may be a man called Charley we ought to be looking for.'

So there was another player on the scene.

'We shall be looking for Charley in Marianna Manners's life,' said Young. 'With luck we will find something.'

Coffin had a sudden memory of Didi's face lying on the muddy grass. Stella's face became superimposed upon it.

But it was impossible that Stella would ever be found lying in the mud.

HE TELEPHONED HER after leaving the Chief Inspector. After some difficulty she was located in the Theatre Workshop talking with the new lighting manager who seemed to have grander ideas than they could afford.

'Darling, I must have known many men called Charles or Charley in my career but I can't recall one in particular nor one that I know at the moment.'

He didn't tell her why he asked, and she was left puzzling, although she could guess.

'What's your second name, dear?' she said to the lighting expert, studying the name badge she wore, as they all did these days for security reasons. Elizabeth C. Rust. 'Not Charlotte or Carlotta?'

'Claire,' said the girl. 'What's the joke?'

'Not laughing,' said Stella. 'Just wanted to know.'

But she felt better today.

No silent, breathy telephone calls, and no feeling that someone was treading quietly behind her. In fact, if only Letty came back (Letty was a problem in herself at the moment; those two thought they were not alike, but they were—both obsessive and capable of rage), and the money things worked out for the Drama School she would have no worries.

Or none other than those all women and all actresses carry with them as luggage.

THE GROUND WHERE Didi had been found had been searched very thoroughly. Her handbag with her small possessions and her diary had been found at once, lying so close to her body that she must have dropped it as she was strangled and the killer hadn't cared.

Robbery was not his motive.

The whole area had been cordoned off and the search had gone on until dark. An alert-eyed constable had found a cassette from a tape-recorder under the arch. It was half hidden behind a pile of old bricks but clearly to be seen once you had your eye in.

The tape was taken back to the Murder Room where it was played. The sounds that came out were blurred. Then after about five minutes of playing time they heard a girl's voice.

The investigating team could hardly believe what they heard.

NINE

Under the arches

THE YOUNG CONSTABLE who had searched among the mud and old bricks and rubbish under the bridge was as amazed as anyone at what he had found.

'I tripped over a brick and there it was. I nearly trod on it trying to right myself but I had my eye on it and knew that even if I broke my neck I must see I didn't damage what was there. No, I remembered to pick it up with a plastic glove.' He shook his head. 'I just knew in my bones it was important.'

He was only on probation as a detective-constable but he felt sure he would make it now. Who could turn away a man who brought back such a valuable bit of evidence?

Knew it for what it was, too. At once. No mucking about.

To his fury, he had not been allowed to carry his find back to the Murder Room himself, but although instructed to go on searching, he had managed to get in to hear it played.

For a few moments he thought he had brought back a booboo after all. First there was nothing, just a running blank, then a few blurred sounds. Traffic noises, a plane going across the sky.

I've bombed, he said to himself (he was his own best friend) but then it came good.

They heard a girl's voice.

'Eddie,' she said. And then once more but clearly enough to be heard. 'Eddie.'

IN WHAT CAME to be known as the Eddie Creeley tape, that was all that could be heard, but it was enough. The tape was rushed to the forensic laboratory to see if more sound could be brought up but no, what they had was what they got.

Archie Young played it over several times before bringing it to the attention of the Chief Commander.

'This is only a copy, sir,' he said. 'Original's over in the lab to see if they could bring up anything else.'

Coffin listened. 'What it has seems to be enough. I suppose it is the girl's voice?'

'I'm betting so. Haven't asked the sister to listen yet.'

'I should leave that for the moment.'

She was liable to be seriously disturbed, hysterical, Coffin thought. He went to his office window and looked out on the early autumn scene. It had been raining in the night, but now the sun was out. The leaves on the trees in the little park beyond were turning a pleasant yellow. 'But what was it doing there?' he said aloud. 'Why was it there? And why was it made?'

Young was too busy with his own thoughts to listen seriously; it was there. He was counting it lucky the tape had been found and been readable. He had the girl's voice and he had a name. That was enough.

So then I had to think again. I haven't forgotten to look for Charley but I'm taking Eddie Creeley in for questioning.

'But how was it made? Why was it made? And why was it there?'

'You're not thinking it's a fake?'

Coffin shook his head. Didi's voice had carried a conviction. 'Just asking questions.'

But Young had the bit between his teeth. 'Those are questions, I admit it,' he said briskly. 'But we will find out the answers when we get the killer.'

EDDIE CREELEY HAD TRIED to call on Annie Briggs as soon as he heard about Didi. It was not an easy decision because he knew how Annie felt about him and how she was likely to behave.

He had taken a job as a hospital porter at Spinnergate General. It was work he enjoyed because it made him feel a valued member of the community, which was not a feeling often allowed to a Creeley. Although there were moments when he felt the responsibility. For instance, the night before last, when he had seen a nurse book in a patient called T. Ashworth, a chap complaining of severe stomach pains, and had heard the same nurse say next day that the man was a fool to discharge himself because he almost certainly had a carcinoma of the stomach.

Should he say anything? Had he an obligation to do so? He felt guilty himself and a bit sick. Death seemed so close and everywhere.

He worked a day and night shift according to a rota and a split shift every third week when he had hours free in the day and then went in again at night. Other weeks he worked all day, and then every fourth week he was on all night and had the day to sleep.

This was a split shift week, always hard on the nerves.

By this time he had his Aunt Lizzie home from prison and back in the house. This was not something that pleased him or a state of affairs that he wanted, but he had no choice. The Creeleys hung together.

Prison had not improved Aunt Lizzie. She had never been an agreeable woman but she was now silently, sullenly unpleasant. She tried, Eddie could see that she was trying, to make herself an easy companion, but if she had ever had the knack she had lost it.

Eddie looked at her as she tried to prepare a meal, which she said she wanted to do to help him. There was something pathetic about a person who was fundamentally horrible trying to be nice.

She cut her finger as she chopped onions and swore. Her cooking skills had not been improved by being banged up, although she said that towards the end the long stay prisoners (of whom she was certainly one, having served beyond her term on account of various nasty things she had done to fellow prisoners and the odd warder while inside) had been allowed the use of a small kitchen.

Curiosity had driven him. 'What did you cook?'

'Oh, this and that. What I could get. I didn't have much cash.' She looked at him accusingly as if it was his fault. Probably she did blame him. 'Beans on toast, mostly. Eggs. But eggs are never very fresh in prison.'

She had heard about Didi's death, and seemed to be treating it as a homecoming present.

He hadn't wanted to tell her. He had collected her from the prison, driven her home, and then had a few quiet days while he assessed what his life was going to be with her in the house. Now when he looked at her he could see his own features duplicated in her eyes. This did not make him feel better.

Then she heard him being sick.

'Why did you do that?'

'It's how I feel,' he had muttered, wishing she hadn't heard. But it was a small house, and what you did in one room was always heard in the next.

'What's up with you? Good luck to whoever did it.' She meant the murder of Didi.

'It wasn't me.' He wasn't sure why he said that. Of course it wasn't him. He felt the vomit rise up in his throat again.

'More's the pity. Shame it wasn't the other one.' This time she meant Annie.

It wasn't as straightforward a matter as calling Lizzie immoral or amoral or evil. She just didn't belong to the human race, that was how Eddie felt.

And he had the same blood in him. Oh, Didi, Didi, if you and I could have made a match of it, perhaps we could have healed ... But no, some wounds were past healing.

'Shut up,' he said savagely and was glad to see her flinch. Prison had taught her something, anyway.

She was glad to be home. 'The old place hasn't changed,' she said looking around. And this was true of the family home whose decorations and furniture had remained the same for some decades. The tenants had not treated it well, they had been people with troubles of their own, but Eddie had touched up the paint and repaired broken chairs in the weeks since he got home while he looked for a paying job. But he had to admit it probably hadn't changed all that much, although he was glad to say he could hardly remember.

But the world outside had changed. There were more cars, and fewer of the old red doubledecker buses that once quartered London. More crime, more violence, some rich people in the Second City, and the old poor... And a new police force.

This was the Second City and in it the Creeley clan were no longer important. He wasn't sure if she understood this.

She knew that Eddie's only sister wasn't there, she had gone to stay with relations in Yorkshire the moment she heard Lizzie was coming out. And his father had died from a heart attack just before they left New Zealand. He and Lizzie were the only ones left, apart from Will.

Lizzie had kept up with the news. 'I was allowed a transistor. I heard about the Marianna Manners murder.' She had taken an interest in that. 'Friend of Job Titus.' She leered. 'We all know what that means. But he's entitled to his pleasures. He helped me. Got in touch with the parole board. I wouldn't be here now if it wasn't for him.'

'I've met him. He called.'

'What did he want?' Lizzie's thoughts were centred about Job Titus.

'I don't know.' But that wasn't true. To himself Eddie said: I think he wanted me to be grateful. But he had another feeling as well; he had had the feeling that Titus had wanted him to do something. Kill someone perhaps, he thought morosely.

'He owed the Creeleys something, Job Titus,' said Lizzie with an evil smile. 'He was born round here, and I know and he knows I know what his family was like. Illegit, he was.'

'That's nothing these days,' said Eddie.

''Tis if your mother is the daughter of your father. That was quite a thing in that family. Oh, I know all about Job Titus,' said Lizzie. 'Incest, that is.'

Goodness knows if it was true, but it was the way she talked and the way he responded that irked him. He had to get out of the house.

'I'm going out.'

Lizzie was content to stay in and she watched him go. She had no desire to go out into the streets of Spinnergate where enemies spied and lurked.

'You've forgotten, Lizzie,' Eddie wanted to say. 'Outside of a small circle you are nothing. And no one knows what you look like.' He could hardly remember from the past but now she had put on weight and gone grey. She dyed her hair herself but that didn't mean it looked natural.

However, he said nothing to her. Her murderous reputation was all she had, let her keep it.

He walked the streets, making up his mind what he should do. A turn to the left, then the next. He knew the way well enough, could see the very tree where he had stood waiting for Didi to come.

'She thinks you're watching her,' Didi had said. 'I told her it was me. Poor Annie.'

Annie's house looked the same, it had always been a closed-up house and being a place of mourning hadn't changed it. Caroline's flat up above looked shuttered too.

He rang the bell and waited. A tall, grey-haired man answered the door. 'Can I speak to Annie, to Mrs Briggs?' He hesitated. 'It's Alex Edwards, isn't it? I'm Eddie Creeley.' He swallowed. 'Didi introduced us once.' *And afterwards she said you were a creep and always hanging round Annie. And I see you still are.*

'I wanted to say...' Eddie suddenly didn't know what he had wanted to say and wished he had brought flowers. 'It's just I'm so sorry.'

Edwards was already closing the door. 'She is resting with friends.'

He was probably a nice man, Eddie thought, seeing Alex's red-rimmed eyes, and knowing well that Didi's judgement was not to be relied upon. Yes, an all right man, but also piss pompous, a prat.

There was only one star in Didi's life and that was the theatre, and that meant St Luke's Drama School and Stella Pinero.

INSIDE HER HOUSE, Annie was talking to Stella Pinero.

Stella had come out of the genuine concern and kindness of her own heart, and also because her husband had asked her to. 'I'm worried about Annie Briggs. Go and see her for me. I can't go myself—it would alarm her.'

Stella had brought with her a small pot of early freesias, she put them on the table without a word. Their fragrance seeped into the room, lightening the frowsty, lived-in smell where it seemed as if no one had been to bed or opened a window.

About right, Stella thought, looking at Annie's face which frightened her. She didn't like the smell of Annie's house, it smelt of female fear and sweat.

'I don't suppose you know who I am,' she began.

'Oh, I do.' Annie started off. 'I saw you as Ophelia in the old Theatre Royal in Swinehouse... Knocked down now and there's a shopping precinct where it used to be.'

'Yes, I was.' *And I was on the old side for Ophelia even then, but I've always made up young. I suppose now I'd have to be Queen Gertrude ... a good role, though.* And Stella's mind divided: one part talking to Annie and the other roving off towards a new production of *Hamlet*.

While Eddie Creeley was still walking Napier Street trying to find the courage to ring Annie's bell, Stella Pinero was inside deciding she had been wrong to come. Alex Edwards was there and doing better at offering comfort than she was. He knew how to manage Annie.

'I'm so sorry about Didi,' Stella was saying in a gentle voice. 'I was hoping she would be one of our first students.'

'She wanted to, it was what she wanted most in the world,' said Annie. 'But I was against it. I knew it would come to no good. Nor has it.'

'Oh, I hope not,' said Stella. I shouldn't have been there, she was to tell her husband later, I was the wrong person. I'm sure I made things worse.

She had seen many a mask of fury and tragedy in her time, especially when she had performed in a cycle of Greek plays, seen Medea face to face, but Annie beat all. There was a kind of energy, almost a sexual light, in her eyes.

'I don't think what's happened had anything to do with her acting.' Alex spoke hastily. 'You mustn't think so, Annie.'

'I know who did it, of course. I told the police sergeant so. Eddie Creeley. Has to be.'

The bell rang, twice.

'Someone at the door.' Annie made no sign of moving. 'They won't let me see Didi, you know. Perhaps it isn't her that's dead. Perhaps that's her come back.'

Stella and Alex exchanged glances. 'I'll do the door,' he said quickly.

This is the woman, Stella thought, who saw murder done as a child and has now had her sister killed violently. And she does not like me; she will not take her eyes off me.

Alex returned. 'Just someone,' he said vaguely; he was not going to say it had been Eddie Creeley. Eddie, as always, had got his timing wrong.

Almost as if she had not stopped speaking, Annie said: 'And of course, he killed Marianna Manners too. I've got my own detective to call upon. He'll find out the truth.'

'You shouldn't have anything to do with that Tom Ashworth. Keep away from him.'

'You're just jealous.' She put her head on one side. 'I asked him to check on the Eddie Creeley and Marianna Manners link.'

'I don't think Eddie knew Marianna,' said Alex Edwards. His face was flushed and he looked as tense and unhappy as Annie herself. He took her hand and patted it. She drew it away without looking at him.

'How do you know?' was all she said.

'I knew Marianna. As a youngster she had a bit of trouble and was one of my cases. I kept in touch.'

'Like with me.'

'No, not like with you.' He was patient.

Annie took hold of the pot of freesias, she put it on her lap, almost nursing it. 'You're very beautiful,' she said to Stella. 'Close to, you are more beautiful than I knew.'

'I take a lot of trouble,' said Stella.

Once again she exchanged glances with Alex Edwards. She stood up. 'I'd better go.'

'I think so,' he murmured. 'She's not herself. But thanks for coming. I'll stay with her.'

As the front door closed behind her, Stella leaned against it, taking a deep breath. *I shouldn't have come. I've made things worse.*

She got into her car and drove back to the theatre, hoping she would find a message from Letty there. Or even

Letty herself. Letty remained obstinately missing, and although you couldn't associate danger and death with someone like Letty, she was worried.

The atmosphere round here was so full of violence and fear that it felt as though anything could happen.

As she drove down Napier Street and took a right turn, she saw a young man whom she did not know being stopped by a police car.

CHIEF INSPECTOR YOUNG had visited the Creeley home himself. He had found only Lizzie Creeley there. She hid when he rang the bell, thinking she was going to be arrested again.

When a detective-sergeant and woman police officer pushed open the back door which was unlocked and let the Chief Inspector in, they found Lizzie hiding under a bed.

She did not recognize Archie Young although he knew her, he had seen recent photographs which gave him the advantage.

When Lizzie was calmed down and restored to this world, all she could say was that Eddie was out.

The woman detective-constable made Lizzie a cup of tea which Archie Young drank with her while the sergeant searched the house.

'Two lumps,' said Lizzie, holding out her mug for sugar, 'and you haven't given me a spoon.'

In spite of the fact that she was a murderer who had never repented, it was Lizzie who was acting the victim now and Young who felt guilty. They were living proof that the division between criminal and policeman was thin, you could see it in their faces: they were both so clearly from the same tribe.

Lizzie announced her intention of calling on Job Titus for protection.

Detective-Sergeant Hill reappeared and reported that Eddie Creeley was not in the house.

'But there's blood in his room.'

'What?' Young stood up.

'Yes, blood. Traces of blood.'

EDDIE CREELEY was picked up by a patrol car and taken to police headquarters while a swarm of police technicians descended like hungry fleas upon his bloody chamber.

Eddie was held for questioning and an interview which the Chief Commander sat in on. 'Hold on until I get there,' he had ordered. 'I want to be in on this.'

Coffin had met Stella and heard what she had to say about Annie Briggs, which did not make him feel better about the part he had played in Annie's earlier life. 'That girl's had too much to bear,' Stella had said. 'She thinks Eddie Creeley killed her sister and she believes he killed Marianna Manners.'

'Does she suggest why? What motive he would have?'

Stella had looked back at Annie's ravaged face, and because she was an actress her own features fell into the same expression so that Coffin saw a frightened woman who had known terrible things.

If any man hurts Stella, I shall kill him, he thought.

And then Stella's face cleared, and the resilient, familiar, lovely Stella came back and was with him again. She spoke with the voice of reason.

'Didi died instead of her, that's what Annie thinks. As for Marianna, I don't know. Perhaps for practice. Are people that wicked?'

'Some are. Or mercenary. Some killers work for money, possibly Creeley did.'

'Is that what you think?'

'It's an idea being handed round. I don't say I accept it.'

Truth, black truth, had many layers, like an onion, and he did not expect any easy answers.

Now he watched Eddie Creeley as Archie Young questioned him. Eddie had tears streaming down his face. Was this too much emotion? Was it real?

'I didn't kill Didi, I loved her.'

'People do kill those they love.'

Eddie turned wild eyes on John Coffin. 'I didn't kill her, I didn't kill.'

'Your name is heard on a tape found near her body. Was she talking to you?'

'I don't know anything about a tape.'

'Did you know Marianna Manners?'

'I did not. You're not going to get me for that.'

There was, as Coffin knew and Young knew, no scrap of forensic evidence to connect Eddie Creeley with Marianna's death.

Someone had come into her life, into her room and into her death.

The same was true of Didi. They were still searching the ground around where her body had been found, asking questions of motorists and anyone who might have witnessed something. But nothing so far. A man had come into her life and taken hers away with him.

'Titus did that. Everyone says so. I'm not standing in for him just because he's rich and an MP.'

'Do you know Job Titus?'

'He asked me for a drink once.'

'What did you talk about?'

'I can't remember. This and that. Auntie, I expect.'

'Did he make any suggestions to you?'

'He's not queer if that's what you think, and neither am I.'

'There are other sorts of suggestions,' said Coffin.

'I don't remember. Ask him yourself.'

'I will.' And get no for an answer. I was just talking to a man whose aunt I had helped to get out of prison, Titus would say. I was interested.

'Do you know the Karnival Club?'

Eddie frowned. 'I've heard of it,' he said without enthusiasm. 'Local place for transvestites, isn't it?'

'Have you ever been there?'

Eddie was quicker on that. 'No.'

Finally Young came to the question that interested him.

'There is blood in your room. Where did it come from?'

Eddie's face changed and he twisted round in his chair. 'I'm not going to tell you about the blood. I'm not going to tell you.'

'Roll your sleeves up and show me your wrists.'

There was no wound, no slices from a knife.

'So where did the blood come from?'

Eddie's voice went high and loud: 'Perhaps it was Aunt Lizzie's. Why don't you ask her?'

'You been beating up your aunt, Eddie?'

'No.'

'Or hanging around street corners and outside windows watching?'

'No, no, and no... Annie thought someone was watching her, and Didi told her it was me. Well, maybe it was someone else. You'd better start looking.'

'Do you know anyone called Charley?'

'No, I bloody don't.'

A few minutes later Young ended the interview and let Eddie Creeley go home. But Eddie knew he was on the end of a piece of rope that Young would pull whenever it suited him.

'What do you think?' asked Young. 'Didn't get much out of him.'

'He's frightened.'

'So he should be.'

'He's in it somewhere,' said Coffin. 'And he knows it.'

EDDIE WALKED BACK to his home, although it hardly felt homely. As he left the police headquarters, he walked firmly while he thought they were watching. As he turned the corner he let himself limp.

As soon as he was inside the house, he pushed Lizzie aside; she was slightly tipsy, having found the gin, and was easy to push.

The police had gone, leaving disorder and signs of their passage everywhere.

He went to his bedroom and sat down on the bed. He could see where the police had been and could see the blood he had left behind on the carpet and on the bedcover. They had stopped short of taking the carpet and cover with them but bits had been cut out. There must be some in the bathroom too, but perhaps they hadn't looked there.

He went to the bathroom to see, locking the door. Yes, they had been in there and had removed several of his possessions, like a razor and some clothes from the linen basket.

He rolled up his trouser leg. A thick plaster covered where he had dug into the artery. The blood had begun to ooze again.

But he wasn't going to die. He hadn't been brave enough to do the job properly.

Lizzie was calling through the keyhole. 'Eddie, the police have been here.' A pause. 'Like bloody flies.'

As if he didn't know.

He didn't answer and the shuffling noises outside suggested that Lizzie was still there.

'Eddie, Eddie?'

He kept quiet.

'Eddie, are you on the lav?'

'No.' His voice was thick.

'The lav can be a comfort when you're frightened,' said Lizzie reminiscently. Prison had taught her strange consolations.

'Are you crying?'

'No, I'm not.'

'Don't be huffy...I saw Stella Pinero's picture in your room. She's been going a long time. I remember her.'

No answer. 'Oh, shut up, piss off.'

Lizzie was not offended. She knew imprecations worse than that. 'Mr Titus telephoned while you were out. He wants you to meet him.'

Oh God. Eddie heaved a sigh. 'What does he want. Where?'

'I wrote it down. He said to.'

She pushed a piece of paper under the door.

The Karnival Club.

COFFIN WAS AT HOME with Stella when the telephone rang. He listened while he drank a glass of wine.

'That's interesting. The two of them.' He listened. 'And him as well? He'll be working. Annie Briggs will be behind that...Yes, I see your point. Thanks, Archie.'

He turned to Stella.

'Feel like going out?'

She looked at him cautiously. 'Doing what?'

'There might be some dancing. A show, that sort of thing.'

She stood up. 'I'll give you the benefit of the doubt.'

'Good. Go and change.'

'Into what?'

'Well, the sort of thing you'd wear if you were watching the show at the Karnival. Say you were casting a show. That sort of thing. I want you as camouflage.'

As he caught the expression in Stella's eyes, he reckoned it was one of the bravest things he had ever said.

She rose quietly, without a word.

TEN

Charley down the river

'NO ONE WILL BELIEVE IT for a moment,' said Stella.

'You look lovely,' said Coffin.

'These are my working clothes. I do rehearsals in these.' Stella looked down at her jeans, expensive and clean, but well worn, bearing the scars of many sessions in church halls and cold back rooms. With it went a silk shirt and a soft tweed jacket. She knew how to put it together.

'You look lovely in your working clothes,' said Coffin patiently.

'I'm dead tired.'

'Come on, I don't often ask you to help out.'

'I'm here aren't I?' Stella swung the car to the right, provoking an angry hoot from a car behind. She was driving because Coffin had been drinking wine and the last thing he wanted at this point in his life was to be breathalysed by his own Force, if there was an accident. They wouldn't want to do it, but they would feel obliged. It would be the Politically Correct action. He suppressed the notion that a certain amount of amusement would accompany it.

Stella drove on unmoved by any hoots from behind. I'll drive my car and you drive yours, was her philosophy. 'It won't work, no one will believe I am casting a play on transvestites or picking up colour. They won't believe it because they will recognize you.'

They both kept silent while she found her route through the streets, still busy in the late evening. Coffin noted that she knew the way. How many times had Stella been there, and with whom? Better not ask.

There was just room in the forecourt of the Karnival for one more car and Stella managed to squeeze into this slice of parking. 'And remember,' she said as she got out of the car, 'if I do see anyone there that I know, they will be my friends and no trouble, please.'

'I'm not going there to arrest anyone.'

'So what are you going to do?'

'Just look. Watch.' And listen if he could.

A strong light shone above the door of the Karnival and when they pushed through to the inner door, this was locked. A deep violet light shone above this door, casting strange shadows on their faces. Stella was tired, Coffin thought, or was it the light?

Stella looked at him. 'You ought to have shaved.'

So he looked different too? 'It's the light.'

There seemed to be a draught coming from somewhere. It was even colder inside than in the courtyard.

Stella said. 'You have to ring.'

'I know that.'

'But you haven't touched the bell.'

'There's someone coming.'

The door opened and before them stood a tall, elegant figure in a purple caftan. In another light it was probably blue.

'I saw you through my little peephole.'

'Hello, Alice, I thought you probably had.' Coffin knew to use that name tonight.

Coffin turned to his wife. 'Can I introduce you: Adam Adamson.'

'I'm Alice tonight,' said Adamson, extending a hand to Stella, 'but you can call me Adam.' He turned back to Coffin, obviously he was a man's man even when he was a woman. 'Didn't expect to see you.'

'Stella's looking for background colour.'

'Of course I know you by sight, Miss Pinero,' said the polite Alice. 'Come along in, and I'll get you a table. I'm on the door tonight. We take turns. Keeps it more friendly.'

He led the way down a short corridor. Stella hung back and gripped her husband's arm. 'Some day I'm going to ask you how you two know each other.'

'Oh, he was one of us,' said Coffin. 'Couldn't you tell?'

'Do you mean what I think you mean?'

'Yes, one of the best young detective-sergeants I ever had.'

Alice-Adam turned round. 'I can hear every word you two are saying.'

The Karnival was essentially one long, narrow room. An orchestra was playing on a platform at one end under a curtained window. The walls were painted a soft pink, which looked comfortable, even cosy, in the light from the lamps on the walls. There was no central light.

Small tables lined the walls and crowded into a crescent around the orchestra. A bar was at the other end of the room. The centre of the room was for dancing, it was already full of slowly moving couples, some anchored to each other and others tenderly apart. One or two circled round alone.

It was a quiet, happy scene.

Alice-Adam put them at a table and advised them to be careful what they drank. Coffin said he would get them a drink.

Alice sat down opposite Stella. 'Can't offer you a cigarette. It's a no smoking club.' He grinned. 'We allow everything else, but not that.'

'Quite right.'

'I miss it, though.'

'What do you do now?'

'I loved what I did,' he said wistfully. 'You might find that difficult to believe. But once I'd let myself out, I realized that was it. We're a more liberal bunch than you might think, and the boss said it was up to me, but I made the decision myself.'

'So what do you do?' Stella persevered. She could see her husband weaving his way through the crowd with the drinks. She was getting a new light on him. He was an amazing man.

Alice-Adam smiled. 'I work for the government... Can't say more.'

Coffin returned with their drinks. 'Didn't spill anything. The décor hasn't changed since I was last here.'

'We can't afford much. What were you doing here?'

'Someone invited me.'

'And perhaps more to the point, what are you doing here today?'

'Accompanying my wife.'

'And what are you really doing?'

'Just looking around.'

Alice gave what might have been a pout, or it could have been a scowl. 'We don't want any trouble.'

'I don't expect to give any.'

'It's not what you give, it's what you bring.'

Stella had been looking with interest from one to the other as this dialogue went on. Like a rally in a tennis match, she decided. Deuce so far.

So much for camouflage. She was irritated that she had been written off so easily as the real reason for anything and thought it unwomanly of Alice. Scratch Alice, she thought, and there was Adam underneath.

But it was going on too long. She put a hand on each. 'It's a draw. I declare you both winners.'

To her annoyance, they took no notice, although her husband reached out for her hand and held it in his. Recognition of a sort, she thought. Maybe the right sort, as she felt the comfort of his warm, dry hand. Hands ought to feel that way. She studied Alice's hand: hard and horny, she thought, in spite of the pale pink nail varnish.

A faint shading of beard was beginning to show on Alice's chin. Stella was diverted at once by the technical problem of what make-up would hide it most successfully. A darker foundation with a lighter powder on top? And of course, a good shave.

Alice finished his drink and stood up; he had seen Stella studying him and didn't mind at all; rather the reverse. He gave her a tender smile and threw a sentence at Coffin. 'The man you're looking for is over there.' He nodded to a table tucked away in a recess.

'I've already seen him,' said Coffin.

Stella watched the tall, blue-draped figure stroll away. 'Handsome lad,' she said. 'I hope he gets the sex thing sorted out, it seems to worry him.'

'I know it does, but only sometimes. Seeing you with me brought it on. He likes you, I could tell.' At that moment Coffin was not pleased at Alice-Adam's attraction to Stella. Nor at her last words.

'And why did you really bring me?'

'Perhaps I wanted you to look around and see if there was anyone here you recognized as Charley.'

Stella licked her lips which suddenly felt dry. She was beginning to get the drift of this Charley business. 'Is the man who watches me called Charley?'

'Maybe.'

'And he's here?'

'Just an idea I had.'

'Well, I have an idea. Did you bring me here in the hopes that I would identify Alice-Adam?' She leaned forward and stared in his face. 'Well?'

'Of course not.'

He wouldn't say if it had been so. Irritably she said: 'I don't know where you got this Charley idea.'

'The name has appeared.'

'And that's all you are going to say?'

'Just look around.'

Stella let her eyes wander round the room. The band was playing a piece of soft music, the lights had gone down to very dim, and the floor was filled with the dancers. Not everyone was cross-dressed, and even if they had been nothing could have altered the strange respectability of the occasion. It was like a dance in an old folks' home and about as sexy. She didn't mean to, but suddenly she felt touched and sympathetic.

She smiled. *I could give them a better party*. Aloud, she said: 'I don't see anyone I know. I don't even know what I'm looking for. Wearing what?'

'Just see if you get any ideas.'

She turned back. 'I don't. I'm tired, let's go home.' She added quietly, 'And that's Job Titus over there. Is he the one you came to watch.'

'Not on his own. He's got Eddie Creeley with him. I just wanted a look. I wish I could lip read.' His eye moved round the room. And a table away was Tom Ashworth: Tash, the detective. Also watching Titus and Eddie Creeley.

'I wish I knew when to believe you or not.'

'You can always believe me.'

'I do. In a way. I think Titus has seen us.'

Coffin nodded. 'He has.'

'You meant him to?'

'I was just interested to see what happened when he did. He's coming over.'

Titus, dressed in the jeans and sweater he wore when visiting his constituency, smiled. 'Chief Commander? I didn't expect to see you here.'

Coffin stood up, he didn't like being loomed over. Upright, he was eye to eye with Titus. 'Do you come here often?'

'I've been here before. As I expect you remember. A number of the men and women here voted for me, and all of them are my constituents. I like to show solidarity with them.'

'You've got Eddie Creeley there.'

'I wanted to talk to him. This seemed a good chance, after my weekly surgery. I don't have a lot of time when the House is sitting. Eddie and I have something in common. We've both lost someone we liked—and I did like Marianna, and we're both under suspicion. We both know it, too.'

He smiled at Stella, who smiled back. Definitely more charming than he had to be, he was turning it on. He won votes, didn't he? Out of the corner of her eye, she saw a faint scowl on her husband's face.

'And you've got Tom Ashworth there,' said Coffin. 'Know who he is?'

'I know. He's watching us too.'

While they were talking, Tash had moved across to talk to Eddie Creeley.

It was interesting, Stella thought, that he and Eddie looked completely out of place here, while Titus, and possibly she herself and Coffin did not. It said something about them. All three adept at dissembling, perhaps?

'Come and join us,' said Titus.

The lights turned pink but the two faces turned towards them were pale. Eddie looked tired, Tash looked ill.

'I don't have to introduce you, do I?' said Titus. 'You both know the Chief Commander. And Miss Pinero.'

'I'm working,' said Tash. 'Not here on a visit. Working for a client.'

Eddie managed a weak smile and took a deep breath. 'Didi liked you a lot, Miss Pinero.'

'I know. I am sorry. But they'll find out who killed her.'

'It's to be hoped,' said Tash in a deep voice.

As they walked down the hall, moving through the dancers, Stella said: 'I'll tell you something for free. None of those three is Charley.'

'No? Never thought one of them was.'

'So what did we come for?'

'I wanted to watch them. Titus and Creeley have some guilt to share between them. And Ashworth is working on them.'

Stella was slowing down. She pushed through the door and leaned against the wall. Her face had gone pale so that her lipstick stood out, blue-red and cold. The lighting out here was harsh above the urn.

'He's been here.'

Coffin put his arm round her. 'What's that?'

'He's been here. May not be here now. But I could smell him.'

But all Coffin could smell was the passage of many sweaty bodies, some wearing scent.

OUTSIDE, Stella got into the car with speed. 'You drive. You didn't drink much.' She had watched him hardly touch his drink, careful as ever, she thought, because he knows that sometimes he can be madly rash. She leaned back in her seat. Without a word, Coffin backed the car into the street. A police patrol car saw them and slowed down, silently watching.

Then the patrol man recognized the car and its driver and drove away. 'What's he up to?' he said to his mate. A bawdy joke passed between them.

Preoccupied with his wife, Coffin barely noticed them. Her colour was coming back. 'I feel better now. Sorry, I was probably imagining it.'

It looked real enough to me, thought Coffin as he drove through the night streets.

Think about it. When did she get close enough to smell Charley? Look at her file and check. Don't ask her. In the mood she's in, she'll come up with wrong answers.

He set himself to amuse and relax his wife.

If she had been another sort of woman he would have tucked her up in bed with a drink of hot milk, but that would not do for his Stella. So he drove to Max's Deli which was still open.

Here he would feed her a cup of coffee and one of Max's rich, imported Belgian cakes. Max claimed that these cream-filled delicacies were flown in from Brussels daily but Coffin thought they came from Slough in a specially chilled van. He fancied he had seen it arrive in the small hours. Challenged, Max said: And wasn't Slough near to Heathrow?

One of the Feather Street ladies was giving a birthday party in a corner of the small inner room. She hailed Stella with delight and offered her a drink and a slice of special chocolate cake.

Coffin watched Stella join them and start to be happy again. The Feather Street ladies could be very exhilarating. For himself, he went to order some coffee.

Max served him himself and wanted to talk about his sister, Letty. 'Have you seen Mrs Bingham lately?' Max sounded worried. 'I've put in my bid for the catering in the Drama School, but I just get silence.'

I'd like to know where Letty is myself, thought Coffin.

'I don't like to worry Miss Pinero.' Although Coffin could see that Max would do just that if need be. 'It's not really her job. She's the Artistic Director.'

'She keeps her eye on things.'

IN THE NIGHT the wheels slowly turned, and the report from the community policeman who had checked Caroline's flat on the top floor of Annie's house was read and digested and a certain importance seen in it. It was passed to Archie Young, who gave it thought.

In the morning, John Coffin saw the fax on his desk.

ELEVEN

Where the river runs backwards

ON THEIR WAY to Max's Deli the pair were observed by another patrol car who reported on the radio that WALKER and MISSUS were nearing home. It was always as well to know where the boss was. Very little about the Chief Commander's life escaped his sharp-eyed Force.

In the patrol car, getting a strictly unofficial lift home, was the community officer who had called on Annie Briggs, searched Caroline's flat for a man, and had initiated the information about a 'suspicious character' seen 'loitering' which was now on Coffin's desk.

The two men were friends, although their careers were taking a different shape. Both were called James, so they were known as Jim and Jimmy. Jim was the driver. The third person in the car was a silent WPC, Jim's partner.

'There he goes,' said Jim, observing Coffin. 'He's been a lot easier since he got hitched.'

'Think so? He doesn't come my way much.' In fact not at all. Jimmy had never spoken to the Chief Commander, although he would have welcomed the chance and thought he could have told him a thing or two. He was deeply sceptical of the bureaucracy of the Force and wondered if any notice was taken of the careful reports he sent in. Straight in the bin was his bet.

Rarely did they talk about police matters. Crime you can live with, you don't have to talk about it. But the current two murders certainly did interest them.

The two men soon got down to discussing Didi's death and comparing it with Marianna Manners's. The same killer for both, they agreed. It happened, not often, sometimes. They avoided the fashionable term of 'serial killer.'

AFTER COFFEE and a slice of Max's special plum and almond cake Stella had recovered her spirits and wanted to forget about smells and so on. She decided it was time to worry about Letty.

'Where is she when I need her?'

'Gone missing,' said Coffin. 'Like her mother. It's in the blood.'

'I hope you won't.'

'No, I'm tethered.' He took her hand and gave it a pat. 'Let's go home.'

She stood up. 'On the way. Your place or mine?'

He was glad she was in an upbeat mood because he was going to have to ask some more questions about the smell; he couldn't leave it alone.

On the way from Max's they met Tiddles the cat, also on his way home. So they followed him and he positioned himself outside Coffin's front door in the Tower and waited.

'Do you know, I've never been quite sure of Tiddles's sex,' said Coffin as he felt for his keys. 'I suppose he's got one.'

'As much as any cat that's been spayed.'

Coffin gave her a wary look. 'Spayed?'

'Yes, Tiddles is a female masquerading as a male. I know you always call her he.'

'I'm not good on sex in cats,' said Coffin humbly.

'I expect you've seriously confused her.'

'Maybe we should send her down to the Karnival Club.'

He had the door open and Tiddles, unsexed but happy, bounced in before them. Bob, the dog, whose sex had never been in question since he was willing to mate with anything that moved, was the other side of the door.

'We ought to talk about this sense you had of Charley being present or having been present at the Karnival.'

'If Charley is this chap who is obsessed with me.'

'I'm just using that as a name,' said Coffin patiently.

'Or if he has anything to do with the killings.'

'I'm not saying so. Just speculating. We can't rule anything out.' *And if he's going for you next, then I want all the details I can get.* But he hoped Stella would not read that thought.

Stella sat down on the big yellow sofa which had been her contribution to his furnishings. 'Come on then, get the questions in and get it over.'

'First, when were you close enough to the fellow to get any personal . . .' He hesitated, fumbling for the words. 'To get any sensation about him.'

'When did I smell him, you mean?' said Stella bleakly.

'All right, yes. When was he close enough for you to get a whiff of him?'

Stella let her gaze go distant. 'Only once. Near St Luke's. Near the Workshop Theatre. I'd been at a meeting. And this figure was in the courtyard. I had to pass through the archway to get home.'

'So what did you notice?'

If he was hoping for details like alcohol, drugs or meths or even shoe polish and cigarette smoke, he was disappointed.

Stella shook her head. 'You know, I didn't notice anything special then. It was only when we walked through the Karnival that I thought I am reminded of something...' Her voice tailed away. 'It seemed very close then, his presence.'

'Perhaps I should have taken you back and made you look at every person there.'

Stella smiled. 'I had had a good look round and no, I didn't recognize anyone. Not to look at. I'm not being a lot of help, am I?'

'We'll dig away at it.'

Stella nodded without enthusiasm. 'I'll go on thinking about it and if anything comes to mind, then I'll tell you.'

But you'd rather not. He could read her face. She was more troubled by all this than she was willing to admit. He didn't want Stella to suffer in any way. He was very protective of her now, more than ever. She was his Stella.

So there was possession there, too. Jealousy as well if it got the chance to raise its head. Which it could do with alarming speed: he had seen Job Titus looking at her.

'What did you make of that little group, Titus and Eddie Creeley? Tom Ashworth too for that matter, he made up a third.'

'He was there on business, I suppose. It's always business with him. We ought to have asked him about Letty. He's in everything, that young man.'

Coffin was glad to hear her call Tom Ashworth 'that young man', it seemed to diminish any threat he might be. He had noticed Tom Ashworth, too, looking at Stella, who had looked back.

He would have to live with that side of Stella, he couldn't keep her on a string. He was not sure where strict faithfulness came in Stella's canon of wifely duties, while being uneasily aware that he had better not ask.

'But I like him better than Job Titus,' continued Stella. 'Did you see Titus eyeing me? He's a swine, that man. But I don't see him as a killer. He might hire someone to do it for him, but not Eddie Creeley. He's got more sense than that. Anyone could see Eddie Creeley is a no-hoper and probably the whole family always were.'

'They usually got caught,' admitted the Chief Commander. 'But they made a living by it. At least, the old generation did. Eddie's got a job in a local hospital, so I'm told. I don't see him as a killer somehow.'

'It's only because of his uncle and aunt,' said Stella. 'But you don't inherit murder like a disease. There isn't a gene for it.'

There might be, thought Coffin. But he had always been puzzled by the elder Creeleys' murder. He had never heard of an adequate motive for it. A little money had been stolen, yes, but surely not enough?

He looked back into the past. 'I never knew why they did it.'

'You mean they were innocent?'

'No, not exactly that,' he mused. 'But something never came out.'

Stella stood up. 'I'm going to bed. I've got a heavy day tomorrow.' She passed her image in a big wall looking-glass and gave an experimental smile. Awful. She'd have to do something about her face. Major cosmetic surgery, possibly. She studied her lips. Or perhaps a new lipstick would do it. Cheaper, certainly.

'About the group of three in the club tonight. Were you just asking my opinion to take my mind off the other thing, or did you really want to know?'

It had been a bit of both. 'Really wanted to know,' he said.

'Well, I'll tell you: they stood out like a sore thumb, didn't they? What were they doing there? What a place to meet.'

'I've been wondering about that. Job Titus called Eddie Creeley there and Ashworth followed them. So it all comes from Titus.'

At the door Stella paused. 'There's something I have to tell you...Job Titus and I, a couple of years ago, before you and I really took up again... There was nothing in it. Not really.'

'As these things go,' said Coffin savagely.

'Do you mind?'

'I'm furious.'

As he was. Hurt and deeply angry.

Stella nodded, and decided to say no more. It was up to him now. 'Coming up to bed?'

'Later.'

Stella hesitated, then picked up her jacket and left.

He sat on. It was something he would have to accept in Stella. And after all, it was in the past.

No comfort really. You can be jealous of the past. He went across to the bureau where he kept drinks and poured some whisky. He might have more than one drink, he felt he needed it. Deserved it. And what was this about the smell of Charley? Was Stella imagining it? Or even inventing it because she was disturbed by the sight of Job Titus?

No, Stella did not invent things, a certain bleak honesty was more her style. As now, for instance, in telling him what she had. She needn't have spoken. In a way he wished she hadn't.

He wished, too, that she did not have her name juxtaposed to that of Charley in the diary of a girl who had been murdered.

He thought about Eddie Creeley, named on a tape by that girl about to die. Just his name and the distant sound that might be traffic. It was puzzling.

Had Eddie Creeley killed Marianna Manners for money, and then killed Didi as part of an old family feud? Eddie certainly had his name in there, but there was no real evidence, circumstantial or forensic.

Not yet.

The blood in his room was being analysed and grouped, all its constituents laid out ready to be labelled. It might prove to be Didi's blood but Coffin guessed it was probably Eddie's own.

It was a point to think about: why had Eddie drawn his own blood? There was something about blood that excited the imagination. Perhaps Eddie was drinking it.

Eddie the Vampire?

I'm drunk, Coffin thought and put the whisky bottle away. He had been down that road before and come back. Eddie was no vampire killer. Or was there a serial killer out there who might be stalking Stella?

He picked up a photograph of her that he liked a lot. She had been appearing in a Coward revival of *Private Lives*. The production had been dressed in the full 'thirties style. Stella wore a long, bias cut satin dress, he knew it was a copy of a Molyneaux original of the period. Black and white with a silver bow on the shoulder. Her hands held a long cigarette holder. He could see her slender fingers and painted fingernails. Stella had lovely hands; she did not bite and never had bitten her nails.

The chewed battered nails of both Marianna and Didi. Did the killer need that?

Or was it a signal to him to choose this one? He walked to the window, enjoying even in his present restless and angry mood the sight of his bit of London spread out before him.

And he never once thought of his sister, Letty, absent now for some days.

IN THE MORNING Coffin went into his office early. He took Stella a cup of coffee in bed. At first he thought she was not going to speak. Then she raised herself on one elbow.

'Friends?'

'A bit more than that.' He sat down on the bed and studied her face with pleasure. Even first thing in the morning, she was good to look at.

'I'm too truthful, that's the trouble.'

'You can hardly be that.' He felt a strong urge to stroke her hair as it fell about her face. 'I've fed the cat and the dog. Tiddles has gone out but you'll have to walk Bob. I don't want to take him with me, he's fallen in love with the leg of my desk and it gets embarrassing.'

'He is a pest,' said Stella fondly. 'I don't know why we keep him.'

'Look after yourself.'

'I will, I always do, and I'll take Bob with me.' Bob was a keen guardian of Stella.

'And if you have any more thoughts about the smell... Let me know, will you?'

'You thought it was important?'

'You were upset. That was real, that meant something.'

'Yes.' Stella thought about it. 'It did hit me. But now it's faded.'

'Try and remember what really got to you. Analyse it.'

She nodded. 'Do something for me: think about Letty. I'm worried about Letty. Don't forget Letty.'

'I've got a busy day.' Several committees, two reports to read and absorb and one to write. As well as a diary heavy with appointments. In addition to a meeting with local journalists from newspapers, Radio Spinnergate and TV London, on whether his Force was dealing with racism and promoting enough women. He didn't delegate enough, he knew it was a fault. 'But when I've got time, then I'll think about Letty.'

'And what about Job Titus?'

'Let's agree to forget him.' Not that he could, professionally, do so. He knew he was doomed to have Job Titus, MP, cropping up in his life. Someone might always kill Titus, of course.

There was a large pool in which swam assorted fish. There was one called Eddie Creeley and another called Charley and another called Tom Ashworth who was swimming side by side (and possibly in competition) with two other fish called John Coffin and Archie Young. And the biggest fish with the sharpest teeth was a shark called Job Titus. He could sense the presence of other fish but not name them.

And floating in the pool were two dead fish, bellies up.

Stella drank her coffee and watched him go through the door. Think about Letty. He probably would and that would be all. But she was worried. She had got to know her sister-in-law pretty well over the formation of St Luke's Theatre and its allied institutions, and the one thing she had learned was that Letty kept her eye on her business.

'Money has to be watched,' she had said to Stella once.
'Or it gets away from you.'

And it was just on this point that Stella was troubled.

She lay back on her pillows and looked at the ceiling.
What she saw there was a question-mark.

IN THE MURDER ROOM where two separate but linked teams
were investigating the deaths of Marianna Manners and Didi
Dunne, Chief Inspector Archie Young, who was the link,
knew that he might have something important.

He had the report of the community policeman for the
area in Spinnergate where Annie Briggs lived telling him that
the neighbours had seen a strange man outside Annie's
house in Napier Street. Coming or going, they were not sure
which. A favourite television programme, from which not
even neighbour-watching could distract them, had claimed
them at the crucial moment. And a quick look later he had
gone.

But they had minded enough, felt nervous enough, to
complain to PC Jimmy Fraser, whom they knew. Archie
Young knew Jimmy Fraser also and trusted his judgement.

Jimmy had gone to Annie Briggs's house, asked to see
over the flat on the top floor where the tenant Caroline
Royal lived. Miss Royal was absent but Annie had, under
pressure, let him look around.

Not much trace of Miss Royal but signs of a man. He had
left clothes there. Jimmy thought this worth a mention.

Did they have Charley here?

He wanted to concentrate on all this but he couldn't think.

The bustle of the room had gone quiet. They were all listening.

Even in here he could hear the screaming.

'Archie,' he said to himself, 'you made a bad move there.'
His wife had told him many times that he was less than per-
ceptive in his handling of women. 'Gentle yes, subtle no.'
Kindly but heavy-handed, she had summed up for him.

I played the tape so she could confirm it was her sister's voice and she went mad. It was unfortunate but I had to do it. Who else could I ask?

Suddenly he realized the noise had stopped. He walked to the door and looked across the ground from the Murder Room to the main building. The woman detective whom he had left with Annie Briggs when she became hysterical saw him and walked across to him.

'The doctor came?'

'Yes, sir. He's quietened her down.'

'I'll go in and see her.'

Detective Winnie Baker hesitated. You didn't usually tell your boss what to do (especially Archie Young who was no angel), or in this case what not to do, but now it seemed wise. She had had half an hour of Annie in full cry and it was nothing to start again.

'I shouldn't, sir,' she said. 'You'll only get her going again.'

'I need to go over Miss Royal's flat. Annie's got the keys. And I'd like her with me.'

He did not say why.

Detective Baker said nothing but her expression said a good deal.

'Go in and ask her.' He just stopped himself saying, 'There's a good girl.' He was of the generation that wanted to say kind and helpful things to women but he knew it was no longer correct.

They ought to invent an expression like the theatre's 'break a leg'. Did people still say that? Probably that was wrong now.

Winnie Baker came back. She shook her head. 'She says only if the other one comes.'

'Who's the other one?'

Winnie hesitated. 'I think it's the Chief Commander, sir.'

Whether you liked it or not, and Archie didn't very much, preferring to be in total control of his own cases, that man got everywhere. You had to admire him. Archie did, and unconsciously modelled himself upon Coffin.

So he would telephone John Coffin or send a message and the great man would come in and say the right thing and ask the right questions and see what was to be seen and everything would be cleared up.

He let the momentary pique die away before saying: 'Right. I'll see what I can do. Stay with her. Have a cup of tea or something.'

But what has he got that I haven't got? he asked himself as he picked up the telephone. A way with women, and a seeing eye. Damn.

QUIETENED by the doctor's injection and soothed by the hot tea, Annie took them into Caroline Royal's apartment in a calm manner. Just a faint remoteness to her gaze suggested she was focusing on some view far, far away.

She had been driven to Napier Street in a police car. Archie Young had followed and the Chief Commander arrived last.

Annie met him at the top of the iron staircase. 'This is a fire escape really, you know.'

'I rather thought so.'

'I didn't put it in. It was here. But it was quite convenient because it meant I could let the top floor to Caroline.' She was unlocking the door as she spoke. 'Well, go in and have a look round, although I don't know why you want to. What's it got to do with Didi? My sister's dead, you know.'

'I did know.'

'Well, of course you did. I don't blame you.'

Coffin waited.

'Although I did tell you Eddie Creeley would kill me. I thought it was me he was after. He got Didi instead.'

Annie's face showed signs of breaking into areas of different expression. Eyes wild, mouth smiling, jaw tense as if inside her mouth her teeth were grinding away.

'Let's have a look round,' said Coffin quickly. Get it over.

'I heard her voice,' said Annie. 'You'll never know what that was like.' She stepped aside. 'Go on, look around. As if it matters now.'

Caroline Royal had left the place very tidy, a few small possessions like an old copy of *Vogue* magazine, a pair of gloves and scarf lay around but the bed was made, the small bathroom tidy and the kitchen bare.

Coffin looked in the refrigerator; an unopened packet of fruit juice and a small jar of honey seemed to be all it contained.

He went back into the bathroom and touched the soap: it was hard and dry.

'Miss Royal away a lot?'

'All the time,' said Annie. 'She's a buyer for a big London store so she has to travel a lot. Buying stuff all over the world.'

'Of course.' He moved back to the bedroom, Archie Young with him. He opened the wall cupboard in which the male clothing had been found.

It was still there. So was a woman's tweed suit, top coat and dressing-gown, all well worn and old.

'She hasn't been back?'

Annie shrugged. 'I don't know, I don't watch. She could have dropped in.'

And dropped out, Coffin thought.

The drawers of the dressing-chest contained make-up and a small amount of underclothes, and tights.

The three of them walked back into the sitting-room. Annie sat down.

'Who's the man?' asked Coffin.

'Don't know,' Annie shrugged. 'Her man.'

'But you've seen him?'

'Not really.'

'You're not being helpful, Annie.'

Annie turned her head away and looked out of the window.

'Oh Annie, Annie, Annie,' said Coffin. 'You aren't trying.'

'Doing what I can.'

Coffin walked to the window. To the Chief Inspector he said: 'Does this look to you as it does to me?'

Young nodded. 'Yes,' he said heavily. 'Wish I'd been in here before.'

Coffin turned back to Annie. 'Miss Royal has not been here for some time, has she?'

Annie licked her lips. 'I suppose not.'

'In fact you haven't seen anything of her for weeks.'

Annie turned her face away as if she didn't want him to read what was in it.

'You know what I think, Annie? I think in fact she could be missing.'

He sat down beside her. 'So we do need to know about that man.'

BACK IN HER OWN HOME with Coffin and the Chief Inspector, a new brew of tea was made and drunk. Annie poured the tea out with an air. It occurred to Coffin that she liked entertaining and got little chance to do it.

After two cups of tea she was persuaded to talk. Under probing, Annie produced a little more information about Caroline Royal and her man friend.

No, she didn't know his name. Caroline never referred to him.

'Didn't like being questioned?'

'She's a reserved person.'

'Perhaps she was ashamed of him? Did he strike you as someone she would be ashamed of? You say she's a sophisticated professional woman, so that would be a bit surprising, wouldn't it?'

'Perhaps he wasn't quite her class,' admitted Annie with reluctance.

Coffin pushed on to another aspect. 'He only left a few clothes here. Overcoat, raincoat, couple of hats.' Clothes that strongly reminded him of the figure that Stella had described: dressed in black, and wearing a hat.

'He didn't live here. Only visited.'

'You'd expect him to have left a dressing-gown, pyjamas.'

'I suppose he didn't wear them,' said Annie without much interest.

'I noticed he left a pair of boots, and inside was a pair of thick woollen socks. Any comment.'

'I suppose he had tender feet. I think he did limp a bit.'

'And no shaving materials.'

'Took them with him. You'll have to ask him.'

'Oh, we will. When we find him.' Which search you are not doing much to help. 'Find out where he works, where he lives. Where does Miss Royal work?' Or where did she work? He was beginning to have a bad feeling about Caroline Royal.

'One of the big Oxford Street stores.'

'But which one, Annie?'

Annie dragged at her memory, and let something come up. 'Ferguson and Dyer, I think.'

'Yes, I saw one of their carrier bags in the cupboard. Miss Royal seems to have nothing but winter clothes in there.' And not many of those.

He waited, and eventually Annie said: 'Well, if she was going to somewhere with a hot climate...'

'She's been gone longer than you admit, hasn't she, Annie?'

Silently Annie nodded. Once started nodding, she kept it up like a doll. Coffin gazed at her in alarm.

'I'll get you a glass of water.'

The doorbell rang and he could hear someone shouting through the letter-box.

'Annie, are you there? Are you all right?'

Annie took a deep breath and stopped nodding her head. 'It's Alex . . . Mr Edwards.'

Archie Young got up. 'I'll let him in,' he said hastily. 'Your social worker, wasn't he?'

'He's a friend now . . . He'll let himself in, he's got a key.'

And sure enough, Alex was in the room with them. He crossed at once to Annie's side.

'Saw your cars,' he said accusingly. 'Can't you leave her alone? Can't you see she's in shock? Are you all right, Annie?' He put his arm round Annie, who flinched away as Coffin noticed. 'Trust me, Annie.'

'Why did you make that racket at the door if you have a key?' said Young.

'I have a key for use in emergency: I don't regard it as my right to enter Annie's house at will,' he said with dignity.

Coffin spoke mildly. 'We're not an emergency.'

'I know you, you're the boss. What are you doing here?'

'I'm a friend of Annie's too,' said Coffin, his voice even gentler. He could see that Alex could barely restrain himself. There was a lot of emotion flaring round Annie's head and it wasn't clear if she realized it. 'We met a long while ago.'

He caught Young's gaze. The man's in love with her, it said.

He stood up. They wouldn't get any more out of Annie now, even if there was any more to get. She didn't know where Caroline Royal was or where she had gone.

'We'll find out where Caroline Royal works. Ferguson and Dyer, you said?' Annie nodded. 'And see what they can tell us.'

Annie's eyes flickered as if in alarm and Alex responded at once. 'What's she got to do with anything?'

'She doesn't seem to be around,' said Coffin. He turned to Annie. 'I'd like to have another look at her place later.' He held out his hand. 'May I have the key?'

Alex said at once: 'I'll come with you.'

'No need.' He kept his eyes on Annie. Silently she handed over the key.

'THAT MAN'S UP IN THE SKY and over the top,' said Young when they got outside. 'Always has been and he's getting worse. I don't think he's in the right job, he's not solid enough.'

'He cares,' said Coffin absently, fingering the key. He hoped Annie had given him the right one.

'Want me with you when you go to the Royal flat?'

'No.' He knew who he did want.

Young considered. He hated being left out when it was his job to be in, but there was nothing he could do. And the Chief had been a good detective in his day. The flair and the intuition were still there. He believed in hard slog and patient attention to detail himself, but there was no doubt a kind of telepathy helped.

He became aware that it was operating now and the Chief had read his mind.

'I'll let you know at once if I pick up anything,' he was saying.

As they parted, each to his own car, Young said: 'I don't think there's anything in the Royal absence. She's just taken off for time on her own.'

Taking most of her wardrobe, Coffin thought, and leaving a motley collection behind.

TO STELLA, over drinks in their sitting-room, he said: 'Tell me, do girls, working women, just take off for time on their own, so-called, these days? Don't they just say Well, I'm off to Paris or Saigon or New York with Tom or Dick or Harry and no business of yours?'

Stella considered. 'Yes, that's about it.'

'What would you have done?'

'Just gone. If I wanted to. Leave the odd message to my agent, maybe.' She knew she would have done so, an offer, an audition (although she was too important to audition these days, or thought she was), it was hard to leave those behind.

'And clothes?'

She thought about it. 'That's more difficult. I might take nothing much at all. Depends how rich the chap was, or how generous.'

'Thanks.' What an insight I'm getting into Stella's life, he thought.

'And don't ask,' Stella said.

'Ask what?'

'If I ever did.'

Then he decided instantly that she certainly had, more than once perhaps, and he was suffused with retrospective jealousy.

Aloud he said: 'Will you come with me to look at something?'

'At what?'

'A property.'

'Don't bite your tongue out telling me details.' But she finished her drink and stood up. 'What is it, are we moving house?'

'Just viewing. I want your opinion.'

STELLA RAISED her eyebrows in surprise as they drew up outside Annie's house. 'So this is it?' But she let him lead her up the steep iron staircase and open the front door.

He stood back to let her in. 'What do you make of it?'

'It's just a place.'

'Use your nose.'

Stella widened her eyes, registering surprise and comprehension at once. 'So?'

'Yes, go around, take your time.'

He watched as she walked slowly round the sitting-room, then the kitchen, finally the bedroom and bathroom. He could read her face. 'There's something, isn't there?'

'Maybe.' She frowned.

'Try the cupboards. Both of them.' His and Hers, he thought.

Stella opened the cupboard which contained Caroline's clothes, or what there was. She shook her head slowly. 'Not what you'd expect from a high flyer. If she was one.' She picked up the carrier bag of deep blue plastic with the name of Ferguson and Dyer spread across it and wrinkled her nose. Beneath it was a smaller paper carrier: Harrison's of New Bond Street. 'That's more like it, that's money. Harrison's is up there with Valentino and Yves St Laurent for my money.'

'Now try the other cupboard.'

This was the cupboard with the few oddments of male clothing and the boots with socks in them.

Stella stood there looking, then put her head closer to the clothes, then she shut the door with a little bang.

'Yes, that could be Charley,' she said. 'That definitely could be Charley... Do you know, I feel quite cold.'

She watched while he locked the front door behind him. 'Is that it?'

'Yes. Do you mind if we call in my office on the way home?'

'No, of course not.' Even if it wasn't her favourite place.

IN HIS OFFICE Coffin quickly typed a note to be delivered at once to Chief Inspector Young, wherever he was.

It was brief.

I am concerned about Caroline Royal. She may have gone off of her own free will but I think the man she had in the flat may have been Charley. I think we need to trace her.

As they drove back to St Luke's Mansions, Stella said: 'You are worried about the girl who owns that flat, aren't you?'

'Yes . . . I don't want to alarm you and I hope your chap never reappears, but if he does, stay well away from him.'

'I always do,' said Stella.

He parked the car neatly in the slot allowed to him beside the Mansions. There was no integral garage.

'Wait a bit,' she said. 'I've got something to tell you. We have trouble of our own. Letty has withdrawn almost all the money in the St Luke's Theatre account. The money has gone and she's gone with it.' She looked her husband straight in the face. 'I don't think she's coming back in a hurry, do you?'

Coffin tightened his hands on the wheel. Letty. Oh God, she's done a runner. Just like our mother.

TWELVE

Still the river runs backwards

DAMN LETTY, she was a complication he could have done without. She had come into his life suddenly, when he had not known she had existed, bringing with her news of his mother, and now she had gone and apparently taken a large sum of money with her.

That looked like panic, which was not something Letty suffered from as a rule.

He remembered how she had claimed that the man watching Stella might really be there for her. And hadn't her daughter come into it somewhere?

His skin prickled. Surely Letty could not be part of this case in any way?

What did he really know about Letty? Except that she was good with money. Too good, as it now seemed. He had liked her, admired her, trusted her. That looked like a mistake now.

And then the alarming, selfish, frightening thought: she could get me into trouble. Letty could get me into big trouble. If there had been any financial misdealings in money or property, the dirt could rub off on him.

For that matter, what did he know about Stella, except he loved her passionately and physically and that did cloud the mind. Then he rejected doubts about Stella with fury. She's honest, is Stella, perhaps more honest than I am. There were gaps in her life he knew nothing about, but weren't there always? You had to trust.

If I don't trust Stella I am nothing.

Towards the end of the case, talking it over with Archie Young, Coffin said that he had realized there were three centres for this crime.

Not centres which created the murders, or where they were done, but which made sense to them. Centres which drew together strands, connected them.

The office of Alex C. Edwards in Britannia Buildings, the unloved block of local government offices, was one; the small office of the Tashworth Detective Agency, Tash, T. Ashworth, Prop., was another.

And, as Stella had alerted him, the Karnival Club. This was the third.

He had been to Tash once, soon after coming into his command here, when it had been run by the elderly man whom he took to be the father or uncle of Tom Ashworth. The set of rooms beside a bookmaker's shop in Spinnergate had struck him as being like the sort of place where you waited for a taxi. There was even the same smell of long dead cigarette smoke.

He had never been to Alex's office but he had seen enough similar places in his career to know that it would be clean, cheaply furnished, and with a dead pot plant next to the coffee machine.

The Karnival changed its décor rarely and was best seen in artificial light, but oddly enough, of the three centres, he found it the most friendly.

These centres had, as he said, the scent of Charley in them: you could smell him there.

It was a rough thought.

Response to scent, the sense of smell, is a curious thing. Exactly what happens inside the brain when you smell something? Seeing colour is the brain's response to the electrical waves set up when we view an object, they beat across the brain and we see colour, which otherwise does not exist, so everyone sees it differently. A bit differently, anyway. Your yellow may not be my yellow, my red different from yours. Is smelling something of the same process? He had to ask the question.

He was in the middle of the boring but crowded committee meeting which he was not chairing and his thoughts were wandering.

So what was it that had stirred up Stella's electrical brain waves and would it do the same for anyone else? It hadn't done the same for him, as he had noticed nothing.

Well, he'd smoked a lot once and that had knocked his sense of smell. Or some of it. Some smells got through...as now...thoroughly masculine smells.

If jealousy had a smell, then he must be reeking of it. Stella had provoked a wave of it.

He yawned, it was hot in the room and the air-conditioning seemed to have given up. But then they were all smoking. The cupboard had smelt just like any other cupboard, a bit more scented than he might have expected.

'Chief Commander, can we ask your opinion?'

He roused himself and tried to think what he had last heard them talking about.

'It's all a question of timing, isn't it?' This being a useful intelligent-sounding holding phrase while he took a deep breath and waited for a helpful response.

...And there was Eddie Creeley. What you could call the Creeley factor. The thing to do was to take Eddie in for questioning again, he decided, and Archie Young had probably done it already.

The room seemed to be waiting for him to say something else.

'But of course, security must be the paramount precaution,' he said cautiously.

He had said the right thing. A murmur of approval rose around the table.

'The President will be sending over his own security advisers,' said a small dark-haired man across the table.

'Naturally,' said Coffin. He was off the hook.

Right, he knew the President, they had met once, long ago, before either held high office. Coffin was still surprised how far he himself had got; he wondered if the President felt the same? He returned to his own thoughts. His mood did not lighten. Sometimes you could sink in deep waters without even knowing you were swimming.

ONE DAY PASSED, two and then three, his mood did not lighten. Stella continued to worry about money and the Drama School with occasional outbursts against Letty. She read a lot of scripts, two for TV and one for film, throwing all aside saying she was worthy of better things. In short, showing less and less of the side that he loved and far too much of the side that had made them quarrel and part in the past.

It began to look as if they might be going that way again.

He started to feel that she blamed him for Letty while at the same time she was worried about Letty, whom she liked. Human nature, and especially Stella's, was never easy to handle. Now surely he himself was easy most of the time? He gave himself a little pat on the back.

He ought to worry about Letty himself but all he could feel at the moment was resentment that she had dropped him in it. He caused a few inquiries to be made about where she was, but nothing came of it. Letty had covered her tracks well.

Or had them covered for her by other hands... He repressed that thought. Pushed it right down below to a level where it gave him hardly any trouble at all.

A thought about her daughter, also out of sight, slid in and out of his mind without raising a wave.

He had long since learnt to keep his private life in separate drawers, so Letty and her daughter had the cover put over them. Even with his first wife he had been able to do this. Only Stella could never be tucked away. It was a measure of his feeling for her.

COFFIN AND STELLA had a dinner engagement across the river in that other London where he had once lived. He had an old friend still working in the Met, now a Chief Superintendent (Crime) who had just remarried. Walter Watson had married an old friend, a widow, after his own wife had died in a car accident.

Stella and Coffin had attended the wedding where Stella had expressed mild doubts about the happiness of two such ill-matched people, one so plump and fair-haired and the other so lean and sinewy. 'It's like Jack Spratt and his wife,' she had said.

'They've known each other a long time. No surprises, I imagine. She knows what she's got and so does he.'

Melinda's first husband had been a police officer and in fact it had been Walter Watson who had broken the news of his death in a shooting, and comforted her afterwards.

'But don't read too much into that.' They both knew the old legend that the officer who comforted the widow was also the first to seduce her. 'Anyway he who tried that with Melinda would get rough treatment: she's a karate expert as well as a first-class cook.'

'I like Melinda,' said Stella. 'Is she really called Melinda?'

'I don't think she was christened it, but she chose it for herself. She thought it suited her. They've asked us to dinner. Do we go?'

Stella nodded. 'Work out a date.' She tossed a book across. 'You can look through my diary and see what I've got free.'

He knew what she was doing. Check on my movements if you like, she was saying. See that I am not misbehaving.

'They suggest this weekend,' he said, not looking at the diary.

'Right, lovely, let's go.'

The Watsons, Wally and Melinda, lived in a comfortable detached house in Camberwell. 'It was my house,' said

Melinda, as she showed Stella where to put her coat. 'And I wanted to stay.'

'You did right. I mean, it was your place.'

Walter Watson had CID authority over an area of London which took in Dulwich, Camberwell and Peckham with a few outlying districts. It was a mixed area with some solidly prosperous streets not too far away from a large estate of poorer housing. The crime was mixed, too. Inventive, was how the Chief Superintendent put it. But it was a good place to live and he had never wanted to move away. He had his contacts there, a network that suited him. He was known, his sinewy, tough figure and blue-eyed face with plump, epicene cheek was easily distinguished as he went about his business. There were jokes about him, but not uttered too loudly.

The two men had kept up a friendship even although their careers had diverged.

The house smelt of new paint.

'Of course I made Wally paint it all through,' said Melinda.

'Quite right.' Melinda's taste ran to soft pinks and blues but Wally had made a good job of the repainting.

'But we bought a new bed.'

'Of course you did.' Stella smoothed her hair. Melinda had a photograph of a youngish man holding a dog on her dressing-table. Her first husband it must be, and Stella wondered if Wally minded seeing it there. As it was there, presumably he didn't. Or had no choice.

'Wally would have settled for the old one, but that didn't seem right.'

'Men have no imagination about some things,' said Stella with feeling. If she had put up pictures of her old loves there would have been quite a gallery. And Coffin would have minded.

'And much too much about others,' said Melinda. She waited to see if Stella laughed and when she did, Melinda laughed herself. She had seen Stella's eyes rest on the photograph. 'That's Wally's son.' She paused. 'Adopted, dear. Lovely boy, isn't he? Lives in Canada, in computers. I didn't have any children.'

There was a question hidden there and Stella answered it. 'I've got a daughter.'

'He had a son, didn't he? Got killed, I heard. I mean, we all hear things in this business, don't we? I was in the Force myself before I married. WPC. I wouldn't have gone any further. It's a man's world. Not so much as it was, of course. But I like being married, I like a man about, and Wally was ideal. He's really no trouble.' She didn't say why but went on: 'You know, I was terrified of meeting you.'

'Me? Of me?'

'You're famous, and you have lovely clothes, and you're so sophisticated.'

'Not very famous.' Mildly famous.

'But now I've met you properly...' Melinda led the way downstairs. 'I just admire you.' She shook her head.

They could hear the two men talking.

'Tell me, does your old man talk shop?'

'If he gets the chance.'

Melinda said thoughtfully: 'I think he'll get it tonight.'

'But you're a marvellous cook,' said Stella as she put her fork into the pâté, so smooth, rich and creamy. No, she wasn't imagining it, Wally Watson was certainly fatter and less scrawny than at his wedding.

The conversation was friendly, not touching on crime, while they ate their way through the duck pâté, and the roast beef, and the chocolate cake with whipped cream.

Starvation tomorrow, thought Stella, as she forked up a rich mouthful of chocolate and almond. Delicious, but God help their cholesterol level. She watched her husband eating the food with gusto, but he never put on weight.

That is my husband, she thought, we are actually married. It was still an amazing and sometimes alarming thought. She had the feeling that as a wife more was expected of her than she was actually delivering.

'I ran across Adam recently,' Coffin said to Wally. 'Remember him?'

'Certainly. What's he up to?'

'Oh, this and that. Calls himself Alice.'

'Heard about that. Not in any trouble, is he?'

Coffin shrugged. 'If he was, it would take a clever man to catch him. He's like a cat who knows how to steal the fish.'

The two men exchanged glances.

Wally poured out some wine. 'Got something that might interest you,' he said to Coffin. He turned to his wife: 'You going to make the coffee, love?'

Melinda stood up at once. 'Stella, give me a hand?'

'Yes, glad to.' Stella followed her to the door. Behind her, she heard Wally say:

'I think we've got something in common. There's a body you ought to take a look at.'

Melinda's face remained cheerful. She's a professional at crime, Stella thought. She realized that she would have to become the same.

WALLY WATSON went across to his desk in one corner of the room, opened a drawer and took out a folder. 'Don't usually bring work home.'

He had it ready, Coffin decided.

'But I wanted you to see this.' Wally laid a photograph on the table.

Coffin stared down. There was a woman's figure, legs drawn up, arms pressed against her, she was lying in a shallow grave, earth had fallen on her face.

'Strangled,' said Wally. 'I know you've got a couple. Thought this might be one of the same. We haven't identified her yet.'

It could be any youngish woman, Coffin thought. He mustn't think of Letty.

'We've sent out all details plus this photograph to all Southern Forces. Archie Young will have one.'

'I hadn't heard,' said Coffin.

'Just today. Coincidence you coming over, but I thought you would want to see.'

'Why do you think it's one for us?'

'Certain details,' said Wally.

'We've got one missing young woman.' Caroline Royal. Not Letty, never Letty.

THEY DROVE HOME in a relaxed mood, the recent tensions between them draining away.

'I'll drive,' said Stella, her voice amiable. 'I don't mind. I feel like it. Food does cheer the spirit. Was it the chocolate cake or the beef?'

'It was the wine and whisky with me,' said Coffin, loosening the seat-belt. 'Yes, you'd better drive.'

She waited until they were across London before asking: 'So what was all that about?'

'They've got a body. Might relate to the two bodies you know about.'

Stella drove on in silence. 'Some distance between them.'

'Yes, that's a point but might not be important.' Murderers might be mobile. Especially serial killers.

Stella thought about it. 'That would rule out Eddie Creeley.'

'I don't know.'

'And I don't see Job Titus popping out to Dulwich for a strangling.'

They both started to laugh.

Surely death could never be funny, so what were they laughing at? Stella parked the car. Just glad to be alive and with each other.

ARCHIE YOUNG was early next morning with news of his own. He telephoned.

'Caroline Royal does not work at Ferguson and Dyer and never has. They know nothing about her and have no contacts to help us find her.'

'Ah.' Coffin considered. He had never expected that Caroline Royal would be easy to track down and this confirmed it. The original disappearing woman. He said: 'Have you had anything from South London?'

'Yes, and I'm interested. Do you think it's Royal?'

'On the cards, isn't it?'

Coffin kept silent about his worry over Letty. 'I'd like to come along myself.'

'Right, right.' If Archie Young was not pleased at the suggestion, he knew better than to show it too obviously. A little doubt in his voice was about right and would be understood.

'And get a car to bring Annie Briggs over. She might be able to identify her.'

A cortege of three cars set out from the Second City, crossed London, was held up by traffic and arrived late. A message from Chief Superintendent Watson led them to the mortuary of the big teaching hospital which cared for the health of the district. The hospital was an old one with a distinguished history going back to the middle of the last century but its buildings showed its age. The local police division had always made use of the pathology department which was, indeed, world famous. Famous it might be, but the yellow brick shed which housed the mortuary was old and grimy, due for rebuilding with the rest of the hospital complex next year. But, as the hospital staff were wont to say: Next year never comes.

Coffin knew the place, as did every South London detective who had handled a murder inquiry. He knew the yellow brick outside and the brown paint inside; he knew the smell of disinfectant and something sweeter and more sickening. The place was fiercely clean and sterile but the human body in decay triumphed.

Oddly enough, there were no ghosts and everyone knew it.

But it did provoke strange thoughts. Coffin looked sideways at Wally Watson (about whose sex life there had been ancient speculation—which he had not mentioned to Stella) and wondered what an autopsy would show of his physical development?

He had taken a deep breath outside to see him through those first minutes before he must breathe again.

They had been met by Walter Watson with his professional face on. After the barest of greetings, he led them into a small side room. On a table lay the victim.

She was decently covered but her face was visible. Now cleaned up, Coffin knew this dead person was not Letty.

One fear put to rest.

'She's been in the ground a few weeks by the look of her,' said Archie Young.

The Chief Superintendent nodded, a matter-of-fact look still in place. 'A month or two maybe, but the conditions there kept her in a fair state.'

'Where was she found?'

'In a patch of open ground by the hospital. Pack of kids and two dogs uncovered her.'

'Nasty for them.' Young had a couple of children of his own.

'More excited than frightened,' said Watson. 'Kids can be quite tough, you know. And I'm not sure they thought the body was human.'

'So it was found by chance?'

'Well, we weren't looking for what we didn't know we had,' snapped Watson tersely. 'But we would have found her eventually, so to that extent the killer was unlucky if hiding her was his game.'

'How's that?'

'A new building for the hospital is going up. But there are remains of a Roman site and the archaeologists were due to go in for a dig. We'd have got her then.'

There was silence for a few moments.

'Our victims are recent,' said Archie Young.

The Chief Superintendent said nothing; he was watching John Coffin.

The young woman's hands had been crossed in front of her. Although the flesh had darkened and shrunk the fingers were delicate and well shaped. Each nail was painted bright red, the colour had withstood its burial better than the skin around it.

Archie Young said: 'Our girls both bit their fingernails. We thought that turned our Jimmy on. He looked for it and then, whammy, she was it.'

Coffin reached down and touched one nail. The red colour lifted and came away.

'I was waiting for you to get that,' said Walter Watson with satisfaction. 'Told you there was a something.'

'False fingernails,' said Coffin. 'Underneath, the natural nails are badly chewed.'

He stood back. 'Get Annie in for a look... Is she prepared?'

'As much as she could be.' Archie Young shrugged. 'She's got one of my best WDCs with her, Winnie Baker, they know each other.'

Coffin went outside to where Annie sat in the car. She was looking out with an anxious expression on her face.

'Good of you to come, Annie.'

'Didn't have much choice.'

'It's important or we would not have put this job on you. I know it's not an easy one.'

He got in the seat next to the driver and turned round to look at her. The driver stared straight ahead, carefully not looking.

'I want to talk with you. It seems necessary. Just a few questions.'

Annie gave a nod. All right, she was saying. Go ahead, but don't expect too much from me. Annie, except once, all those years ago, had never trusted the police. Perhaps she trusted this one, John Coffin, as much as anyone.

'Do you know where Caroline Royal is?'

'No.' She said it again, 'No.'

'But you know something?'

'No, I don't. Told you all I know. Must have.'

'She's been gone some time, hasn't she?'

'Looks like it,' said Annie who was finding difficulty in speaking.

'You must have been concerned?'

'I suppose I was ... but she travelled a lot.'

'Still ... as time passed.' He studied her face, she was white.

'Did you kill her, Annie? You can tell me.'

Annie shook her head violently.

'I don't believe that you did.'

'Thank you for nothing.'

'I don't believe women commit serial murders of this sort. If that's what we're seeing ... But you're an unusual sort of woman, aren't you, Annie?'

Annie bit her lip. A small bead of blood, red and shiny, appeared on her lip. Through her bloody lips she muttered something about Lizzie and Eddie Creeley.

'Oh, they aren't out of the picture,' agreed Coffin mildly, 'although I think Lizzie must be, as she was in prison at the time of the first murder.' Or the second, if this new body now counted as the first.

He sat back. There was a moment of silence. Annie, Annie, Coffin thought. I wish I could understand you better.

Annie licked at the blood on her lip. 'I'd like a drink of water.'

'We'll get you one. You know what you have to do? You know what you're in for?'

Annie nodded towards the woman detective. 'She explained.'

'And you're willing? Can't make you do it, Annie.'

There was a lot unsaid between them. He was remembering the frightened child who had seen two dead people being buried, who had faced a murderer.

Annie did not dwell on the dead old couple, whom she hardly remembered now except as two rolled-up envelopes being deposited in the earth, but she thought of Lizzie Creeley who was still alive and Eddie whom she hated. She found it easy to hate Eddie. He had killed Didi.

'Have you told anyone that you were coming here today?'

'I didn't have time.' Annie wished she had spoken to Ashworth and Alex Edwards, both of whom she regarded as her protectors. Alex occasionally sent in emotional bills, Ashworth had so far presented no account. But it was money on results with him, he said, and so far he had done nothing. 'I wish I had now. You've been rough with me.'

He didn't apologize, he knew he might have to be rough again. He also knew that there was a sturdiness inside Annie that could take it.

'I want you to promise to keep it to yourself until I say,' said Coffin.

Annie nodded. 'All right.' But she would tell Ashworth, that was a professional matter. A woman shouldn't come as close to murder as she seemed to do without telling someone.

Coffin stood back to let her out of the car. 'I respect you, Annie.'

Respects me but doesn't like me, Annie thought. And he was right, she was not likeable; what had happened to her when aged eight had made her unlikeable. Perhaps she always had been unlikeable and perhaps that was why life had elected her to see those bodies all those years ago. Annie had a profound superstition that life had a plan for you and her plan included death.

From that all else flowed.

He took her arm. At the door, Annie paused, she turned to him as if suddenly confused. 'Why are you here, why am I here?'

I'm here because I thought the dead woman might be my sister Letty; you are here because she might be Caroline Royal.

He shook his head but did not answer.

Annie was led in, white of face but resolute.

Coffin let her look. Then:

'Is this Caroline Royal?'

Annie fainted.

THIRTEEN

Fishing as the river is running backwards

THE PROCESSION OF CARS turned back to the Second City. Coffin drove with Chief Inspector Archie Young, whose subordinates followed in another car. Annie, somewhat recovered but very pale, was driven home by the woman detective, with whom she had now established a friendly relationship on the basis that any woman was better than almost any man.

She was grateful that the body was not Caroline, but knew she had not seen the end of any questions.

I didn't know the girl at all, she told herself and all who would listen. It was her face that made me faint. So human and so dead. It might almost have been myself.

'Now calm down, dear,' the woman detective said. So Annie knew she must have spoken aloud. 'You didn't know who it was and that's all for the moment.'

They'll be after me again about Caroline. But this time, Annie was careful not to say it aloud. *That's not over with.* She knew it with a sad conviction.

'SO SHE'S MISS NOBODY,' said Archie Young in an unusually poetic vein. He had been moved by the body, so young, so very dead.

'Oh, she's somebody all right,' said Coffin. 'Miss No Name, though.' Certainly not Caroline Royal, if Annie was to be believed. Nor was she Letty Bingham, his own sister, thank God, but of course it never could have been Letty. He was just being over-anxious. A woman like Letty did not turn up dead in Dulwich, South London.

'Very young, she's younger than the others.'

Younger even than Didi. Not a child but not far away.

'Yes, that in itself ought to have told us she wasn't Caroline Royal . . . Who remains missing.'

Young was not so interested in Caroline Royal as his superior was. 'She'll turn up. They do in the end.' Dead women, he meant, murdered women.

'This one is one for us, though. No rape, no signs of attack from the murderer or resistance from the victim. She put up her head and said yes, just like the other two. Strangled. Same method of killing.'

'And of course, the chewed fingernails.'

'That's what turns him on.'

The traffic was dense in the tunnel as they went through to the other side. Like the entrance to Hell, Coffin thought, as they drove in. Dante would have been able to describe it, although he might have been disconcerted by the strong smell of diesel oil and by the noise of pop music from the car radios, and the faint, very faint, smell of death and corruption.

Or was he bringing that with him from the mortuary? Some smells do stay in your nose.

'Does it strike you that there is a difference, with this unidentified body?'

The Chief Inspector tried to concentrate. The Old Man's got something on his mind. Had had for some time. Might be Stella, his own Alison had hinted that certain stresses were taking place. And what wonder, he thought, neither character being of the easiest.

'Bound to be some, aren't there?' Abstracted but polite, he avoided a small car that was weaving in and out of the traffic lanes.

'But I think these might be important... Don't you get the impression that the other two bodies were meant to be found? Found soon and found...' He paused. 'As arranged.' This time it was not a question he was asking but a thoughtful statement.

Archie did not answer for a moment. 'Hard to say.'

Coffin could hear Wally Watson's voice, repeating an earlier statement: Only found by chance, boys playing in the wood near the hospital, their dog dug her up. Bit of her anyway. An arm sticking out... We'd have found her in the end, though, because that bit is going to be developed as part of the hospital. And then, as I said, it was due for an archaeological dig. Roman and possibly early Saxon.

All this would be well known.

And again: Some poor kid that's run away from home and got caught. No one will claim her. Or not for some time. Maybe never.

Coffin wondered if that would prove to be true. Somehow he thought this girl was one who would be claimed.

'It's one of the series, though,' said Archie confidently.

'Think so?'

'The nails prove it to my mind. It's little things like that that give it away. It's what he's looking for. It's the mark.' He added, 'This death brings in the Met and that's a help.' Not that he liked sharing, of course, he was like an alley cat in that; what was his, was his.

And a nuisance, thought Coffin, reading his mind accurately; rivalry between the two Forces was not unknown.

'And we've got to accept that there may be other bodies.'

'Could be.'

Outside it was beginning to rain and even inside the tunnel the temperature was dropping. Coffin felt cold. 'You've known Wally Watson for some time?' asked Archie Young as he drove out of the tunnel and felt the fresh air.

'For years.'

'He's a good sort. In his way.'

'He's a good copper. Could have risen higher if he'd wanted but he likes it where he is.'

'Nice place, Dulwich. Thought of living there myself once. Alison's got an aunt who says she's going to leave us her house, but it would have been difficult for work. Long drive.'

'What will you do about the house?' inquired Coffin absently, his thoughts still running on the series of murders.

'Sell it, I expect.'

'Property is always useful.' Letty had taught him that much.

'About the chewed nails,' he said. 'Doesn't it strike you that the killer must have known about her nails?'

Covered, the nails had been with bright red falsies, but the killer had known what was underneath.

Was he straining the logic there, or was it so?

'Might have done,' said Archie Young, as if he didn't think it important.

They drove on in silence. Presently Young said: 'There's your good lady...' He had this tiresome way of talking sometimes, Coffin thought it was the result of some awkwardness when he had to mention personal relationships. 'Heading for the Spinnergate Tube Station.'

There was Stella, wearing dark spectacles, a striped woolly cap on her head and jeans with a tweed jacket. My camouflage clothes, she called them.

Also, her working gear. 'She's off to a rehearsal,' he said.

She had her head down and was moving away fast.

The Chief Inspector slowed down, watching Stella who had stopped to buy a newspaper from the stall hard by the Underground station. She looked up, saw her husband and waved.

'Let me out, Archie, thanks. I think she wants something.' And Coffin shot across the road.

'Bless you, and good luck to you, Buster,' murmured Archie Young to himself, with sympathy and irony. He knew a husband whose marriage was under stress when he saw one. He'd been there himself.

Coffin caught up with Stella.

'Got a minute?' she said. 'Something to tell.' She looked at her watch. 'I'm in a hurry, though.'

'I'll walk beside you... It's important?'

Coffin got his wife a ticket from the machine, then went down the escalator beside her.

'It's Letty, I've had a message from her. It was on my answering machine. I don't know when she left it... I've been upstairs with you and didn't check the machine all day yesterday.'

This was unusual for an actress, ever hopeful for that big new offer, that angel in the wings.

'Well?'

'So that's it, really.' A train was already approaching, moving the air in front of it down the tunnel. 'She didn't say anything much, just that she was well and would be in touch... The message is there for you to hear.'

'Where is she?'

'Didn't say.'

'Damn.'

'Sorry, I know you've got a lot on at the moment... And there's something else, isn't there?'

'Yes, another body. Stella...' A train was already approaching. 'Stella, the smell thing. Think about it and let me know if you have anything to add.'

'I think I have already.'

He could see she didn't want to talk about it. 'Have a try. Think people, Stella.'

Stella stepped through the open door of the train, turned and waved. 'I will. Promise.'

Before the doors could close, Coffin said: 'Stella, what was the name of the shop on the other carrier bag in Caroline's cupboard?'

'Harrison's of Bond Street,' she called out as the doors came together. Then she was gone, the train speeding on into the tunnel towards central London.

Coffin walked towards his office, where, under the firm eye of his secretary, he set about clearing his desk.

When he had a gap, he spoke to Archie Young on the telephone. 'Inquire at Harrison's of Bond Street if Caroline Royal worked there.' There was a mutter across the line. 'Just an idea...'

He could imagine what Archie Young was saying to his Inspector: 'The boss is having one of his psychic turns.' He wouldn't laugh, though, because he had met this trick of Coffin's before, been sceptical and then found it had worked.

And it was no trick, it was based, as he knew, on seeing further into the wood than he did himself. That was the difference between Archie Young and the Chief Commander and why John Coffin was where he was.

COFFIN WENT into his outer office about to say to his secretary that he was going for a walk (his code name was not WALKER for nothing), only to find himself confronted with Job Titus, MP, and Eddie Creeley. Titus looked as usual, nothing seemed to dent his ebullience, but Eddie Creeley's face was white.

Coffin sent a reproachful look at his secretary, but she was new in the post, a career move for one helper and pregnancy for the other had left him naked to the world for a few weeks with only temporary help. Frances, his new secretary, had not yet learnt all the rules, the foremost of which was: Keep them all out. His assistant, young Andrew, was on a course, his office was understaffed.

However, he admitted that Job Titus would be a hard man to turn away. He himself found it difficult, but he played the card he had in his hand.

'I'm afraid that I'm just going out.'

Titus took no notice, he brushed past Coffin. 'Won't keep you a minute. Come on, Creeley.' He didn't look behind to see but he had Eddie Creeley on a string and he knew it. Creeley followed meekly. Last came John Coffin.

He closed the door behind them. 'Well?' He did not ask them to sit down.

Job Titus drew up a chair and sank down, Eddie remained standing, so did Coffin.

'You've got another body.'

'How do you know that?' Into his mind shot a picture of Miss Nobody, the girl with the tumbled black hair and the chewed nails. Titus should not know about her yet.

'It doesn't matter.'

You worry me, Coffin decided. You have sources of information I don't control, I don't trust you, and I don't like you. And you don't like me.

'It does matter, it matters to me, but we won't go into that now. What do you want? Why are you here?' He didn't sit down. A faint sense of the ridiculousness of the situation was beginning to seep into him. He'd count to three and then he would sit down. Invite Eddie Creeley to do the same.

'If there's another body and it forms a series, then I'm not guilty of killing Marianna, and Eddie here is not guilty of killing Didi.'

'I loved Didi,' said Eddie hoarsely. 'Wouldn't have touched her.'

'And for what it's worth, I was fond of Marianna... All right, she could be a pain, so can most women, but you don't kill them just for being themselves.'

'It's true that another body, strangled like the first two, has been found, but no conclusions can be drawn yet.'

'Then let me draw them for you: if you have a multiple murderer, then it's not me and it's not Eddie. I did not kill Marianna, Eddie did not kill Didi and Eddie did not kill Marianna for money for me... Yes, I know you thought that.'

Once again, he knew too much.

'So you can stop digging into my life looking for muck.'

'I'm not digging into your life.'

'No, but your men are.'

Coffin looked at his hands and masked what might have grown into a smile. Good for you, Archie Young, so you have been looking into Job Titus.

Titus saw him. 'Well, damn you for being smug.'

Coffin jerked upright.

'Nothing in your life that you've ever been ashamed of?' Titus was an angry man.

'We all have.'

'Of course you have. So have I. More than I'm proud of, I expect. They'll find things there if they dig hard enough, but that is not what your job should be. I did not kill Marianna. Must I say it again?'

'I heard the first time.'

'And perhaps it has never occurred to you that I was seeing Eddie because I was sorry for him. Because I think the Creeley family are a sad lot who could do with a helping hand. Apart from anything else, I am their MP, they are my constituents, it's my duty to look out for them. Lizzie Creeley wrote to me. What she and her brother did all those years ago was wrong, but she's paid. I was sorry for her.'

Coffin took a deep breath.

He didn't like Titus, he never had, but he had to admit there was a genuine note to all this. It would be intolerable if he was obliged to like the man or even to respect him.

He stood up, walked across to a wall cabinet. 'Let me offer you a drink.'

FIFTEEN MINUTES LATER he saw them out himself. Eddie Creeley shook his hand several times, muttering thanks. He was limping slightly.

'How's your leg, Eddie?' asked Coffin.

Eddie blushed. 'Better. My own fault. I did it myself, I thought I could kill myself...cut a vein. Didn't work. Wasn't brave enough, hadn't the stomach, felt sick.'

'Dying can be a harder job than it looks, Eddie. I'd steer clear of it if I were you.'

Job Titus had moved ahead. 'Come on, Eddie, I'll drive you home.'

When they had gone, his secretary said: 'Are you still going for a walk?'

'No, I don't think so.'

'I'm sorry I let them in.'

'It didn't matter.'

'Oh, good, I thought you were really angry, but now you're not.'

He leaned against the door, admitting with reluctance that Titus had altered his mood. That's charm in operation, he admitted, and I'm not sure if it's honest or if you can trust it.

He straightened up. 'I've changed my mind. I will go for a walk.'

THE MESSAGE went around: WALKER is on the prowl.

The Chief Commander did not go far, he walked a few hundred yards to a small park which perched on a hill so that it looked down on the river. He sat on a bench thinking.

He enjoyed surveying this Second City for whose peace he was responsible, and from where he sat he could see the top of St Luke's Mansion, his own tower was unmistakable. He could make out the curve of Napier Street where Annie Briggs lived, and if he used his imagination he could see where the roof of the Karnival Club must be.

He thought about the three dead girls; he thought about the tape with Eddie's name on it. If Eddie had not been the killer, not been named by the soon-to-be-killed Didi because he was there, then he had been named deliberately.

He thought about the new body whose chewed nails had been covered. The killer had known about them.

That must mean that the killer was not a man picking at random, this killer was working deliberately, choosing victims and casting suspicion on purpose.

This killer was at home among them.

The wind blew from the river bringing dampness on its breath. He got up, walking down the path to the gate.

Out there, the police machine was working on. Interviews were being passed to the Locating Officer. The computers would be working overtime (if they didn't break down) and now it was an inter-force investigation, the Metropolitan CID would be involved.

With all this concentrated work, they ought to nail the killer.

But luck came into it too, you always needed that special bit of luck.

HE WALKED BACK to the office, checked the latest letters and faxes and calls that had come in. All routine, nothing fresh as yet from Archie Young and his team.

He went home, his mind calling up his other current worry: sister Letty. He had a key to Stella's flat, so he let himself in to listen to Letty's message on her recording machine.

Letty had not had much to say and had probably chosen her time when Stella would be out so that she would not speak to her directly.

Don't worry about me, she said, I'm all right and will be in touch. Trust me.

He listened carefully. She had been speaking on a public telephone in a noisy place.

He ran it again. Voices and movements in the background. A voice speaking on a public address system. The speaker was making an announcement of some sort.

A railway station? And if so, where?

He left Stella's place and climbed his own staircase. It might be possible to bring up the voice, hear what it had to say, and identify the location.

Possibly. Science was magic. But then Letty herself was still on the loose and doing what?

The whole place was dark with no sign of Stella. The dog was asleep on the bed and the cat was looking out of the window, so there was life around.

He made himself some coffee and considered a strong nip of whisky but he had gone that way once too often in the past and it was better avoided.

As he went to the refrigerator he found a note from Stella stuck to the door. 'I will cook dinner,' it said.

Fat chance, he thought, looking around the bare room. There might be food there but it was well hidden. He sat down in the kitchen to drink his coffee and continue to think.

But when Stella arrived within the hour, she confounded him: she was followed by a trio of helpers from Max's Delicatessen, each bearing dishes.

She smiled at him and kissed his cheek. 'Friends?' She had never quite understood why she had been cast into darkness after telling about Job Titus, but she was glad to be back in the warm. She felt sure she was.

'Did you say cook?' said Coffin, looking over her shoulder.

'It counts as cooking.' She waved her hand as her supporters deposited dishes on the table. 'Beef en croûte, salad and garlic bread. I think there are mushrooms in that dish.' She lifted a lid. 'And orange pudding in this.' She distributed tips and smiles lavishly to the dish-bearers, then took up the conversation begun in the Underground as if they had only just parted.

'So what about Harrison's of Bond Street?'

Coffin broke off a lump of garlic bread. 'I don't know yet. Just an idea... There's enough garlic in here to keep off vampires.'

'Perhaps that was my idea.'

He looked at her sharply. 'What's that?'

Stella sat down, facing him. The cat leapt on to her lap where she stroked it. 'My follower was back today.'

'What?'

'Yes, just as I came out of the Tube... Must have been waiting. There's a dark corner there, good to lurk in.'

'He, she or it threw something at me.'

She saw the alarm in his face. 'No, it wasn't a bomb although it could have been. It was this.' She reached into her pocket and put a rose on the table.

'If that's from Charley, then I think it's goodbye.'

FOURTEEN

In the murky river

NO ONE DISTURBED THEM that night except the cat demanding to be let out and then in again.

'Stella, I am going to take the tape from your answering machine and see if I can get the background noises brought up. It should be possible, technically... It might help to work out where Letty is.' God knows what she was up to.

'I wish you would. I'm worried about her.' Stella studied her face in the looking-glass on her dressing-table while she considered what shade of lipstick would give her most uplift today. Sometimes a bright colour destroyed you, whereas on another day it was just what you needed. Soft colour today, she thought. Then she said, as if one decision made released another, 'About the smell. It wasn't totally masculine. Men and women do smell differently, you know, and I don't just mean aftershave and toilet water. It's the hormones.'

'I know,' said Coffin. Did he though?

'And the figure that came near me that day... Well, the clothes smelt of a man, smoky and masculine, but there was the smell of a woman too.'

'And that's what you picked up in the Karnival Club?'

'Yes. Similar.'

'Thank you,' he said. He knew where that thought led him.

But in the morning, as soon as he arrived in his office he got the telephone call he had been hoping for about Caroline Royal.

'Yes,' said Chief Inspector Young. 'Yes and yes. Harrison's of Bond Street do know Caroline Royal, they have employed her for years and she still works for them. I don't know how you knew.'

'Just something I saw.'

'It's a pity my lot didn't draw the right conclusions, eyes and no eyes,' said Archie Young somewhat sourly. He did not enjoy being set on the right track too often by the boss. Just once, he prayed to his anonymous God who sounded very like his former headmaster at school, just once, let it be me.

'And you have an address?'

'We have an address for her. South London.' Then he added: 'They haven't seen her for some time. She'd been on a business trip to America and since then has had a bit of leave.'

'Have they spoken to her?'

'Not recently.'

'Well, good luck to you.' Coffin hesitated and the Chief Inspector crossed his fingers. 'I wish I could come with you but I can't.'

The Chief Inspector uncrossed his fingers and said cheerfully that he would keep in touch.

Middle of the day and the river running fast

CAROLINE ROYAL was not expecting a visitor, she was lying in bed reading. By her side was a mug of coffee and some fruit. Breakfast as a meal was out; she was a tall, well-built young woman who dared not put on weight. She wore trouser suits a lot, all the travelling she did made it convenient, but her clothes were tailored, made for her at Harrison's and she could not risk expanding out of them. No one was allowed to get fat at Harrison's.

She looked down at her legs stretched out on the bed. Nice around the ankles, a bit thick on the thighs, put on more weight and she would look like a middle-aged man in that latest tweed. Lovely colour, of course, like ripe mulberries, and delicious texture, you couldn't beat the Italians.

But not to look like a man, although she did admit that she had had fun once or twice, wearing a tie and putting on a felt hat. Which had been a mistake in one way, clearly a mistake, because it gave certain people the wrong idea. One certain person, anyway.

I am Caroline Royal, she said to herself. She said it again, like a mantra. Caroline Royal, Caroline Royal.

It was as well to remember it, because she hadn't been christened it, had sort of invented herself. The fashion world was a tough business and the power to invent yourself and reinvent yourself was important.

She had done it more than once and thought she might soon be moving on again.

When the doorbell rang she was under the shower, she considered ignoring the summons, but it rang again with the sort of energy that forced an answer from you.

She wrapped herself up and got there before the next ring. 'What do you want?' she said aggressively. The sight of three men there both alarmed and got the adrenalin rising at the same time.

Chief Inspector Young and a sergeant from the Second City investigating team, together with a man from the local CID because this street was in the Met's territory, stood there. Politely he identified himself before asking if she was Miss Royal and could they come in?

'Why me?'

He murmured something about a murder inquiry but he was watching her with interest. As Caroline stepped back into the room, he summed her up as a masculine-looking girl who could probably look after herself.

'Wait while I get dressed.'

She returned wearing a pleated skirt with a silk shirt in which she looked entirely feminine. Women could always surprise you, Young thought.

She seemed startled to be asked about Napier Street and Annie Briggs, who had not, she implied, been an ideal landlady.

'No,' said Caroline Royal. 'No, I haven't lived there for weeks. Months. I paid my rent and cleared out. I didn't like my landlady, she was creepy. And no, I didn't leave male clothes behind. And I didn't have a man there. Not once, not ever.'

I have no sex life to speak of, except in the odd hotel room in Paris or Rome or New York. I am always on the move, and even then it is usually to cement a deal. They are not celebrations of sex but a kind of business arrangement.

'She had a man about the place, more than one possibly. I caught the odd glimpse.'

Caroline did not think she could identify the man, just the odd flash, they knew how it was.

'No, it was not the reason I moved, it was not my sort of place, not as near the City Airport as I'd thought, and miles from Heathrow. I travel a lot, just back now... It's how I come to have heard of the murder. I liked Didi.' She frowned. She was right to have got out. It might have been her.

'Was it Annie?' she asked. 'I mean... is it Annie who killed Didi and the other one?'

'Why do you say that?'

Caroline paused, shrugged and looked doubtful. 'Don't know. Just came into my mind. She's that sort, could be anything.'

Late afternoon. Low tide on the Thames

ARCHIE YOUNG WENT BACK and made his report to the Chief Commander. 'So Caroline is alive and well, has not lived in Napier Street for some time, and she fingered Annie for the murders.'

'You thought she was honest? Telling the truth?'

'I did. A tough young woman, but honest.' A touch masculine, but attractive.

And Annie had lied. Lied up down and round about. Had them for fools. Coffin found he resented this treatment, and he knew what to do about it.

'Better see Annie, then.'

'She's playing the same card as before. Won't see anyone if you aren't there.'

Coffin looked at his diary: 'This evening, then. Keep her in play until then.'

IT WAS TRUE that the Chief Commander was busy with the routine duties of his office, but he needed time to think. He hoped Archie Young was doing the same.

He allowed himself an hour which he called his Think Session.

He read through the file that contained all the up-to-date reports on the deaths of Marianna Manners and Didi Dunne. He had nothing yet on the new and unidentified victim.

As far as he could see, there was no circumstantial evidence that connected any known suspect with the death of either girl. No fingerprints, no discernible body traces, no forensic evidence of any kind. The killer had been clever or lucky.

Job Titus was clever, Eddie Creeley was not. Job Titus might be lucky, Eddie Creeley belonged to a family that passed on bad luck like a legacy.

He knew what Young would say. 'When we know who it is, then we will get the forensic evidence,' and he would think: Oh, Archie, Archie, those days are done. Evidence first, please, and then the arrest. Not the arrest and then dig out the evidence that convicted. Tempting but dangerous.

So they had two dead bodies, and a third, and nowhere to look. He knew the police machine was rolling on and any moment now might produce a vital piece of information.

But at this moment there was nothing but questions.

The tape with Eddie's name on it.

The chewed fingernails.

The fact that the last victim had been the first killed.

These were interesting facts that had to be explained.

In all cases, there were left questions unanswered, puzzles with no easy answer, and perhaps this was what they had there.

He drank some cold coffee, which tasted rank on his tongue. A long while since he'd dealt with a poisoning case, he thought, but cold coffee would be a way to administer it. If you could get the victim to drink.

What was he thinking then: that the three deaths were connected, one killer involved? Yes, he accepted that as real.

So they had a serial killer?

Why then did he have this uneasy feeling that this was not a serial crime in the classic sense?

Because he had the strong feeling that all the deaths were meant to be discovered and the first death was to be found last.

It might be they had found the last girl too soon for the murderer. Was that a feasible thought?

The power of analysis and then of synthesis that had given him such power as a detective was forcing him now to break down the events into various pieces, not just as previously seen, and he was putting them together in another mosaic.

A killer with a plan. A Charley, not sexually driven but otherwise motivated.

What motive? Love, hate, revenge, money, malice, these were good sign words.

He supposed you could fit Annie out with revenge. She had long given signs of wanting revenge on the world.

As ARCHIE YOUNG MET HIM, walking across the pavement on Napier Street to that tall, ugly house with the empty top floor, he said: 'One more thing: Caroline Royal said, ''Ask Annie about the Karnival Club.'' She seemed to think it meant something.'

'I bet it does.' That place seemed to fit into everything. But Caroline Royal's words echoed his own thoughts. Young's too, judging by the look on his face.

Without another word, they went in to see Annie together. The door was opened by a uniformed woman police officer who had the tired, baffled look that contact with Annie seemed to bring on.

When they got there, Annie was supported by Tom Ashworth and Alex Edwards.

'Hello, Annie. You wanted me, here I am.' Coffin nodded towards the two men.

'I asked them to come.' Annie jerked her head defiantly. Go on, blame me, send them away if you dare, she was saying.

No one was better at body language, thought Coffin, a natural performer. Or was dissembler a better word?

'So, Annie, you know why we are here? To get the truth about Caroline Royal. She has not lived in the flat above for some weeks, has she? She gave notice and left and you knew it.'

Annie remained quiet.

'Come on, Annie, the male clothes found there were not hers. Nothing to do with her. Whose were they?'

Alex Edwards went across to where Annie sat and put his arm round her. 'Don't bully her.'

'Am I bullying you, Annie?'

'Don't Annie me.'

'Let's go up the stairs and look around, examine the clothes. Shall we?'

Alex said loudly: 'I call that bullying. Don't go, Annie.'

'I don't want to go,' said Annie.

'I think we'd better, Annie.' Coffin's voice was cold. He held out his hand. Still Annie stayed where she was. 'Or shall we bring them down to you.'

'Don't go,' said Alex.

Annie stood up suddenly. 'Shut up.' The Annie underneath, who was not so docile and good and gentle as the Annie on top suddenly showed. 'Let's get this over.'

All four trailed up the iron staircase. 'You've got a key,' Annie said. 'Must have. I gave you one.'

Archie Young produced a key and unlocked the front door. Inside, the flat smelt damp and empty. Easy to believe now that it had been unlived in for weeks.

Coffin said: 'Let's get those clothes from the cupboard. You do it, Annie.'

She didn't move.

'All right, I will.' Coffin went into the bedroom, brought out the dark overcoat, boots and hat. He held them out. 'Try them on, Annie, try them on for size.'

She took them and threw them on the ground.

'They are yours, aren't they? You wore them. My wife and others saw you in them. You like dressing in them. Annie here, Charley at the Karnival Club.'

Tash said, 'Say nothing, Annie.'

'My wife saw you. You hung around. You frightened her.'

In a rough quick voice, Annie said: 'I didn't harm her, I love her, I just looked.'

'Looks can be a threat,' said Coffin.

'I wanted a part of her.'

Coffin winced. Poor Stella, many wanted a part of her, unlikely vultures. Perhaps he was one.

'Let's go back downstairs,' said Tom Ashworth.

But Annie, having started to talk, could not stop. 'I knew when I saw those two Creeleys burying the old man and woman that I was different. Not like other children. It took me a time to realize what it was, years really, although I was always worried. Then I knew. I didn't have one sex, I had two. I could be what I liked. But don't get me wrong, I was a good wife and mother. Only I suppose my husband could tell . . . But I'm a good mother.'

'I'm sure you are,' said Coffin gently. 'Where's the child now?'

'She's with her gran, my husband's mother. They get on. I sent her away.'

'Annie, be quiet,' said Tash.

'I'm advising her,' said Alex Edwards. 'I do that.'

'You be quiet too.'

'I didn't kill anyone,' said Annie. 'I didn't, I didn't.' She started to scream at the top of her voice. 'Get out, all of you.'

The noisy, violent unstable Annie was out in the open.

FIFTEEN

Dead water

CHIEF INSPECTOR Archie Young meditated aloud: 'So we've got an occasional transvestite who has an obsession with your wife and possibly other ladies but who probably didn't kill anyone.'

'I think she could kill someone,' said Coffin, who had been alarmed by the look in Annie's eyes. 'But it might be herself.'

'She has friends, helpers. Alex Edwards for one, although he's an odd bloke and I wouldn't choose him as my own best friend, but she seems to like him. Or perhaps she hasn't got much choice, he does hang around. And there's the chap from Tash. I suppose she's paying him?'

'He likes payment,' said Coffin, thinking of the substantial bill for Stella's divorce. And no doubt Letty, *in absentia,* was clocking one up also.

'You can tell Mrs Coffin to stop worrying now.'

'I think she was telling me herself,' said the Chief Commander, remembering the look on Stella's face when they had talked about the scents of men and women. How long had she known?

'I'm afraid I haven't helped much in this case,' he went on. 'All I seem to have done so far is eliminate one suspect after another.'

Job Titus was gone, Eddie Creeley was out, now Caroline Royal and Annie. Had they ever been serious suspects?

'You've been interested, sir,' said Archie smoothly, 'and that always encourages chaps in the field.' He was being tactful and he knew it.

'Did I tell you I had a conversation with Titus and Creeley?' Not that Creeley had said much. 'All bluster and puff and as much oil as the water would bear.'

'You don't like Titus.' Young was reflective. 'But who does?'

'His constituents seem to. And a fair number of women.'

'It's his face,' said Young. 'He looks like a chastened angel.'

Poetry from Archie Young was always a surprise. Coffin gave a moment's consideration to whether Archie had picked up any gossip about Stella and Job Titus; it was about fifty-fifty that he had done.

'I'd like to get him for something,' he heard himself say. 'Corruption or unfair pressure in getting the Creeley pair out of prison.' Titus made him feel wicked.

'Did you really say that aloud, sir?' asked Young politely.

'You didn't hear me.'

They walked into Police Headquarters side by side. 'I'll just go into the Murder Room to see what they've got that's new,' said Young.

'Let's have a drink first. In my room.'

Once inside the Chief Commander's comfortable room, Young relaxed, enjoyed his whisky and wondered what was coming.

'I seem to have lost my sister,' said Coffin. 'Mislaid her, anyway.'

'I had heard something of that sort.'

Coffin nodded. 'Thought you might have.' Of course. Little in his life was secret from these professionals, from his relations with Stella to what he had for lunch.

'I've met her once or twice. She struck me as a very sensible, rational lady. Down to earth in a nice kind of way. Not one to do anything without good reason.'

'That's what worries me.'

Archie Young studied the whisky at the bottom of his glass. 'Forgive me for asking, but is money involved?'

Ah, so you've heard about that too? 'Yes.'

'Opens up possibilities.'

'And all of them nasty.' Blackmail, ransom, or just plain doing a bunk with her money.

But he was sure that Letty had never run away from anything in her life.

They finished the drink in silence. Then the Chief Inspector stood up. 'Thanks for the refreshment. I'll push off and see what's going on. Nothing much is how I feel. Unless the Met comes up with something on the body they've got, we're in dead water.'

BUT LIFE HAS its own momentum.

There is a mathematical theory of cluster which can be tested any day on a motorway exit. Life knows all about it, too. Events hang together.

Two days passed during which the Chief Commander attended to routine matters: he had an interview with the deputy spokesperson from the Second City Equal Opportunities Group who was tough but eventually friendly and accepted a drink before departing, the next major engagement was to be guest speaker at a bankers' luncheon, before returning home to see the dress rehearsal of the Christie play for which Marianna and Didi, among many others, had been auditioning. It was interesting, that link.

He was with Stella. In the audience, which was packed with friends and relations of the performers, he saw Annie Briggs in the company of Alex Edwards.

He looked around for Job Titus. 'Asked but couldn't come,' said Stella, examining her programme with a professional air.

But to his surprise he saw Eddie and Lizzie Creeley. Lizzie looked happy and excited as if this was a good night out. She seemed to change as each day passed.

When they moved at the interval to seek a drink at the bar, he saw Tom Ashworth sitting in the back row.

Stella raised an eyebrow. 'What's he doing here?'

'Likes the theatre. Didn't he try for a part?'

'May have done. He's got the face, very mobile.'

Coffin said carefully: 'But what I think he is doing is watching.'

'Whom?'

'Probably Annie and Alex Edwards.'

'On the job?' Stella sounded exasperated. 'That man must know all there is to know about quite a lot of us.'

'He may be worried about Edwards.'

Stella was horrified. 'You don't mean that?'

'I may do.' The killer had known details about his victims that could not come by chance. And after all, who knew more about certain people and was in a good position to find out more than a social worker with access to personal files? 'And no, before you ask, we don't seem near to finding the killer.'

'I guessed that for myself,' she said as they sat down.

'Stella, I know that Annie hung around you, was watching you, and she says she loves you...but don't trust her. She may be wicked.'

'That's an old-fashioned word.'

'Wickedness is always with us.' He reached out and took her hand. They sat, hand in hand, watching the play. It was a comfort to them both.

He thought that Didi's murder had not cast a gloom over the performance, the cast was enjoying itself as amateurs always did, but Stella said no, they were just being brave and more than one of them had been in tears.

At the end of the performance, and as the applause died away, a great wreath of roses was quietly laid on the stage as the curtain fell.

'For Didi,' said Stella.

NEXT DAY movement began.

'News just in,' said Archie Young cheerfully. 'Things may be on the roll. The girl is identified. Nothing on the body, except underneath her was found her library card. In a plastic case, so that it was not too damaged. Must have fallen out of her bag or pocket. Bit of luck, isn't it?'

'Yes, very lucky,' said Coffin thoughtfully.

'Even has her address on it.'

'Really useful.'

'Well, it's a start.'

'So who was she?'

'Mary Andrews, Seven Larch Court, Selly Oak. That's her ID. Has to be her, sounds right.'

'Any idea what she was doing in Dulwich?'

'If Wally Watson knows, he isn't telling,' said Young regretfully.

But it was just what we need to know, Coffin thought, if any way forward was to be found.

The murderer too was beginning to sense moving water, which did not please him. He was the fish who swam in deep still water.

He had a kind of mantra that he said to protect himself: Caroline, Annie, Letty, Stella.

The police finding Caroline so soon had been a nuisance, she could have stayed lost.

THAT SAME DAY, the technician entrusted with the tape bearing Letty's voice telephoned.

'We have brought the sounds up... Seems to be a railway station. The background voice is a public announcement system, as you guessed.'

'So?'

'Echoes are bad and the voice itself not clear but...' He read out what it said and Coffin wrote it down on the pad in front of him.

Thirteen-forty train for Dudley and Wolverhampton will leave from platform 4.

'So which station?'

'At a guess: Birmingham.'

Coffin's guess too. So Letty had telephoned from a large and very busy station at the centre of a huge conurbation. Not easy to locate her. And she could have been changing trains.

'Shall I return the tape to you?' At the back of the technician's voice was a hint of amusement which caused John Coffin to remember that on the tape would be several loving messages from him to Stella.

'Yes,' he said.

'Just one more thing. Not this tape, but I've been working on the other tape. The Didi Dunne tape, and I think it's interesting that it is a completely new tape. Never been used... It'll be in my report.'

'Thanks for telling me.' *Like the rest of them, you know I am passionately interested and interfere all the time. Only you aren't saying.*

He worked on, talking to his deputy, reading reports, making several telephone calls, but underneath it all he was rolling over and over his two problems till they seemed to become one.

Letty and Didi, Didi and Marianna, Marianna and the new girl to join the band: Mary Andrews.

He was surprised when the telephone rang on his private line, jerking him out of his thoughts.

'Stella, anything wrong?'

She rarely phoned when he was working.

'I decided that I must talk to Tom Ashworth at Tash to see what he knew about Letty. He was looking for Elissa... He thinks she's in trouble.'

'The girl or Letty?'

'Both of them.'

'Does he know where they are?'

'No, but he got something that helped Letty. A card from the girl telling him to fuck off. Lovely, wasn't it? She realized he was searching for her. The card was postmarked Birmingham. He thinks Letty may have heard herself and have gone after her. We must find her.'

'She's a grown-up lady.'

'Please! I got the impression that some scandal might break, there was great stress in her voice. I don't want that, and neither do you. Do you?'

No, any scandal that involved his sister could so easily rub off on him, which would give all those people looking for a reason to attack him just what they needed. He had his enemies, as had all heads of police forces at the moment, they were not popular men. He was as respected as most, possibly more popular than some, but his nature, his way of work, his very career had attracted criticism.

He sat at his desk. It looked as though someone ought to go to Birmingham and find Letty. That person had better be John Coffin in person and alone. Letty was his private problem.

But to find her he would need help. The right sort of help.

For a second he considered Tom Ashworth, but he knew that on the desk in front of him, discreetly tucked away among other papers, was the invitation from Phœbe. So far unanswered.

He could go and see her, unofficially, and she would help. Just in a friendly way.

NEXT MORNING, having told his office he was not about and given instructions to his deputy, he packed an overnight bag while Stella watched murmuring words of encouragement.

'Do you think you'll find her?'

'I don't know, but I shall try.'

'Do you want me to come with you?'

'You've got rehearsals all day, haven't you? And other business.' Stella nodded. 'There you are, then.' And there was Phoebe to see; he had not mentioned her to his wife.

He was throwing things into his bag. 'You'll leave something behind,' said Stella.

'It won't matter.' He kissed her warmly, affection when parting being absolutely essential in marriage, he had decided. 'I'll keep in touch, of course, and I will be back tomorrow anyway, earlier if I can. I must be.' It didn't seem much time in which to find Letty.

He drove westwards out of London, towards Oxford and Banbury and thus finally into Birmingham, that huge, sprawling industrial complex. The day was fine and sunny so that after Oxford he got off the motorway and took the country route which lay through gentle, wooded hills. He was a city dweller, could never be anything else, but he enjoyed the countryside with the pleasure of someone who did not work in it or expect it to provide him with a living. He began to feel happy. Whatever happened to him once he got to Birmingham, the journey was a holiday.

He switched on the radio, turning it high so that the joyous Beethoven chorus sung by the prisoners emerging into the sunlight in his opera *Leonora* filled all his space.

And behind in St Luke's Mansions, Stella had picked up the card from Phoebe which he had dropped.

ON THE OUTSKIRTS of Birmingham John Coffin stopped to consult a map, buy a drink, then consider how best to talk to Phoebe. He drank weak lager while he consulted his memories. Phoebe was a direct, energetic, and clever woman, attractive without being beautiful. She had that innovating spark that created the best police work, but he knew that her sex precluded her from the highest positions.

Ah yes, sex, for in that sphere too, Phoebe had been direct, energetic and innovative. He would have been glad to be assured, as Miss Austen might have said, that she was happily married and bedded.

He looked around for a telephone; Phoebe was not the sort of woman that you called on unannounced. He did not know this part of Birmingham, in fact he knew the city very little, but he could tell from his map that he was not far from Phoebe's office. If she was in it.

'Is there a telephone?'

The elderly barmaid ceased from polishing a glass and blew on it, then she looked at Coffin. 'Payphone round the corner,' she said, and went back to her blow and polish technique. 'But it won't take money, you'll need a CARD.' She spoke as if phone card was some strange animal that might bite.

He had one, and the phone, in a niche between the bar and the lavatory, worked. 'Hello, Phoebe.'

She recognized his voice at once. 'Ho, John...you're coming to my party.' A statement and not a question.

'Lovely invitation.'

'Thought you'd be glad to have it.'

'Can you help me, Phoebe?'

'Ah, I knew something was coming.'

There was no need to lie to Phoebe and perhaps better not. 'I'm looking for my sister.' He held back most of the details but in a few words he explained the situation. He wanted to find Letty Bingham, his sister.

Phoebe took a grasp of the situation at once. 'She doesn't sound the sort to take rooms or live in a caravan.'

'If she's here, then she'll be in a hotel.'

'Plenty of them,' said Phoebe.

'I've considered that fact and, knowing Letty, I know that whatever her state of mind, she will go for the best.'

'Quite a number of those too, remember we have the National Exhibition Centre here. Come round and we'll talk... Wait a minute, name and description first and I can make a start.'

'Thanks, Phoebe. Well, I think she'll be using her own name. She's tall, about five foot eight, about a hundred and twenty pounds, dark eyes, dark hair worn long, creamy dark skin; she wears big earrings, real jewels.'

'Doesn't sound much like you.'

'We had different fathers,' he said briefly. 'Younger than me and looks younger still.'

As he left the pub, he read the headline on a newspaper that someone had left behind.

SERIAL KILLER LOOSE IN SOUTH LONDON, he read.

Phoebe was unchanged, except perhaps a little fatter. She shook his hand briskly and then planted a kiss on his cheek. 'She is not at the Albany, the Holiday Inn or the Grand. Not as far as a few telephone calls can tell. No one of that description. But cheer up, I have more on the list.'

He was pleased to see her, there had always been an exhilarating quality about Phoebe, she had so much energy and inner happiness that some of it rubbed off on her friends.

He could see that he would have to watch himself.

'Sit down and have a sandwich and a drink.' There was a tray on her desk. 'You're convinced she'll only be in a four star hotel?'

They drank, ate and gossiped while other hands made the calls. As he had expected, the subject of the series of murders in the Second City and South London came up soon.

'Heard about the latest,' said Phoebe, putting mustard on a ham sandwich. 'We had a case like it when I first started here. Four women, one after the other, always on Wednesdays in successive weeks. Soon got the man, though, he worked in an old people's home and Wednesday was his day off. One of the residents fingered him, said he always smelt of women on Thursday mornings. Useful, that was. We do get lucky sometimes.'

'And did the man smell?'

'I didn't try sniffing myself. Have another sandwich? No, I will, looks like being a long day. An officer from the Met is coming up today and I shall have to show him round. Just got the word.'

'I thought there would be someone soon. Is it Wally Watson?'

'No, a chap I don't know, one of the new young ones.' Presently a young uniformed officer appeared.

'Down to two-star places now, ma'am, and you said not to bother.'

'And no likelies?'

'No. Don't think trade is too good just now. Half empty, some of these places.'

'Thank you,' said Coffin. 'Both of you.'

At the door the young man said: 'There's a smart new place opened out towards Harbourne... one of these country house places, so-called. Didn't try there.'

Coffin stood up. 'I'll do that myself. Thanks.' It sounded made for Letty.

'Let me check first, sir.'

He was back in a short time. 'Bingo. A lady of the description you want registered over a week ago, she is there now... She is calling herself Mrs Brown.'

'Thank you.' Coffin stood up.

'The Arden Court Hotel,' said the young officer. 'Forest Road, Harbourne.'

'Want me to come?' said Phoebe.

'No. But I'll be in touch.'

'You better be.'

THE ARDEN COURT HOTEL looked to be the sort of place which Letty would have chosen: it was quiet, set back in wooded grounds, and appeared expensive.

Across the road was a public park with a botanical garden; a large notice said this was an Open Day, which the number of cars outside bore out.

He parked his own car before the porticoed front door, walked through swing doors framed in gold that moved silently before him, and went across to the curving walnut desk on which rested a golden disk saying: *Please Register Here*. The desk was in the charge of a girl in good tweeds and pearls who was attended by a red setter.

'I want Mrs Brown, please.'

The red setter yawned while the tweeded girl fingered her pearls, but she smiled and was polite. 'Who shall I say, sir?'

'Smith, John Smith.'

'I'll see for you.' Her smile was still polite but more fixed as she picked up the telephone and spoke. She knew enough to be wary of these Smiths and Browns. 'You can go up. Room 12, the first floor. Shall I get the porter to take you?'

'I'll find my way.'

Coffin walked up the heavy carpeted stairs. There were flowers in big vases on the landing, big, heavy-headed chrysanthemums. He touched one sceptically as he passed, but it was real.

He knocked, a voice called him to come in. He pushed open the door.

'Good afternoon, Mrs Brown.'

The room was large, with chintz curtains and a fourposter bed; about this room were scattered various possessions, like a travelling bag and a dark crocodile handbag which he recognized as Letty's. On the air hung the sharp green citrus note of the expensive scent he associated with his sister.

Letty was standing in the middle of the room, staring towards him.

'You! I expected—' She stopped short, pressing her lips together in a gesture new to her but which spoke of tension. There were new lines on her face as well.

'Whom did you expect, Letty?'

Instead of answering, she said: 'How did you find me?'

'It wasn't difficult.'

'I didn't want you here.'

'That was obvious... Come on, Letty, what are you doing here and whom are you expecting?'

She put her hands to her eyes, she was crying. 'You've ruined everything. You haven't the least idea what you've done.'

'I can see you're in trouble, Letty, and you'd better let me help.'

'Just go.'

'I didn't come all this way to be turned back.' He was looking round the room as he spoke. It was tidy enough, but on the bed was Letty's red top coat and by it a briefcase. Either she was on the point of going out or she had just come in. He went to the window and took a look. Her room was in the front from which he could see the park and botanical garden. 'You'd better tell me what it's all about.'

Before she could speak, the telephone by the bed started to ring. Letty froze.

'Answer it, Letty.'

Letty was breathing in shallow gasps, she did not move.

'Answer it, or I will.'

Coffin took her by the arm and gently led her across to the telephone, he picked up the receiver. Then Letty grabbed it from him quickly. 'Hello. Yes, speaking... Thank you.' Tension drained from her voice. 'Just room service. Some laundry being returned.'

'So it wasn't the call you were expecting?' He went over to the bed, lifted the briefcase and handed it to his sister. 'Open this, will you?'

'Put it back, leave it alone.'

Coffin returned the case to the bed where he opened it. Inside it was stuffed with banknotes. He turned back to his sister. 'A telephone call that's expected and that alarms you, a bag full of money. Who are you paying off, Letty?' He sat down on the bed. 'Come on, Letty, talk. I know the signs, it's either blackmail or ransom money and you aren't the sort to give in to blackmail. So that makes it ransom and that makes it Elissa. Am I right?'

She did not answer, and he showed his anger. 'Where did you get all this money? I know you emptied the Drama School Trust Deposit account because Stella told me.' He shook her shoulder. 'Come on now, tell me.'

'I mortgaged some property.'

Letty turned away, showing irritation. 'Haven't you got a murder or two you ought to be getting on with? A committee on racial equality or some protest group you ought to attend to?'

'I'm attending to you.'

The two of them faced each other like combatants. 'Come on, out with it.'

Letty threw out her hands, as if she was giving in. 'I've been worried about Elissa for some time, you know that much. She seemed to be behaving so oddly, out of character, she's always been a sweet, docile child, but suddenly she was spending too much money, using money that she should not have touched because it was not hers. I thought she might be into drugs, although she denied it. I thought she was using Ecstasy, which alarmed me, it can change people.'

'It can kill.'

'Yes, I thought of that, don't think I didn't. Then she dropped out of sight, which was when I hired Tash. He didn't do much, said she was still in London. Perhaps she was then. She rang me once, so I thought: At least she's alive.' Her breath was coming in gasps.

Coffin let her take a rest.

'I do love her, but perhaps I haven't been a good mother, I've had too many other interests.'

'I think you've been a very good mother.'

'Do you really? That's a comfort... Then, about ten days ago, I got a letter. It said that the writer had Elissa and I was to wait for the next letter. That came the day following and said I was to take a hundred thousand in cash and go to Birmingham, book at this hotel and wait. That was when I sent the message to you, I knew you and Stella would be anxious. I suppose I knew you would try to trace me.'

'Underneath you wanted me to, didn't you? You shouldn't have tried to manage this on your own, it was stupid.'

'There were the usual threats about what would happen if I got in touch with the police,' Letty muttered. 'I couldn't risk it.'

'And you were instructed to use this hotel?'

'I did exactly what I was told.'

Coffin got up. 'Where's that laundry? It's taking a long time to come,' he said suddenly.

As if in answer there was a tap on the door. A soft Irish voice said it was the chambermaid.

'Let her in.'

Letty opened the door and took a pile of clean clothes from the arms of the girl. 'A boy left this note for you,' she said. 'Said you were expecting it.'

Letty closed the door, leaning against it clutching the washing. 'I feel sick.'

'Open the letter.'

'I should have asked her about the boy.'

'It wouldn't have done any good, it would be just a lad chosen at random and paid to deliver it.'

Letty opened the letter.

'It says that I've got a man here and must get rid of him or else ... They must be watching me.'

The car park across the road would provide good cover for anyone sitting in a van or car and using binoculars; he had been unwise to look out, he had been seen, Coffin thought. Seen but not recognized for what he was, he hoped.

'Anything else?'

Letty was still staring at the note. 'I am to go to the callbox round the corner and wait for a call.'

'Taking the money?'

'Yes.'

'Is that all?'

For a moment she did not answer, as if she was far away in some terrible world of her own. 'I'm not to tell anyone.'

She looked at her brother, he could see terror and bewilderment in her eyes, she was very close to real panic. He felt sick himself but he controlled it. He was not neutral here, this was his niece, Letty's child. He remembered the last time he had seen her. She had been a leggy adolescent in black tights and a white sweater, but there was a promise of beauty in the fine bones and huge dark eyes. In spite of the brown eyes there was a hint of red in her hair which made him wonder if this was how his mother had looked.

No, I am not neutral, he told himself, I am not detached, I mind about Elissa, but all the more must I be professional.

For some reason, the face of Didi appeared before him and he remembered how Marianna Manners had looked as she lay dead, and the dirt and mouldering leaves in the hair of the first dead and last found girl, Mary Andrews, local Birmingham girl.

Letty spoke out of her despair: 'I don't know what to do.'

Coffin told her.

SIXTEEN

The river is running cold

LETTY LEANED against the wall of the telephone booth which was one of the old-fashioned red boxes, she was glad of the relative protection it gave her. She closed her eyes and said a prayer under her breath; she spoke to a nameless, faceless god who must have love for mothers. Plenty of work for a god like that, she thought, he must keep busy. 'Don't forget me and Elissa,' she was saying inside. 'I know you have a lot of applications and I'm not a deserving case but keep me in mind. Do it for Elissa.'

She was following the instructions laid down in the note, standing in the box and waiting for the caller to ring.

Five minutes had passed, now six minutes, now seven. Still the phone did not ring. Perhaps it was all a game and it never would. No, her brother had said, it will be slow, this is to break your nerve.

I have news for you, brother, it is already broken. She stared at a stain in the floor, a dark irregular stain as if someone had bled there. They might have done, the phone-box smelt like a mixture between a misused lavatory and a charnel house. The new open booths with their plastic hoods may be open to the world but they are cleaner.

The stain reminded her of her life: irregular in shape and bits of it unpleasant. *There was so much I have never told you of my life, brother. I have only let you see the shiny successful outside, not showed you the uglier bits. You don't get where I have without a struggle.*

I have never told you of my growing, brought up in children's home, have I?

I told Stella but swore her to secrecy. It wasn't that I didn't want to tell you but you never asked. Do you realize that you have never asked me? A brother and sister who had to learn to know each other, and yet you never asked any questions.

I thought it might be British reserve, but Stella said no, you were frightened. He had been alone so long, she explained, he had invented himself and invented his past and now he feared what he might really find out. He was in any case, she said, a hard man to know.

You can say that again, Mr Chief Commander. People who don't ask questions don't get answers. I know I puzzled you, but Stella saw through me at once. She knew that it had been hard for me, that I had battled to find an education and then to graduate with a first class degree, I'm not an intellectual, so it was tough. Then I had to create my looks; you called me beautiful once, but Stella knew I was manmade. I know now how to dress and how to put on make-up to create an illusion. She does it herself.

Stella said to me once: 'What happened to you when you were a girl to give you that scar?' She knew it was a man, said she herself had suffered more than once; of course, she was in control now, she had learnt how. That's what she said, but not quite and of course I never discuss it with John, men don't have the right reaction, they just get fierce and angry and that's not what you want, is it?

Oh well, maybe my business was not a rape but a quick and rough seduction. So I don't like men all that much, I just like Me. ME in capital letters. But I wanted Elissa to avoid all that hassle, I wanted to give her a perfect beginning. A perfect life no one can guarantee. Now this has happened.

I am waiting for this telephone call, and I am getting orders from a man again which does something to my stomach. The bell is ringing.

Letty felt sick as she reached out to answer it. The line was live, humming, but no voice uttered.

'Hello, hello?'

Still silence. She tried again. 'I'm here, I know you are listening, please answer me. I'll do anything you want, just answer me.'

The line went dead.

Her brother had warned her about this being likely to happen. 'They are testing you all the time and they will try this way and that. Hang in there, the phone will ring again, you bet.'

You are not the sort of woman who hangs around waiting for a telephone call, Letty told herself, you trained yourself not to be. It's humiliating.

They want to humiliate you, Coffin had said briskly, it's part of the process. Accept it and get on with it. *Thank you, brother.*

'Yes, here I am. Yes, I can hear you but your voice is not clear.'

'You disobeyed orders. Who was the man with you?'

'What man?' Don't admit I was there, Coffin had said.

'The man who stood at your window.'

Letty said: 'That wasn't any visitor, just a workman inspecting the window.' They had agreed she should say this.

The voice will be disguised, Coffin had told her. Keep him in play, tell him you couldn't get all the money.

'No, I couldn't manage all that money, there wasn't time. I would have to borrow it and that takes... Yes, I am listening, I promise you I tried. I will go on trying if you give me time.'

Coffin had said: Tell him you want a photograph of Elissa showing that she is alive and well. The photograph must be backed up by something that gives a date, say a newspaper.

'Where is the money?'

'I have it with me.' This was untrue. Do not take the money, Coffin had said.

'I'm not bargaining,' said the man. 'The price must be paid in full. Get it or else.'

'I want to hear my daughter, is she there? Put her on the phone. Elissa, can you hear me?' She was shouting.

'Get the money and you can have her back unharmed. You have twenty-four hours to get all the money as asked. Go back to the hotel. You will get another message.'

Letty pushed open the door, drawing in great gulps of fresh air. It was over for the time being, she had done what her brother had told her, she had held on. Without noticing what she was doing, she walked across to the park, where she found an empty bench under a tree. Here she sat.

Two people sitting in a van watched her. One held a mobile telephone, the other was crying.

Letty was crying too. She wished it had been Stella Pinero who had found her and not her brother. Coffin might be right with his advice but she wanted sympathy and he hadn't offered much of that.

I'm just a job to him now like those murders.

She had discovered something that was interesting, perhaps she ought to tell him, but it could have no possible connection with the killers of the two girls.

In a more normal state of mind she would probably have told him already and laughed about it. But the whole bright golden fabric of her life, constructed and polished by her with so much care, was collapsing.

She got up, crossed out of the park and back to her room. The van had gone.

The hotel foyer was empty except for the receptionist's dog; she knew that Coffin had quietly departed.

Life was a tangled skein and perhaps her fact was important. I was just poking around, she could say, I've always been curious and I've found it paid.

JOHN COFFIN had driven himself to Phoebe's office, he took a roundabout route, losing himself for a time in Birming-

ham's one-way system of streets, but his circuit allowed him
to check that he was not being followed. Phœbe did not
seem surprised to see him, and although he could see she was
busy, she came out of her office with her hand outstretched.

'Thought you'd be back. You'll be here for my party yet.'

'Love to, but you know how it is, life gets in the way.'

'Don't I know it,' said Phœbe. She looked amused. 'So
what's on your mind?'

'Is it obvious? I've got a problem.' He let her take this in,
then he said: 'And now so have you.'

'You've found your sister?'

'Yes, I think she meant to be found. If I hadn't got to her,
she would have found some other way.'

'So what's up?'

In a few words, he told her. Her face grew gloomy. 'Is this
for real?'

'She thinks it is,' he said cautiously. 'I'm not sure.'

Phœbe said: 'We'll treat it as real. What will she do now?'

'If she's done as I advised, then she will have gained a bit
of time, held off the kidnapper, and then she will wait for
you to get in touch.'

'Right, well, it's not actually my sphere.'

Coffin nodded. 'But you know where to go?'

'Sure, we have a special unit which we activate when
needed. You have the same, I imagine? I'm not part of it but
I will set it in motion. Do you want to be part of the operation?' It was a courtesy question only, due to his rank, she
did not expect him to say yes. Relatives of the missing were
better not involved.

He knew the rules. 'No, I'd rather be left out of it. I've
done what I can. I was seen but I think not identified. Since
then I have been careful. I was not followed coming here.'

'Good.' They were still on the threshold of her office, she
pushed the door open more widely. 'Go on in, I'll set the

ball rolling... Oh, by the way, there's someone in there that you might want to talk to.'

A tall thin young man was standing by Phoebe's desk, staring at her CLEAN AIR notice as if he would like to smoke but dare not. He turned round when Coffin came in.

''Afternoon, sir. Sergeant Downey. M'Guv'nor, Walter Watson sent me up.'

'I know why you are here.' Do we shake hands on it or not, thought Coffin. What is my position here? In some ways, I shouldn't be here at all. He knows and so do I.

'Yes, sir, visiting the address we have for Mary Andrews.' Sergeant Downey added hastily: 'But not cutting across the Second City's investigation, they've been kept fully in touch.'

He feels as awkward as I do, thought Coffin, and probably not too pleased to run across me in Phoebe's room. Coffin saw he would have to ask the questions; in spite of his air of amiable cooperation, it was clear that Downey would not volunteer anything and had probably been told not to. Chief Superintendent Watson might be a friend but he guarded his territory like a tom cat.

'You've been to the address? It checked out?'

'Yes, oh yes, she lived there all right.'

That's it then? 'So who else lives there?'

'That's just it, sir. No one does. The place is empty. Not cleared of furniture, that's still there although it must be getting pretty damp, but the owner is an old, sick man.'

It was the usual getting-blood-out-of-a-stone task, the Met would never change. What was theirs was theirs and theirs only. He decided to pull rank.

'Come on, Sergeant, what's the name of the old, sick man? What did he have to do with Mary and where is he now?'

Like a well-trained dog, Sergeant Downey responded to the touch of the leash. 'Henry French, sir, he's in hospital, and he's Mary's maternal grandfather. She lived with him.'

I suppose I will find out which hospital, Coffin thought. 'You talked to him?' *What I mean is, what did you get?*

Sergeant Downey said regretfully: 'He can't talk, sir. Dying, out of this world, far away.' He pushed a piece of paper across the table. 'That's the hospital and the ward, but he's no help.'

A touch irritable, Coffin said: 'What about the neighbours? Any help there?'

'No neighbours, they've all moved out, the whole area is due for redevelopment.'

Lovely, lovely, thought Coffin, we have an address only no one lives there any more. Poor Mary, poor child, she really was Miss Nobody.

Sergeant Downey tried to read his expression. 'One of those promising leads that come to nothing,' he said regretfully. Quite clearly he was already thinking of his journey back, the roads would be getting busy, he had made good time up here, but he might be slower back.

Phoebe returned, nodded at Coffin, a nod which said: Your business is under way. 'Had your talk, you two?' she said jovially.

'Yes,' said Downey quickly. That was it. Over.

Phoebe turned to John Coffin. 'I think Inspector Evans, he's the man in charge of the squad, would be glad to have a word with you. Get your impression of the situation, anything you may have observed, that sort of thing.'

'Right, I'll go.'

'Third door on the left ... Want me to come?'

'I'll find the way.'

As soon as the door closed behind him, the Sergeant said: 'What's up with him?'

'He's got worries.'

'Haven't we all?' Downey thought about his wife, and the meal she had planned because this was one of their anniversaries, and for which he was going to be late.

'Did you tell him?'

'No. Not yet.'

'But you're going to.' It wasn't a question. A statement of what must be, or she'd know the reason why and the Sergeant responded.

'Yes.'

I know you hate to share, thought Phœbe, you'll hang on to a bit of information like some precious pearl.

IN A ROOM down the corridor, Coffin met Inspector Evans, a neat, square Welshman. Evans held out his hand and gave Coffin a warm, hard shake. He was a man who liked to get a grip on things. He knew about John Coffin, Chief Commander of the Second City Force, but he was in no way intimidated.

'It's the usual routine, sir, you know how it goes. The telephone lines to the hotel are covered already and after that it's what you might call ad hoc, we have to respond to the situation as it develops.'

'Have you got anyone in the hotel itself?'

'That's more difficult in case the kidnapper has someone planted on the staff, but they employ contract cleaners and I think we can put a woman in that way. One of my best WDs, she's middle-aged and just right. She hates housework but never mind that.'

Coffin could tell that Evans was being deliberately cheerful and talkative. Or perhaps he was always easy with the conversation.

'Have you been in touch with my sister?'

'Yes, we've got a message to her about the telephone tap—' he didn't say how—'but we haven't told her about Sergeant Miller in the cleaning department, we thought it better not.'

'I'm glad she's got a woman around. Letty's not as tough as she acts.'

'Do you want to talk to your sister? There's a protected line that is safe.'

'Yes, I would like to talk to Letty.'

The Inspector spoke down the telephone on his desk, issued a few instructions, and then handed the instrument to Coffin. 'I'll leave you to it.' He went out of the room, closing the door silently behind him.

The room seemed suddenly quiet.

Letty's voice, when he spoke to her, sounded faint and strained. Yes, she was all right, coping, and waiting for the next order from the kidnapper.

No, he couldn't do anything else for her, just leave her to go through what lay ahead, she had to bear it on her own.

'I just wanted to say, about those killings in Spinnergate, the two girls...' No one had told her about the third body, for her there were just the two. 'I just wanted to tell you that the box has something different inside...'

'You're not making sense, Letty.'

But that was it; she had cut the line. She left him with a few words he could not understand. What box?

When he rejoined Phoebe and Sergeant Downey, they were both standing by the window, obviously waiting for him. He was surprised to see Downey still there.

'Was that all right?' asked Phoebe.

'Fine.' He turned to Downey. 'I thought you'd be off.'

'I am just going, but I had something to tell you. The library ticket found with the girl... the forensic brought up a fingerprint on the plastic. Not the girl's, so the chances are, or could be, that it belongs to the killer.'

No use now but if we pick up a suspect... well, it would come in handy.

'I'LL STAY AROUND,' Coffin said to Phoebe, 'get a room somewhere. There are things I want to do.'

'Really?' Phoebe leaned back in her chair and studied him. 'And here was me thinking you came here to find your sister or possibly just to see me.'

'Now, Phoebe.'

'And all this time you really had other things to do.'

'You're a devil, Phoebe.'

'Yes, but I'm a clever devil.' She laughed. 'And I saw your face when Downey was talking ... You're not letting go, are you?'

'Just a feeling that Downey may not have got all he could out of his visit here.'

'I can recommend several places to stay. Or you could stay with me.'

'I think I'll be better on my own.'

Phoebe laughed again, tolerantly and affectionately. 'I never thought otherwise. And as it happens I've got two kids, a large dog and a larger husband cluttering up the place. But I expect we could have tucked you in.'

He wasn't sure if he believed a word of all that, but Phoebe had always known how to deliver a parting line.

He got himself a room in a dim lodging-house on the Edgbaston Road. He took a small room from which an even smaller bathroom had been gouged, but it had a telephone by the bed, if it worked, and the water was hot. He felt anonymous here, which was what he wanted.

From this lodging he telephoned Stella.

'I'm staying on one night, you don't mind? I'll keep in touch. Yes, I've seen Letty, I can't talk too much but it's trouble with her daughter but I'm getting it sorted. You don't mind? Sure, my darling?'

'Dearest, no,' said Stella, staring down at Phoebe's invitation which was now in her possession.

SEVENTEEN

The river lets go some of its burden

STELLA, LEFT ALONE with only the cat and dog for company, found herself worrying more and more about St Luke's Theatre and its finances which now looked shaky in the extreme. She called a meeting of her trusted lieutenants: Alison, Rebecca, and Albert, Frederico (who was not Italian but liked the name), Celia and Joseph. Stage manager, assistant stage manager, lighting supremo, wardrobe head, the exploitation manager and front of house manager. They were all young, all keen, all in their first jobs pretty well, all on short contracts, and all would leave to go on to better jobs if they could get them when they had been trained. Stella paid very little but she was a good trainer.

She would hold a separate meeting with the teachers and the Administrator of the fledgling Drama School because this involved different problems.

The meeting was quiet and serious; they had picked up rumours of financial stringency. Almost all managements ran into problems of this sort these days but they had trusted Stella Pinero and Letty Bingham. No one mentioned the word bankruptcy so they avoided each other's worried faces.

And what could she say to them? My partner in this enterprise, Letty Bingham, has skipped off with most of the money in our joint theatre account. We are in trouble.

The murders didn't help. They had all known Didi, who had hung around both the main theatre and the Theatre Workshop picking up odd pieces of employment as she could, all temporary and all poorly paid, but it hadn't mattered to Didi, what had counted to her was to be in contact with the theatre world she loved. And that chance of getting a place at the Drama School.

Alison had seen most of her, since stage managers always need extra help especially if they get it for almost no pay. 'The sad thing is she would never have been a success, she had no talent.'

'You can't be sure about that,' said Frederico, who had a kind heart. 'She was so young, people do develop, you know.' He was all of twenty-one himself.

'She was so naïve,' said Rebecca. 'She would take up with anyone who offered an opportunity to act or work in the theatre.'

There was a mutter of assent from round the table. Stella felt both sad and amused, this bunch was not as sophisticated as they thought. Oh, granted there was a surface slickness, but every one of them would do almost anything to hang on to work in the theatre. They had as many illusions and dreams as Didi ever had, their worldliness was one thin layer deep; if it had not been they would never have entered a profession where their chances of being unemployed were infinitely greater than their chances of being a star.

Take her own life. Stella was a success, could call herself a star figure, was a household name, but she had known the feeling that came to every out of work performer and would come to all those in the room in their turn: that this was the end and they would never get another part, and would join the ranks of the permanently, terminally resting.

Every one of the group now sitting round the table and drinking Coke had been questioned by the police and not found it enjoyable. 'Not like a Miss Marple movie,' Rebecca had said. 'Great fat man who smoked all the time.' Rebecca was very Clean Air and Stella could see that Sergeant Fish, who had also questioned her while still smoking, had not made a good impression. 'Sharp, too, acted as if he didn't believe a word I said.'

'That's just manner,' said Frederico. 'You know, being professional.' He was the only one who had enjoyed the experience; he had mingled with the police team, spoken to uniformed as well as plain clothes men and had, as he said, 'picked up a new mate'. Frederico picked up mates rather often, probably too often for his own safety, and was a worry to them all.

'Who?' said Rebecca quickly; she had constituted herself his guardian, or, as Frederico put it, his Maiden Aunt.

'Ask no questions,' he said.

Although the group had had no connection with the amateur production of *Witness for the Prosecution,* they knew most of the ladies of Feather Street who made up the Friends of St Luke's Theatre and they had seen a lot of what was going on. They knew the crucial part that it was meant to play in the birth of the Drama School. There was a general feeling that the murder of Didi could be blamed for a lot of their financial troubles, and that the amateur production could be blamed for the murder.

'It did bring in a lot of weirdies,' said Rebecca. 'Look at some of those who auditioned. The Creeley man, for one. I mean, he comes from a family of killers, I suppose he thought that gave him a chance. He couldn't act, couldn't even speak a line, I don't suppose.'

'He was in love with Didi, that's why he came,' said Alison. 'But she wasn't in love with him.' She frowned. 'I sat in on some of the auditions, just for the experience.' She hoped to get into producing, she knew she was not ace at acting. 'And I agree with you, I certainly saw some unexpected faces, the people who turned up.'

'Perhaps you saw the murderer,' said Frederico.

'I hope they catch him,' said someone. 'Or her. Or them. Might be a group.'

'No, this is a serial murderer and that's always singular.'

For a moment it looked as though the meeting would descend into an argument about semantics or capital punishment but Stella called it to order.

'That's enough now. I'm going to talk and you're going to listen.' They turned attentive faces towards her. Stella put the facts to them, suitably edited, and gave them her usual pep talk. She did not say: I have the money to pay wages for this week and next but nothing beyond.

The group drifted away, talking among themselves in half way to cheerful voices because Stella hadn't made it sound too bad.

Afterwards Alison, who had more financial savvy than the others, came up. 'It's tight, isn't it? Tighter than you said.' Although Alison never talked about it, Stella knew that her father was a distinguished economist.

She looked with trust at Alison with whom she had a good working relationship, without being close. She liked Alison, who was large, strong and reliable, all of which a stage manager needs to be.

Stella said: 'Well, you know how it is, I didn't want to cast gloom on the others.' Or not too much.

'I think they know, really... I might get my father to put some money in.'

'Let's see how things go.' It was not wise to accept investment from one of the company even if their father was a wealthy man. If it came off and you pulled through, then you might be saddled with that person for life; she had seen it happen. She liked Alison, but she would not want to work with her forever.

'Of course, he wouldn't expect a profit.' Or even to get his money back. Alison repressed her father's expressed opinion that the theatre was a financial *Titanic*. It would be her money anyway, out of her trust fund.

Stella laughed. No other comment was necessary. She didn't even have to make it a bitter or a noisy laugh, one short hoot was enough.

'Yes, well,' said Alison. 'Have we got a future?' Has the company, has the Drama School (in which a lot of her own hopes for future work rested) got a life to come, was what she meant.

'Yes, oh yes,' said Stella. She would see they had somehow. Alison nodded. 'Good, I hoped you would say that... It's not why I hung back, though.' She dug into the huge soft bag which hung from her shoulder and which looked as though it could carry her to New York and back with several changes of clothes and make-up. All the girls had such bags and Stella had, on occasion, seen hair dryers, cats and even one baby extracted from them.

'You know Didi did odd jobs for me? She was a great one for leaving her possessions about, and she left this behind among other things. It's not a diary, in a way more personal than that, a book, but full of private things, I meant to remind her when we met again...' Alison stopped, then went on: 'But we never did, she never came back.'

Alison put on the table in front of Stella a notebook which seemed thick with odd papers and letters, all bound up with an elastic band.

'She used to make notes in it and that sort of thing...I haven't looked... Well, I have,' she added honestly, 'but I didn't read it, I could see it was personal stuff. The letters are from boyfriends, all ages old. I didn't know what to do with it.'

'Perhaps you should give it to the police. Or to her sister.'

'I wondered if you would?'

Stella hesitated, and Alison hurried on: 'Or if it was necessary to do anything with it at all...I mean, I know she's
dead but it was private to Didi.'

'I thought you said there was nothing much in it?'

'No, but it's about dates, and notes about dates and letters from boyfriends... It's the sort of thing I would hate to
go public if I was dead.'

But the murdered have no privacy.

Stella stretched out her hand for the book. 'All right, I'll
do something with it.'

STELLA CARRIED the notebook round with her in her handbag for the rest of the day, not looking at it.

Her husband had telephoned her to say that he was still
in Birmingham. 'I've found Letty,' he had said. 'It was not
very hard to do. I think she wanted me to find her.'

Beyond that he had not said very much. She had no telephone number to reach him, from which she supposed he
did not want a call. 'How is Letty? Anything I can do?'

'She's all right and being looked after. Leave it at that for
the moment, Stella.'

Stella liked her sister-in-law, whom she admired and respected, but she had reservations about Elissa. Too beautiful, too spoilt, and most dangerous of all, not so clever as
her brilliant mother. Poor Letty.

Finally, at the end of the day, she took the notebook
which Alison had produced, opened the book and let the
bundle of letters and photographs fall on to the table.
Should she take what she had to Annie?

She avoided reading the letters but could not help seeing
the signatures on one or two. Eddie Creeley, of course, several times, complaining about Didi seeing other men. Stella
did read that bit: Call him a man, Eddie had written. It
sounded more like a threat than a question.

At the back was a list of addresses and telephone numbers which included her own. The girl got around, she saw with surprise.

She would visit Annie, tell her what she had, but not give anything to her, not the shoes, nor the woolly sweater, nor the comb and lipstick, she knew these ought to go to the investigating team. At the same time, she felt a sympathy for Annie.

Keep away from Annie, Coffin had said, she may be wicked.

ANNIE HAD REALIZED that what she called Didi's 'little book' was missing. She had tidied Didi's room when the police unsealed it, cleaned away all the mess they had left, and arranged Didi's books and papers. Stanislavsky and a book on Edith Evans were there but the little notebook was not.

There were several programmes from St Luke's Theatre, even more from the Theatre Workshop which Didi had attended regularly, like a church; there was the prospectus of the Drama School, and several photographs of Didi's favourite performers which included one of Stella Pinero.

Annie now had mixed feelings about Stella. She loved her still but was fearful. Love was a dangerous commodity, dangerous to the giver, dangerous to her who received it.

She had given up wearing her masculine clothing but she knew she was still the same inside. What's on the outside, is not what I am inside, she told herself. I am packaged one way, but exist in another. This made her fractious, difficult and unpredictable, with something wilder underneath: what Coffin had called wicked.

She was puzzled that Didi's notebook, which had been such a prominent part of her life (carried everywhere, always in use: 'I must write it down' being daily words with her), was not around where she might have expected to find it. Silly to mind, but she did, because it was part of Didi that was missing.

Had the police taken it?

She had the nerve to ring them up and ask them. No, they hadn't.

She was alone in the house, her daughter still with her grandparents. The police had stopped visiting, but the neighbours had been kind, calling with messages of help, although showing caution: after all, a woman whom murder had touched twice was dangerous company and better kept at a distance.

It was sad having no friends, she knew she had none, although she had several enemies and was herself an enemy to some: the Creeleys being the most prominent, and whosoever had killed Didi.

She had one professional friend: Tom Ashworth, Tash, and him she called daily, because you had to talk to someone. He was not always at the end of his telephone, but he had an answering machine and he was good about calling back. Annie wanted to ring him now to tell him she was puzzled about Didi's notebook, but she teased herself by not dialling, like not eating a cream bun when your mouth is watering. He was her luxury.

But she did ring.

'I shouldn't worry,' he said, sounding uninterested, 'it can't be lost. It'll turn up.'

'I don't know where.'

'Want me to come and look?'

'No.' Another day perhaps. You had to stagger luxuries, take little bites.

'Let me know if it turns up.'

'She wrote everything in it.'

'Did she? Dangerous girl.'

Annie was silent. Cream buns were not meant to bite back, cream buns were for comfort.

Didi wasn't killed because she had secrets, she was killed because she was my sister, Eddie Creeley killed her. She stuck to that thought, certainly Eddie had done it.

Creeley. Saying the name always gave her a thrill, it was like sex.

When she saw the Creeleys in her mind, two dead old people had shuffled behind, wrapped in bandages, earth-stained. Now when she thought of them, Didi walked behind them.

She was seeing the trio as she listened to Tash.

'I really hate what you are doing to yourself, Annie,' he said, his voice sounding warm and sympathetic, which is exactly what Didi always said he was and Annie never quite believed, because there must always be a bill.

What was she doing to herself? Still holding the telephone she looked at her face in a wall mirror. She had lost weight, and she hadn't washed her hair lately, so it must be that what she was doing was not eating and not washing.

When she returned her attention to the telephone, Tash had stopped speaking and gone away, the line was dead. It was early evening; she went into the kitchen to make some tea, or coffee, they both tasted the same to her now. Didi had been dead and unburied for days, the police still retaining her body, for what services she dare not think. There had been an inquest which had been adjourned.

She believed the same was true for Marianna Manners, who was just camouflage, poor soul. Didi was the real victim. Didi was the only victim, the other poor girl was just trimming.

For some reason this reminded her of the Karnival Club and she smiled, she had liked that place, it was friendly and no one questioned you. She would miss it. Might go back, they didn't judge you there.

While she was drinking what appeared to be from the colour of it weak tea, the phone rang again. She picked it up with a smile.

'I knew you'd ring back.' After all, he had her name on his bill.

'Hello,' said Stella, her voice husky. 'It's Stella Pinero. I expect you are surprised to hear me.'

'Yes.' Annie managed to get the words out. 'How could you? Can't you leave me alone?'

Stella felt breathless, but she kept control. 'I have some possessions belonging to Didi to give you. Some shoes, odds and ends, a notebook.'

Annie's aggression and anger melted. 'I was looking for that book. I wondered where it was.'

'Didi left it with the stage manager.' Stella added: 'It must go to the police, so should the other things, but I thought I ought to tell you.'

'I want it.'

'No... I suppose you could look,' said Stella with reluctance.

'I'll come and collect it. Now, tonight. Tell me where to come. And I am sorry if I shouted just now. I was upset. I love you really, admire you so much, you know that. Where shall I come? St Luke's Mansions? I know the place.'

Naturally you do, you ought to, you've stood looking at it often enough. 'No, don't come here.' Stella was alone in Coffin's tower, she was standing by the bookcase in the sitting-room, looking out at the view he loved, in a room he had been happy to create with rugs, pictures, and books. She had the clear idea he would not want Annie to set foot in it. 'I will come to you.'

Annie might be wicked. As well to remember what her husband had said.

STELLA CALLED the taxi service that the theatre always used. It was a comfort to be greeted by one of the drivers she knew best: old Bert.

She gave him the address. 'Napier Street, and wait outside for me. I won't be long.'

'Wait for you for ever, Miss Pinero,' said old Bert with a smile, setting back in the seat. He was a fan. He watched her walk to the front door. 'Lovely lady.'

Stella had had a long day, she was tired, she was worried about her husband, worried about Letty, worried about her own working life, but long training had ensured that she was well groomed, and if her clothes were casual, jeans and tweed jacket, she wore them with style.

Annie, on the other hand, was a wreck. Her hair was stringy and lank, and her eyes were puffy as if she had been crying. She was wearing grey flannel trousers and a flowery silk blouse so both sides of her persona were showing.

'Come in.' Annie stood back to let Stella pass. She led the way to the kitchen which was tidy except for the sink filled with unwashed china. It looked as though it had been there for some time and might start growing things soon.

Stella had Didi's possessions in a carrier bag. 'I just brought them to show you before I take them to the police.' She could tell Annie was displeased. She opened the bag. 'Here, you can look.'

'Yes, all that belonged to Didi, I recognize it. Leave it with me.'

'I can't do that,' said Stella, thinking she shouldn't be here. 'But I thought you had a right to know.'

'Thank you... You know about me, what I was doing? It was serious, not a game.'

'It didn't feel like a game to me,' said Stella with some feeling.

'I wanted to be...like you, be you.' Annie stared at Stella hungrily. She put her hand on Stella's arm. 'Don't be nervous with me.'

'I don't like being touched.'

'Ah, that's a serious fault,' said Annie. 'But I never got very close, did I? You never felt I would hurt you.' She was looking hard at the bag.

'I wasn't sure.' Now she could study this thin, tense woman, Stella felt only sympathy. Annie became not a thing, but another human being. She wanted to say: 'I understand, don't hate yourself so much. We all want to change our sex occasionally, put on another one like a new overcoat, I have myself. I've been to the Karnival Club myself and enjoyed it.'

While she was thinking this, Annie grabbed the book and picked up a knife.

'Now get out. If you think I won't cut you, then you're wrong.'

If the chap is bigger than you and has a weapon, don't be brave, Coffin had told Stella.

The look in Annie's face told her not to be brave, Annie meant it. 'I shall have to tell my husband.'

'Tell him and good luck to you.' Annie opened the door. 'You go now and don't come back.'

The cab-driver gave Stella a curious look as she got in. 'You all right, ma'am?'

'Yes, I'm fine.' Only I'm a fool. So she went back in her cab, leaving the notebook with Annie, feeling that in doing so she had betrayed her husband.

Annie watched the cab drive away, then she opened the notebook, spreading the pages wide and giving them a shake.

A photograph of Eddie Creeley fell out. 'Love, Eddie,' he had written.

'Love, Eddie,' said Annie loudly. 'I'll give you love, Eddie Creeley, my sort of love. Events don't stop, just because you stop thinking about them, or hide your eyes. No, there is a pattern to be worked out. I am still working it out. It's called revenge.'

IT WAS HARD LUCK being Eddie Creeley, although the patients seemed to like him well enough at the hospital where he worked.

The amazing thing was that he was getting fond of Lizzie. For her sake he had turned into a home-maker. Before his parents died, he had left it all to them, or to his mother, not a man's job. Now he saw that sex did not come into it, that you had to make people comfortable, it was a right thing to do. It satisfied something deep inside him that was neither male nor female but a mixture of both. A well-dusted table, the window-panes polished till they shone, the old leather sofa and armchair repaired, the smell of cooking in the kitchen, these things were good in themselves and you were glad to be where they were.

Lizzie was very glad.

She looked out of the window every day about the time when he could be expected home, waiting for him. She looked forward to Eddie coming home.

He knew she did and although he had resented it at first, now he liked it. He brought her little presents, the sort of present a father or a grandfather would bring home to a child: a packet of sweets, a coloured magazine, or a plant in a pot.

Deep down he knew that this would not last, that one day he would walk away from Lizzie. He would recover from Didi, fall in love again, marry and be an ordinary man, but he would always be grateful to Lizzie, because she had taught him to be kind.

'Lizzie,' he said, that same evening when John Coffin was in Birmingham and Stella was visiting Annie who was meditating revenge, and the tide of events was dropping bits of evidence about the murders all over the place. 'Lizzie, when I have saved up a bit of money we will have a new suite of furniture.' He was sitting on a spring on the old sofa.

'Yes, please.' She was enthusiastic. 'Made of that lovely soft velvety stuff.'

'Dralon, it's called.'

'Is it? And pink, let's have it in pink. I saw a pink chair in a window.' She did a great deal of window-shopping, creeping silently and slowly past shop after shop, taking it all in, clothes, furnishings, make-up. If she had the good luck to live long, she would be very knowledgeable about what to wear and what to sit on.

'I prefer red.'

'Not blood red.'

Impossible not to know what she was thinking. 'No, not blood red. Say ruby.'

'About the murders, Eddie... they won't get you for them?'

'They've had a try.'

She nodded. 'They'll try again. I know how it goes.'

As she did indeed, thought Eddie. 'I didn't do it.'

'You'd say that anyway. We did.'

He allowed her these lapses from the usual cant, she had earned that right.

'But I didn't.'

'In a way, we didn't either.'

Tell me which way, Auntie, but he did not say this aloud. He did not allow to himself some of the ways of speech that were licensed in Lizzie. He was a man, had not been to prison, was young.

'In a way, you never do,' said Lizzie. 'It's an accident or self-defence or execution . . .' She paused in her murderer's apologia and watched his face.

'Come on, Auntie, don't leave it there.'

'We did an execution, it was deserved. The old man, well, he abused me.' She blinked. 'You know, did things, nasty things, and she laughed. She only laughed, his wife did, that was worse, wasn't it?'

'I don't know what to say. You've shocked me.'

'So that's why we did it. Only way, only to stop him.' She nodded her head up and down. 'It was a good thing we did, 'cause he might have done it to others. I expect he had.'

'But did you tell anyone? Why didn't you say?'

'I couldn't do that, couldn't say, couldn't mention it . . . and no one would have believed me.'

'Oh, they would have done.'

'No, no, you're wrong, Eddie. The old man said he would say it was all me, it was what I wanted, that I made him. Can you make men do that?'

'God knows,' said Eddie. 'Don't ask me.'

'And his wife said she'd say so too, that I was a wicked girl.' Her eyes, a blue now faded almost into whiteness, filled with tears. She began to sob. 'I wasn't a wicked girl.'

Eddie put his arm round her. *So you are a member of the human race, after all, you poor old thing.* 'Long ago, Auntie,' he said. 'Long ago. Let's have some of that sherry you like so much.'

Lizzie leaned against him gratefully. 'You're so clever, Eddie.'

'No, I'm not clever, but I can see how things join up. The old man abused you, you killed him, Annie saw you, and now it's got to Didi.' Where did it start. And where would it end?

'You've got an enemy, Eddie.'

'Yes, Annie herself.'

Perhaps he was to be the end, punished, killed somehow, and that would be it, the long chain of horror would be over. It seemed unfair on him.

'No, I'm not clever, or I wouldn't be here.'

'But you're good.' She nestled against him, comforted.

'Not even that, Auntie.' I'll probably let you down in the end, he thought. Pity, but true.

'Not many people are clever and good,' went on Lizzie, pursuing her own train of thought. 'There was one in prison, she was clever and good.'

'What was she in for, Auntie?'

'Fraud, I think.'

It seemed right. 'At least you've known one.'

'I think that policeman is good and clever.'

'Oh, go on, which one?' His mind rejected the group he had met.

'The one who arrested us all those years ago, he was young then, older now, but I've seen him, I know his face.'

John Coffin, she meant. Eddie found he could accept that. One good fraud merchant and one good copper in the great pattern of life.

EIGHTEEN

The river gives up its dead

JOHN COFFIN slept uneasily in his rented bed; he missed Stella, he even missed the cat who usually rested heavily on his feet. It was strange already to be alone in your bed. The room was very small with an even smaller bathroom attached, everything was lined with a pale plastic oak that felt as thin as cardboard. The door shivered as you opened it, but the bedclothes and towels were clean, even if the duvet was thin and synthetic. The telephone, as it turned out, did not work.

He made himself some tea from the tray provided while he considered the day.

Letty first, he must check what went on there. Phœbe had offered to be the go-between, she had promised to find out and pass it all on.

Then he would be off on his own particular mission for which he could afford only one day. Downey was a good man, no doubt, but he did not trust him to see what was not obvious.

HE DRANK SOME MORE TEA while he planned his operation. Drive to No. 7 Larch Court where the girl Mary had lived, walk around the house, talk to the neighbours, and stand looking and thinking. Contemplation had helped him before, and might do so again.

The tea was lukewarm, it had not been very good in the beginning, the teabags were weak and stale, the little carton of milk too long away from the cow and the victim of heat treatment, but it was certainly providing no uplift now. There was a packet of sweet biscuits, so he chewed one while he finished dressing. No great surge of energy followed but he went on chewing.

Anxious to be on with the day, he tried the telephone. Not working yesterday, it was still dead today.

Damn.

Was it worth it, he asked himself, to give yourself an uncomfortable night just to poke around investigating a case that you not only could leave to others but ought to do so.

This is not your job.

The accusing faces of Walter Watson, of Archie Young and even of Sergeant Downey moved in front of him, each one saying KEEP OUT and LEAVE IT TO US.

So why was he doing it? He had the answer: I enjoy it and I do it better than anyone else; I see further into the picture. Call it intuition or call it long experience, but it happens.

Here, watch it, he told himself, you're getting above yourself, this is not the way to think. A little modesty here, please.

THERE WAS A TELEPHONE in the hotel lobby and Phoebe answered at the second ring.

'Phoebe? John Coffin here.'

'I know who you are.' That meant Phoebe in one of her more difficult to handle moods.

'Anything to report about my sister?'

'I can give you the latest: she had a message late last night: she's to take what money she's put together, stow it in a plastic carrier bag, Marks and Spencer's for choice, she can go out and do some shopping if she hasn't got one to hand.'

'And where is the meeting?'

'Coming to that: in the botanical gardens, where the birds sing in cages.'

He ignored the touch of poetry. 'Is it a good spot to catch him? Is it all laid on?'

'If he turns up, then he, or she, will be captured... But they don't think he will. It's a try-on, testing her, watching to see who comes with her.'

'Damn, I wanted it all tied up.'

'You're in a rotten mood. Bad night?'

'No,' he lied.

'You know you're behaving just like a relative.'

'I am a relative.'

'It's going well, the way Evans expected. He's quite happy. Just relax. You have to be patient with these operations, you know that as well as I do.'

'How is my sister?'

Phoebe paused. 'I'm told she's in a bad temper just like you. I think she's got more excuse.'

'Sorry, Phoebe.'

'I'd like to meet your wife. I think you must give her a bad time.'

'I love Stella,' he protested. And didn't Stella give him a hard time? He hadn't forgotten Job Titus, all in the past, of course. As far as he knew. Not that retrospective jealousy was any easier to bear.

'And you think that makes it better? How like a man.'

'Oh, come on, Phoebe, let's forgive each other. I apologize for anything I did, past, present or future.'

She laughed. 'You're a clever devil too, clever but fair. And here's a bit of news. Sergeant Downey said to tell you if you rang and were interested.' The ironic note in her voice could not be missed. One and all, they knew he was interested. 'To tell you, if you were interested that it had been established that the girl did not put up a fight. Went willingly, as it were... Oh, and she was not sexually attacked. Mean anything to you?'

It fitted in, the same pattern of docility as the other two.
And no sex. Yes, it meant something to him.

'And there's more.'

'Don't hand it out in little parcels, Phoebe.'

'Whoa there, I'm doing you a favour, remember... Her
stomach was empty, she had not eaten for some time. I don't
know what that suggests to you.'

Imprisoned, tied up possibly, a hostage to murder. It was
the thing that separated this victim from the other two. She
was the first in time, and the worst treated.

He walked round the corner to where he had parked his
car and set off. He had a fair idea of which way to go, but
he wanted to take a back route. He liked small side roads,
you learnt so much more about a neighbourhood than from
the large busy arteries leading through the city.

Pershore Road, Sellywick Drive, Eden Road, Roper's
Passage... You probably couldn't drive through that last
street, too narrow. Stetchly Road, Cat Street, and then, at
last, Larch Court where Mary had lived.

The unthinkable thought comes upon you when least expected.

He started the car and found his way blocked by a big
lorry. He groaned. It isn't worth it, I should retire from the
game and grow roses or keep bees like Sherlock Holmes.

There, the word popped out, the forbidden word, under
the guise of a joke.

Retire.

The lorry full of frozen meat moved away and Coffin
drove forward. No roses, with him they would have green-
fly from the word go. You couldn't keep bees in his church
tower apartment in Spinnergate.

The traffic was slow and patchy but he found his way to
where Mary Andrews had lived with her grandfather, Henry
French, with no trouble except for a bad move down a one-
way street.

He drove round a corner, then stopped the car to sit looking. Sergeant Downey had prepared him for what he might find, but all the same it was a shock to see only one inhabited home in a row of deserted, empty houses.

Henry French had lived in the middle of the terrace but the curtains were drawn here too, and for ever. He would not be back, nor would Mary.

Behind the houses was a wasteland where a factory had once stood. Remains of the factory were stuck there still, so you could see the skeleton of a great red brick monster. The men and women who worked in the factory had probably lived in the streets around here. At the time when Reilly's Ironworks had gone up, men walked to work from close at hand. Those days were over and the whole area was due to be redeveloped.

A big notice said:

CITY DEVELOPMENT AREA.
NEW SHOPPING PRECINCT.

There was the developer's name which he recognized and the architect's also, which he did not. It was going to be a big enterprise and Mr French's reluctance to sell must be holding it up.

While increasing the value of the houses. Don't forget that, he told himself.

Coffin parked his car in the dead street, walking down the garden to the house. This was dead too. The garden was not dead but was busy finding its way back to a primaeval wilderness. It had been heavily planted with shrubs and bushes, all now in vigorous, unrestrained growth, he had to push his way between two rose-trees which had spread out towards each other. Nature, left alone, always overdoes it.

The nylon curtains masking the windows had gone grey with dirt, they would never wash clean now; a line of dead flies lay on the inner window-sill. Even they had given up the struggle for life.

As he walked back to his car, he imagined how Mary Andrews had lived with her grandfather. A small job somewhere, responsible for the cooking and laundry at home, watching television and going to the library. He might call there to see if they knew anything of her, but he already knew what he wanted to know.

She was a girl with expectations. She could be a small heiress. When her grandfather died and the house was hers (if that was what he intended, but in Coffin's imagination it was how it went: Mary was the next of kin and would inherit if there was a will or not), she could sell it for whatever the next developer would pay.

Birmingham was the city of the future, everyone said so, and what Mary might inherit would be valuable, especially if you know how to play the game.

Only an unknown had moved out of the shadows to kill her.

Mary was different from the other two victims, this was what struck him. The first of the series to die, and the last to be discovered.

But the very nature of her death and burial ruled out, in Coffin's view, the idea of the serial murderer.

Sex, obsession, madness, the drive to kill, he rejected those as motives in favour of something harder and more grasping. Somehow gain to the killer came into it.

THE DRIVE to the Sheldon Park Hospital was not long. He found his way there and tucked his car away in a visitors' car park. Several blocks of buildings spread out around him which were built of brick, solid and not handsome but serviceable. The hospital had the air of having once been something else and he would not have been surprised if he had been told it had started out as a workhouse or a barracks.

But when he walked into the entrance hall it felt to him like a good hospital, one doing its best to heal. Among all the mingled spells of antiseptics, drugs, floor polish and the ghostly smells of departed patients, he smelt kindness.

The feeling was reinforced when he was led into the small side ward where Henry French was in bed. Here he introduced himself to the nurse for what he was, a policeman.

Henry French was in a corner bed with a window behind him. A blue and white flowered curtain was drawn around the bed, separating him from the other two patients so that he had, in effect, a little private room. He was curled up, eyes closed, breathing quietly in short, shallow breaths. His hands on the counterpane were neatly manicured and his thick white hair had been brushed into a quiff. Blue pyjamas and a little soft shawl around his shoulders showed under the sheets.

'He looks comfortable,' Coffin said spontaneously. 'Is he asleep?'

'No, just very far away.'

'Can I talk to him?'

The young nurse replaced the shawl which had slipped a little. 'He may be able to hear you, I believe he can, but he will not answer.'

'I had hoped to ask him about his granddaughter, and about some property he owns.'

'You can try.'

Coffin bent down, he took Henry French's hand. 'About your granddaughter Mary,' he began. 'She lived with you, I understand.' He felt a faint, a very faint, pressure on his own hand.

'Did she go to London?'

Was there a movement of a finger against his own?

'Did she ever write? Did you have a letter?'

A letter could mean an address.

This time he could not feel a response, nothing. He tried again. Then he patted Henry French's hand, said: 'Thank you, sir,' and moved a few paces away.

'I'm sorry,' said the nurse. 'I did warn you.'

They were speaking quietly, but stood close to the bed. On a table by the bed on which were flowers and a comb and hairbrush, he saw two photographs in silver frames. One was of a girl, young, plump and pretty, the other of a very young man, and one judging by the flowing hair style taken a few years ago, for fashions change.

Coffin thought: I know that face. Younger, hair different, even a different colour, but the same features.

My God, to think of it being him. And yet in a way, always a likely candidate. Close to Annie Briggs, close to Didi. There with a chance to watch, and so respectable.

He turned in question to the nurse. 'His family?'

'Yes, that's his granddaughter and his grandson, all the family he has. I think he was proud of them both, especially the girl, she hoped to be an actress and he wanted to help. I had thought they would have come to visit him, but neither has.'

No, thought Coffin, because one is dead and the other one killed her.

He took Henry French's hand again. 'Goodbye, sir,' he said. This time there was no answering pressure. Possibly he had imagined it the first time.

As he drove away, he decided that a meeting must be set up between Archie Young and Wally Watson at which he would preside. He thought: Wally Watson has a fingerprint and I have the face. We've got him.

HE STOPPED in a quiet side street where there was one of those cafés in which Birmingham seemed rich to make another telephone call. He was in better spirits. Even the coffee tasted good, and the girl who poured it was polite about letting him use the telephone.

'Phoebe, I'm off, I've finished my business here.'

'I won't ask.'

'You'll hear. But thanks for your help... What news of Letty's affair?' He was anxious, all the feeling about his sister that he had suppressed that day came raging back.

'He didn't turn up to the meeting. Or so your sister believes. In fact, a man was observed watching her and followed back. A house in Edgbaston, not too far from the hotel. It's thought the girl, Elissa, is there. She's been seen.' Phoebe added: 'And not as a prisoner.'

'So she's cooperating?'

'Could be. Looks like it.'

'Perhaps I should collect Letty, take her back to London.'

'No, I'd leave her, let her see it through. From what I hear, I don't believe she'd go. But she's beginning to suspect her daughter.'

Perhaps she always had done, thought Coffin, as he said goodbye to Phoebe. His second call was to Walter Watson in South London. 'Wally, this is your job: get the Birmingham CID to seal the house in Larch Grove so that no one can get in. I'll explain when I get back. I want to meet you in company with Archie Young and his team.'

His next call was to Archie Young. 'I'm on my way back, I think I have a result, but I'm uneasy, this killer is unpredictable, chancy, and there's a lot of malice. Keep an eye on things.'

'Can't run a twenty-four-hour watch on them all.' He totted them up in his head: Annie Briggs, Eddie, and Lizzie Creeley, Job Titus, Alex C. Edwards, Tash and others... What did the boss want? And Edwards, was that necessary?

The Chief Commander's other request to Archie Young was that he must fix a meeting with Chief Superintendent Watson in the Second City. On John Coffin's territory.

The last call was to Stella. It took some time to track her down since she was not at home, but he found her in Max's at last, where she was having a late lunch.

'I'm coming home. In fact, I'm on the way now. I'll see you in a few hours. Will you be home?'

'I'm working this evening: doing an interview on TV. And I've got one or two things set up, but I promise to hurry.' But he could tell from her voice that she was glad to hear from him. 'And Letty? What's happening?'

'I won't talk about it now, but you can relax, Letty will be back, and she'll have her money with her.' Then he said: 'And about the other business, the murders, I think that's tidied up. I know now who killed the girls.'

Stella went back into Max's where she whispered to Alison who was there too that the murderer was known. Normally Stella was very discreet but her relief at the news was so great that she found herself wanting to talk about it.

Their coffee was being served by one of Max's daughters, the lovely one (but going off a bit already) whom they called Beauty.

Beauty was a great gossip and heard this nugget of news with pleasure. She too had known Didi, had been at school with her.

She passed the news round everywhere.

'Stella knows, yes, I think she knows WHO, but she didn't say. She couldn't really, could she? But it will all come out soon. There will be an arrest, won't there? We shall all feel a lot easier then, it's been horrible here.'

'But don't go out after dark,' was her joke.

A lot of people came into Max's that afternoon and heard what Beauty so willingly volunteered, then they in their turn went out into Spinnergate to pass on what they had heard.

Job Titus heard all about it as he travelled home, so did Alex C. Edwards, who telephoned Annie, who told Tom Ashworth. Annie had been doing some digging on her own account since receiving Didi's notebook with Eddie Creeley's signed photograph. Didi had kept a rough diary of an intimate nature which told Annie more than she had expected. Lizzie Creeley heard the news while she was shopping in the chemist for some headache tablets and something to cure sickness. She hadn't told Eddie yet because he wasn't up to it.

NINETEEN

The river in flood

THE MURDERER was saying Relax to Annie; he suspected her
of blackmailing him in an Annie-ish sort of way, in other
words, mad and muddled. She couldn't focus, that woman,
but he was in charge; he had made his plans, wasn't really
here at all. Packed and on the way. Early retirement. You
could call it that.

It wasn't that he liked killing, it was a business matter.
Anyone might do the same for his reason, and a number
had, but he had found it surprisingly easy to get women to
agree to be murdered. Except the first one, Mary Andrews,
the bitch; he had had to lure her south with a few lies, such
as 'I can help you with your acting career. I know it's what
you've always wanted, get you a foothold in the theatre
down here.' He did the same later with Marianna and Didi.

All women are gullible when it is news they want to hear.
Maybe they think: Well, he's lying but let's give it a go, and
that's their weak point. The window of opportunity. And by
the time he had got them planting the false clues, Eddie,
Eddie, they were dying without knowing it.

Mary had to be imprisoned for a bit because Grandpa was
not dead and she might get in touch. Food and drink had
been a problem but he had solved that by not giving her any.
She soon went quiet, damn her, let her eat her nails. She always had chewed them, he remembered those chewed hands
that had slapped his face.

None of this came out in his smooth flow of talk. 'Annie, you're a great girl, I love you.'

Annie listened to his soothing words, and went on with her talk. 'Like HER,' she was saying, and then: 'Did like HIM but he betrayed me.'

'Never,' said the killer sardonically. 'Cops never do that.'

'Can't trust him. Can't trust people. Can't trust you. It's because I don't trust you, I can use you.'

'Well, thanks. That is a vote of confidence. I always thought you were loyal. Loyal Annie, I called you.' *Stupid woman, stupid woman, I am a tiger in the undergrowth, you can never trust a tiger, especially a hungry tiger, because he waits and he watches, chooses his prey, then pounces.* This tiger did observe his victims; if they thought they watched, then they were watched.

'I've been pushed around too much,' said Annie. 'Now I want to get my own back on some people. They patronize you, HE did, SHE did, I won't have that. You can help me.' She did not say Revenge, but he smelt it on her breath like gin.

'I don't know,' said the murderer, with his false smile, 'it's not really my job. I'm supposed to be neutral.'

'But you'd do it for me,' said Annie beguilingly, 'especially because of what I know.'

Dangerous talk.

'For instance, I know, you dye your hair.'

'I do not dye my hair.'

'I know what's natural and what's not. It's a wig or dyed, you are dark, not fair, I can see it in your eyes. And perhaps I know even more about you than you think,' she said. 'I've been reading Didi's notebook.'

'So it's turned up.' Not good news.

'And I've got it.' She pointed to the table on which rested the notebook with the scatter of photographs. 'I'm not saying you killed Didi, but you were seeing her and I didn't know. I hate being betrayed.' She put her head on one side. 'So?'

'I'll help.'

'No choice, have you?' Then she slid in that remark which doomed another woman. 'By the way, Stella had the note-book.'

'Is that so?'

'Said she didn't look in it, but...' Annie shrugged. 'Who knows?'

Damn, and Damn.

He had heard that the identity of the murderer was known, the rumour had reached him, but he was about to disappear in any case, his time was up.

Thoughts circled as Annie talked. They discussed plans of how to settle scores all round. She really was crazy now, her friend decided.

'We might use Eddie Creeley.'

'Eddie, Eddie, oh, I do like the sound of that,' said Annie. Her eyes glittered.

Mad, he thought, over the top and waving a flag as she goes.

'I don't want to hurt HER. Not really. Just frighten HIM.'

'It won't hurt her.' Or not for long, but Eddie would be incriminated again. 'And you have to think of yourself here, what is due to you.'

'If you say so.'

'I do.'

'So what about the Eddie bit?'

'We write his name on a bit of paper, anything will do, just something she grabbed and managed to scrawl be-fore...' He left that open.

'Wouldn't he take it away?'

He would, of course.

'Hide it underneath her body as if she fell on it.' The killer was used to hiding little bits of evidence to turn up as he de-sired. He had done it with Marianna, and with Didi and with Mary, who had to be found if his plan was to work, and had been found just a touch too soon. But he'd be off, over the hills and far away.

'But it won't look like Stella's writing. They can check.'

Annie was being difficult now, it was time for her turn at dying.

'Big block letters, harder to identify.'

'Are you sure?' Annie tried, scrawling the letters as he suggested. 'Oh yes, I see what you mean.' But she still had doubts. 'I don't mind her being frightened, chilled a bit, you know, but not hurt.' And she had another worry. 'Won't she see me, then tell?'

'You won't be seen, you'll be invisible.'

'Will I?'

There was no doubt that Annie could be a nuisance. But he smiled on her and spoke gently: 'I'll show you how it's done, and you will know for yourself. Stand there. Head back. That's right.'

We all have our little madnesses, we need them to carry through a strong enterprise. And my madness has at least been profitable. Yes, on the whole I am in favour of madness.

The matter of the fingernails, well, that was something to admit to: useful because it made the police latch on to the serial murder idea, but chewed fingernails did turn a man on. Hard to say why, like the smell of female sweat really, something hormonal.

Mary had chewed fingernails, particularly ragged on the right hand, and she had slapped his face with that hand, on which was a scar he had given her with a knife as a child. He had marched about the business of murder wearing two heads and he had come through. He gave his head a shake.

I am sane again.

Goodbye, Annie.

had been found just a touch too rough, but he dove off into
the hills and far away.

'But it won't back up anything.' They sat there.

Anita was resting on their minds as was Letty too hidden in
a device.

Big trouble when barrier to identity.

'Are you sure?' And it isn't so.

please tell. 'Do you see what you mean? And she still had

TWENTY

The river is very cold

COFFIN GOT BACK to London before dark, he went straight
to his office where he at once telephoned Stella. She did not
answer nor had she put her answerphone on.

'Keep on trying,' he said to his secretary. He wanted to
hear Stella's voice, he needed her warmth, her sanity.

Then he looked for news of Letty and her daughter, but
Birmingham was silent still on this matter. It was probably
too soon for a resolution.

His secretary said: 'Chief Inspector Young was asking for
you, he's got Chief Superintendent Watson with him.'

Good, that was what he wanted to hear.

'Where are they?'

'In the Chief Inspector's room. Shall I ask them to walk
across?'

'Yes, please, and order some coffee and sandwiches.'
Suddenly he was very hungry. Archie Young and Wally
Watson came in together at the same time as the sand-
wiches and coffee.

After a look at Wally Watson's face, Coffin produced
some whisky as well. He poured each man a good measure,
but took none himself. He had to do the talking and he had
to convince two practised, hard-headed professionals.

'Glad to see you back.' Wally Watson supped his whisky.
'Downey said he saw you.'

'Have the Birmingham team put a watch on the house, as
I asked?'

'The house is important, is it?'

Coffin considered his words: 'Very important. It's the motive for everything, and in it there should be proof of the murderer's identity.'

Archie Young cleared his throat in a way familiar to Coffin, expressing at once doubt and a desire to be convinced.

'Oh yes, it's the motive for the murder of Mary Andrews, just as her murder provides the motive for the deaths of the other two women: to establish that we were dealing with a serial murderer, whereas in fact the murderer was out for money.'

Watson put down his sandwich. 'Was the girl rich?'

'No, but when her grandfather died, I believe she would have inherited his house, and that house is going to be a valuable profit—'

'A house? Is that enough of a motive?'

'Murders have taken place for a few pounds, and one way and another this house is going to be worth a lot more than that.' And the killer may have hated Mary, Coffin had picked up the smell of hate. She had been imprisoned and starved before dying, that had to count for something personal.

Wally Watson said: 'We've had a call from the next of kin, says he's willing to do the formal identification.'

'I bet,' said Coffin. 'What did he sound like?'

'Nice young man. Bit of a Brummie accent.'

'There would be,' said Coffin. He could act, this chap.

'What name?'

'Charles French, a cousin, all that's left of the family. He said he is the grandfather's executor.'

'Oh, the old man's dead, is he? He wasn't earlier today.'

Wally Watson shrugged. 'He seemed to know about the will.'

'I'm sure he did.'

The other two men looked at him, and he knew what they were asking: Out with it, enlarge on these hints, explain.

The Chief Commander got up and started to walk up and down the room, talking as he went. 'You, Wally, have a fingerprint, I have a picture of the murderer's face, and you—' he stopped in front of Archie Young—'you have the murderer living here in Spinnergate.'

He poured some more whisky for the others, this time taking some himself.

'And I'll tell you where to go to find him.' He might be still there, a working day, after all, and he had no reason as yet to believe himself a suspect. Or so Coffin hoped.

'I'll just try to get my wife on the telephone, and then we will go on talking.'

He went to his outer office to telephone Stella. He longed to hear her voice but there was still silence.

LIZZIE CREELEY was ministering to her nephew Eddie who was sick in bed. Every so often he would go to the bathroom to lie groaning before trying to vomit.

Lizzie fussed around. 'You're doing yourself no good.'

'I know I'm going to be sick. I want to get it over,' he moaned.

'You'll feel better when you have been sick,' said Lizzie hopefully. She helped him back to bed. 'Why don't you try these tablets I got you?'

'They won't help.'

'They might, the chemist said they would. He's got migraine, I said, so try these, he said.' Lizzie was enjoying being a nurse, she was beginning to feel a real person again, as if her young self and her old self had joined up again after being separated for so many years.

Eddie groaned and rolled out of bed. 'I believe I really shall be sick this time.'

'Oh good,' said Lizzie, following him to the bathroom door. 'There you are, you see, you are clever, Eddie, although you say you are not, because you have migraine. Only clever people have migraine.'

'Then I wish I wasn't,' said Eddie, returning from the bathroom. 'I wasn't sick.' He groaned.

'Better luck next time,' said Lizzie. She helped him back to bed.

'Thanks, Lizzie, you're an angel.' What a thing to say to a murderess, he thought, and at once felt sicker than ever. I believe I shall manage to be sick next time, he told himself, and then I shall feel better. He groaned again.

'It's nerves that brought it on. You're highly strung.'

'I don't think I am. But I do keep thinking of Didi, I'm not out of that wood yet, Auntie.'

'I blame Annie Briggs,' said Lizzie, who had been in that wood herself.

'It's not her fault.'

Later, when Eddie had been sick and sick again and then fallen asleep, Lizzie put on her coat.

'I'm going to see that Annie for myself and have it out with her.'

The distance between the two houses was not great, Lizzie was soon in Napier Street. Annie's house was dark, with no light showing in any of the front rooms.

'Doesn't mean she's out, though,' said Lizzie. She rang the bell. In the old days when they had been neighbours, doors had not always been locked. So it was no surprise to Lizzie to find the door opened when she gave it a push.

'Annie? Annie, are you there? It's Lizzie, you remember Lizzie.' She walked into the hall. 'Annie?'

Then her foot touched something, she looked down, and in the light from the street she could see Annie on the floor, her face puffy and discoloured with a belt drawn tight round her neck. Lizzie bent down to touch Annie's face. It was still warm.

Lizzie did not scream, her life had toughened her, but she gave a little cry before picking up the bit of paper with Eddie's name on it.

Thank God, my boy's been home all day and I can swear to it, she thought.

She leaned against the front door, breathing deeply. What to do. Go away, say nothing? Burn the piece of paper. But she had given up lies, and these days even preferred the truth, because it always stayed the same and did not turn into something when you took your eyes off it, as lies sometimes did. For this reason, her mind turned to John Coffin. He could be bleak and hard but he was straight.

'It'll have to be the police.'

JOHN COFFIN had convinced the two other policemen.

'So what next?' asked Young.

'Take him in,' muttered Wally Watson.

'But can we charge him yet?'

'There's the fingerprint,' said Coffin.

Young looked doubtful. 'That could be explained away.'

'It'll do for a start.'

'We have the address to go to, his office.'

'Will he still be there?' questioned Wally Watson. 'What about the telephone call from Birmingham?'

'I don't suppose he really rang from there,' said Coffin. 'I think he's still here. But not for long. Let's go.'

Two cars set out, Coffin and Walter Watson in front, with Archie Young and a sergeant following.

They drove through Spinnergate to the small building with dirty windows and a basement with iron bars next to a betting shop. Coffin had been there before and did not like it any better this time. He stared down into the basement and felt cold: Mary Andrews had been kept there, and starved.

He felt the chill of malice and evil in that starvation. Hatred of a person. Money was not the only motive, he thought, there was hate, evil, inside this man.

They pushed inside without waiting for an invitation.

A pleasant-faced young man with dark hair got up from behind a desk. 'What can I do for you?' He hesitated. 'You're police officers, aren't you?'

'And who are you?' asked Coffin.

'Tash. T. Ashworth,' the young man said.

Coffin nodded. 'And how long have you been using that name?'

'For about forty-eight hours. It's not illegal, I've bought the business. It's my professional name. It's not my real name, nor was it the last chap's, there hasn't been an Ashworth for the last ten years.'

'So where is the last Tom Ashworth?'

'I don't know. My solicitor must do, he arranged the contract. Indemnity and all that. The chap's out there somewhere.' He was blithe about it.

Then he looked anxious. 'What's up?'

'Nothing that you've done. But I am afraid that we will have to turn you out and seal up the premises. You'll get back in, don't worry... Archie, leave the sergeant here to do what's necessary.'

The sergeant licked his lips in anticipation. If he played this well, he could see a chance of promotion. He nodded. 'I know what to do, sir.'

Other teams of experts would be surging in, fingerprinting, photographing, searching the very dust of the place, but he had the luck, he was here first.

'Be careful with the basement,' said Coffin. 'I want that dealt with inch by inch, and nothing missed.' I'll get that bastard, he thought. Hanging would have been too good for him, frying would have been better.

The two cars drove back together, but this time the Chief Inspector drove with Coffin so that they could talk.

'He's got away. Too carefree altogether, that young man who bought the firm.' Coffin was tense.

'But we know where he must go,' said Young. 'To that other identity he will claim. Charles French, where are you?'

When they got back to Headquarters, they heard the news that Lizzie Creeley was waiting for them: she had made her report.

'I suppose forensics are in Napier Street,' said Coffin to himself. To his surprise, Lizzie answered: 'I don't know. I went with Annie to hospital.'

'Hospital?'

'Well, someone had to.'

'Then she wasn't dead?'

'Not sure,' said Lizzie. 'I thought she was.'

But she would not have gone to hospital, dead bodies do not go to hospital.

Coffin and Archie Young consulted. 'I'll go,' said Young. 'On my way.'

'Right.' At that moment Coffin's secretary arrived. 'Oh, sir, your wife telephoned and left a message. She's on her way home. About forty minutes, she said.'

'Thank you.' Coffin turned to Young. 'I'm coming with you.'

'She's probably dead by now,' said Young as they drove. 'Just our luck.'

But she was not.

'That's a tough lady,' said the doctor who met them. 'She must have a different constitution from most. But enough oxygen must have got through to the brain to keep her going.'

'I think that's a fair description,' agreed the Chief Commander.

'Of course, she may be brain damaged.'

But Annie proved them wrong. She opened her eyes, closed them again, and said: 'Stella.'

STELLA PINERO had driven herself home to St Luke's Mansions after a happy day. She was convinced that she had secured a new backer for St Luke's Theatre, and one who was prepared also to be patron to the new Drama School. With such a patroness, the school would surely get all the certifications necessary to tap all possible funds. Money was the game, but she must practise her curtsies.

She got out of her car and was locking it when she looked over her shoulder, there was a dark figure lurking behind her. Damn, surely that lark was over.

'Annie, is that you?'

But she knew at once that this was not Annie: the smell was all wrong, this smell was totally masculine. But there was another smell as well. It was petrol.

Her shoulders were gripped and then something leather and hard slid round her neck. She began to choke. She felt herself pulled backwards, and her feet began to slip beneath her. She fell against her attacker who silently dragged her backwards.

Silently, silently.

The smell of petrol began to be stronger, she was choking and gasping for air. I am being doused in petrol, Stella thought, I am going to be burnt alive.

The body has its own survival instincts. Her arms and legs were constricted, she could hardly breathe, but she had the use of her legs. Performers know how to use every part of their body, Stella kicked backwards at her opponent.

Her attack seemed unavailing, he was dragging her into the darkness of St Luke's courtyard, where he would set her alight and deposit her on her own doorstep.

I'm not going to let him, thought Stella. Anger gave her new strength.

The leather thong round her neck was biting into her skin. She heard the click of cigarette lighter, smelt the flame. Then suddenly headlights flared as a big car shot into the street, she and her attacker were caught in the beam. With new energy she thrust herself against the man, kicking with her high heels, struggling to free herself. One kick went home, she delivered another.

He swore at her: 'Bitch!'

Then, with the sinuousness of a body trained in exercise, Stella swung round, pushing him as far away as she could. The man staggered against the wall of St Luke's, the petrol bottle fell to the ground, splashing him as it went.

Flames leapt all over him in one sudden eager movement. He was a flaming torch, reeling, rolling round the courtyard, screaming.

Stella's coat was burning, she tried to tear it from her back, but she was restricted by the belt round her throat and could hardly breathe, she wrenched at the leather, dragging it loose. Then she was pulling at her coat, staggering against the wall, still hearing the screams.

Coughing, she saw a figure leaving the car, dragging a smaller figure by the arm. She knew that car.

'Letty...' it was all she whispered. 'Letty! Help me! I'm on fire.'

LATER, LYING DOWN in her bedroom, with Letty and the doctor, and somewhere in the room, her husband, she heard herself say: 'Letty, what were you doing?'

'I've come bloody home,' said Letty, who never swore. 'And with my rotten, lousy daughter.'

Stella was breathing deeply. 'Don't be too hard on yourself ... I think you two saved me from being incinerated.'

TWENTY-ONE

The tide has turned

STELLA SAT IN FRONT of her dressing-table mirror examining her neck where a blue bruise was forming. The skin was torn where the buckle on the belt had bitten into her. There were patches of blisters, covered with dressing, lower down the neck, her hair had been singed and she needed a hairdresser, but on the whole, her condition several days later was not too bad. She had been scorched but not burnt.

Tash had gone up like a fireball and with eighty per cent burns had died within the day.

'I shall need make-up on that,' she said, looking at what she could see of her neck.

Thank God her face was unmarked, thought Coffin. He had a tightness in his throat that would not go away.

'Dark cream, I think,' she went on, picking up a stick of make-up and beginning to pat on little blobs of colour. 'I believe I like this tint. I last used it when I was in a Maugham play, I believe I came from somewhere south of Rangoon and was not quite a good woman... You know we hardly use make-up now, it's all meant to be so natural. Of course, if you're playing a corpse or an old man, you have to use slap.'

Her husband was sitting watching her. 'You're talking too much,' he said in a fond voice. 'Let her talk,' the doctor had said.

'I know, that's because I'm feeling emotional. I smelt him burning, you know, I smelt burning hair and flesh.'

Coffin took her in his arms, but gently because her skin was tender.

'I was nearly victim number five.'

'Annie's still with us,' said Coffin. 'So you would have been number four.' He wasn't joking, though, and he kept his eyes on her as if he could not let her out of his sight. 'Annie's palled up with Lizzie, of all things.' You could hardly call it a friendship, but it was a relationship. Lizzie did the shopping for Annie while she was recovering, and they both watched television while Annie talked.

'A complete waste, it would have been,' Coffin went on. 'I feel vengeful about that: I hadn't read Didi's notes about getting help in her acting from Tom Ashworth who had trained actors and knew how to audition.'

'Had he?'

'He might have done a bit of acting, he was blond as Tash, in nature it seems he is dark-haired and wore spectacles. The strange thing was that he had run the Tash agency for one whole year, establishing his identity. Back in Coventry he had worked in an estate agency, which is presumably where he got the idea of the big way to make money.'

'If you'd arrived a bit earlier, you could have rescued me and not Letty.' But she had really saved herself with that last kick at the killer which threw him away. Still, Letty had wrapped Stella in her own coat, putting out her smouldering clothing. Yes, Letty had helped.

'It's time Letty did something.' He was not feeling forgiving towards his darling sister. 'She knew about Tom Ashworth, or guessed something.' That was what she had meant about the box and what was inside being something different. 'And she never spoke clearly. Never came out with it.'

'She had her own worries,' said Stella tolerantly, glad that the money bags were back. 'Will Elissa and the boyfriend be charged?'

Coffin shrugged. 'I'm not interfering. But yes, with several things, I expect, and so will the girl. He attacked a police officer, young thug, so there's that for a start.'

He got up. 'All right, I'll mend fences with Letty, but the girl has to take what's coming to her.'

'You ought to be grateful to her. If you hadn't gone to Birmingham you would never have found the murderer's identity.'

'Letty was my excuse for going, not my reason. I was looking for what I found. I knew there had to be something like that behind the killings: money, I knew it the moment I saw that it had been intended that the first girl should be found and identified . . . she was in a site that was going to be excavated and she had her name tucked underneath her.'

'What a great deal of detail he knew about places and people.'

'Who better than a detective? Always had my eye on him, although I suspected the social worker for a bit. He seemed to fit.'

Stella dusted her neck with powder. 'So the other two girls were just a cover-up? That's horrible. Where did he get the idea?'

'I don't know,' said Coffin. 'Read it in a book, I expect. Agatha Christie. I dare say. I expect we will find a row of crime books on the shelves when we search where he lived.'

'Where did he live? Apart from here as Tom Ashworth . . . Oh, he was good-looking,' she said sadly.

'He had a flat in Coventry.' He had looked like a cigarette burned at both ends by the time he got to hospital. The gods do a thorough job once they start. On the other hand, he had been found to have a huge cancer inside him, so who knew what games the gods were playing?

'Poor Didi,' said Stella, 'but she has people who grieve for her. Those other two girls, Marianna Manners and Mary Andrews, who grieves for them?'

'I won't forget,' said Coffin. 'And somehow, I think Annie will remember them all. She said she is going to pray for them. Lizzie with her, I expect. They seem to do things together now.'

Stella laughed. 'Shall we give a party and ask them?'

'Heaven forbid. She might come as Charley.'

But Charley had died, gone up in smoke.

Coffin looked at his wife. 'Should I change my life? Should I retire?'

Stella put down the stick of Leichner. 'You're not serious? What would you do?'

'I might put in an offer for Tash. I would be with you a lot more.'

'Darling, I love you dearly, but I think we are both better working . . . Oh, by the way.' She pulled a card from behind a bottle of scent. She held it out to Coffin. 'Phoebe? Who is Phoebe?'

Her eyes were alight with amusement, and something else as well. Me and Job Titus, she was saying, so what about you?

'Ah,' said Coffin.

Attack was the best method of defence. 'We've got Job Titus,' he said. 'He was picked up this evening . . . For kerb-crawling.'